*This Darkening Universe*

*Books by Lloyd Biggle, Jr.*

THIS DARKENING UNIVERSE
MONUMENT
THE METALLIC MUSE
THE LIGHT THAT NEVER WAS
THE WORLD MENDERS
THE STILL, SMALL VOICE OF TRUMPETS
THE RULE OF THE DOOR AND OTHER FANCIFUL REGULATIONS
WATCHERS OF THE DARK
THE FURY OUT OF TIME
ALL THE COLORS OF DARKNESS
THE ANGRY ESPERS

*Edited by Lloyd Biggle, Jr.*

NEBULA AWARD STORIES SEVEN

# This Darkening Universe

## LLOYD BIGGLE, JR.

DOUBLEDAY & COMPANY, INC.

GARDEN CITY, NEW YORK

1975

All of the characters in this book
are fictitious, and any resemblance
to actual persons, living or dead,
is purely coincidental.

Library of Congress Cataloging in Publication Data

Biggle, Lloyd, 1923–
This darkening universe

I. Title.
PZ4.B593Th  [PS3552.I43]  813′.5′4
ISBN 0-385-08676-8
Library of Congress Catalog Card Number 75–11070

*This Darkening Universe*

# 1

# JAN DARZEK

Among the myriads of dead worlds in the universe, few had numbered a private detective among their mourners. This world was one of the rare exceptions—because it had been murdered.

The cracked and eroded street was dotted with irregularly shaped traffic islands, where flame-colored shrubs thrust up unruly masses of large, brittle leaves that tinkled like metal in the dry wind. Around the islands, in clusters—also irregularly shaped—lay heaps of crumbling bones.

Jan Darzek, standing on a world remote beyond his comprehension (for he was no astronomer) and confronting a catastrophe whose dimensions defied his understanding, could find no expression for impotent anger except to gape stupidly at the magnificently disproportional artifacts of an extinct civilization while with one heavily booted foot he clumsily sifted the crumbling remains of the civilized.

URSGworl, his acting chief assistant, stood nearby, waiting respectfully for the next wish that would be his command. Finally he spoke. "Razonl says their ground vehicles were electrically powered. The storage system utilizes a new principle."

Darzek made no comment.

"Wusqom thinks the beams in those buildings are an alloy he's not familiar with. He'd like to take samples."

Again Darzek made no comment. Wusqom knew better than to ask. They had no evidence that disease had done this thing, and Darzek felt certain that it had not; but until they knew, they would garb themselves in protective clothing and take no risks whatsoever.

Once more he tentatively extended a boot, this time to touch a bulging rib cage located in the vicinity of an oddly structured pelvis. The blackening bones suggested, to Darzek's untutored eye, a skeletal system based on something other than calcium, but so unimportant was the chemistry of these remains that he did not bother to ask the nearest chemist, who stood nearby.

The ribs crumbled at his touch, but that, too, was irrelevant—as was the curiosity Darzek felt about an intelligent race that found symmetry abhorrent and produced exquisitely lopsided buildings and ridiculously unbalanced designs and yet lived in cell-like rooms whose symmetry was absolute.

A remarkable world-wide civilization, in full flower, had been brutally plucked and trampled on. Every major life form on the entire planet had been exterminated. Darzek's own ancestors had survived overwhelming disasters and massive tragedies on their planet Earth, including many of their own making, but none of that compared with the mind-shattering stupendousness of world catastrophe.

And this world was one of many. Someone, or something, was systematically laying waste a galaxy. Darzek's self-appointed task was to track it down and stop it. Thus far he had found only the weathered ruins of one civilization after another, each gruesomely ornamented with random heaps of decaying bones.

"These remains are no fresher than the last," Darzek said. "We'll leave a message beacon for URSDwad and take some long jumps and try again."

They formed a line and moved through the transmitter frame to the decontamination chamber on their spaceship. No one, not even Jan Darzek, had a backward glance for a devastated world too long dead to tell them what they so urgently needed to know.


# ROK WLLON

He was EIGHT, the Eighth Councilor, the eighth member of the Council of Supreme, and so secretive was the galaxy's ruling body in all of its endeavors that only three other members of the council knew his natural name.

He had convoked an emergency meeting of the council, as was his right as a councilor, and now he anxiously awaited the response.

Gul Darr, who was ONE, the First Councilor, had sent an emissary to ask that this meeting be called, and Rok Wllon had done so despite deep misgivings. Gul Darr was an admirably competent person when action was called for, especially violent action. No one was better aware of that than Rok Wllon, who had known Gul Darr since he was a private detective named Jan Darzek, on the planet Earth.

Unfortunately, Gul Darr was much more inclined to exaggerated dramatization than to a dispassionate evaluation of facts. He had furnished a message for presentation to the council, and Rok Wllon knew that the moment the council heard it, at least four members would disgustedly move for adjournment.

A *ping* sounded. On Rok Wllon's communications console, the second segment of a circle had lighted. Another *ping;* another segment. When Rok Wllon had counted five, a quorum, he got to his feet and began to don his robes. This was a time-consuming ceremony because of his insistence that they hang precisely at the angle he favored. By the time he had them arranged correctly, the glowing circle of light was seven eighths complete.

He flashed the signal of assembly.

His own mind was made up. He did not doubt that Gul Darr had discovered a serious problem, and very likely the fate of a number of distant worlds hung in the balance. His request was reasonable enough; it was his manner of asking that offended.

Rok Wllon would revise the message. If Gul Darr received what he asked, he should have no complaint. If he did complain, Rok Wllon would speak frankly to him. For the real issue before the council was vastly more important than Gul Darr's discovery in the Lesser Galaxy. The real issue was the leadership of the Council of Supreme.

Gul Darr had furnished him with an opportunity, and he intended to make the most of it.

With a final glance at his robe lines, he stepped through his private transmitter to the Hall of Deliberations.

## DOCTOR MALINA DARR

She sat in her shabby office and contemplated the day's mail with stark despair. It contained five bills—four of them long past due—and one small remittance. Creditors sometimes made allowances for a young widow with children, especially one with professional status, but eventually they wanted their money.

The year 1994 had been a financial disaster, but at least the future seemed bright, and she had faced it with cheerful confidence. Now 1995 was proving only slightly less disastrous, and the one remaining question was which would come first: 1996, or her bankruptcy.

Abruptly she brought her meditation to a halt. A middle-aged woman and a teen-aged boy were coming up the walk. Even at that distance, she could diagnose a rampaging case of *acne vulgaris,* and the woman looked prosperous enough to pay cash for the consultation and medication.

If she did, for the first time in a week Malina and her children could drop their diet of dehydrates and have fresh food for dinner.

## MISS EFFIE SCHLUPE

Jan Darzek's former secretary and partner in galactic intrigue had retired with what she considered the perfect exit line: "I'm glad I saw the galaxy, but I want to die in Brooklyn."

But in Brooklyn there was little for her to do except cultivate her rocking chair, and her urge to make something happen became irresistible. It was either that or be consumed by boredom.

So Miss Schlupe became the proprietress of the Greater Brooklyn Natural Health Food Store, a tiny hole-in-the-wall shop offering tastily packaged, nutritious tidbits as well as such staples for cleansing and fumigating the digestive tract as desiccated ragweed, extract of octopus bile, and pine cone flour. In one corner Miss Schlupe operated a small health bar where she prepared whimsically contrived blends of juices squashed from complacent fruits and vegetables of certified good health. Food faddists had not discovered the place, or perhaps there weren't many food faddists in 1995 Brooklyn. Miss Schlupe did very little front-door business, for which she was grateful.

It left her more time for her alley trade in illegal homemade beers and wines, and that business was booming. She brewed and fermented them from the purest ingredients and lavished loving care upon them, and all of them were excellent except her rhubarb beer, which was superb.

She had hoped that an occasional raid by the local revenuers would add spice and variety to her existence, and she derived no small amount of amusement from her elaborate preparations for such an eventuality. Unfortunately, except for the cop on her beat— one of her best customers—no official had viewed her establishment as anything except a yogurt emporium operated by a lively little gray-haired woman.

Confronted with such an ultimate humiliation, Miss Schlupe again felt an irresistible urge to make something happen.

# SUPREME

It made galactic government possible.

No individual, no bureaucratic army of individuals, could administer a governmental synthesis consisting of millions of worlds. Supreme could. Supreme was the ultimate computer. Its location was Primores, an artificial world that orbited the central sun of the Milky Way Galaxy. Supreme *was* Primores—a computer the size of a world.

Supreme maintained the records of a galaxy—the vital statistics, the cultural and historical records, the business records, the legal records. It handled and recorded exchanges of property and solvency transactions, from the inconsequential to the infinitely complex, and maintained the code to the solvency or identification credentials by which the uncounted (except by Supreme) citizens of the uncounted (except by Supreme) worlds of the Galactic Synthesis were able to pursue an orderly existence. Supreme was the ultimate reference and legal library for a galaxy and the final authority on the laws and statistics of all of its millions of member worlds. It also was the repository of information concerning non-member worlds, such as the planet Earth, and its tersely summarized rendition of Earth's history coincided with no version extant or even imagined among Earthmen.

Supreme recorded laws, and it interpreted and explained them, but it could not make laws. It could not issue orders or instructions except to those engaged in undertakings specifically authorized by the Council of Supreme.

Being unique, Supreme had no position to maintain. Being emotionless, it had no pride. It did what it was built to do, and it did that superbly. It had no conception of error, or of blame, or of guilt. Nor was it capable of a sense of responsibility if its conclusions or suggestions misled or were incomprehensible because the facts upon which they were based had long since been forgotten—except by Supreme —and its reasoning processes, entwined as they were through the labyrinthine interior of its world-sized mass, frequently were as difficult to follow logically as they would have been to trace physically.

Supreme's builders had carefully prevented it from issuing instructions except under carefully defined conditions. It was not their fault, and Supreme was totally unaware of the fact, that by a process of slow evolution some governmental officials had begun to accord Supreme's suggestions the full impact of law.

## URSDWAD

He waited.

He was a native Primorian, with a head that protruded from his chest and a body that terminated above it in a bulging hump. His tiny face, with large eyes surrounding a single enfolded nostril and a mouth hidden under the chin, would have won him no awards for pulchritude even in galactic circles; but the misshapen body hump housed an enormous brain, and despite his quiet, meditative manner, he possessed superb powers of intellect.

He had served Gul Darr faithfully and well for many years, and now Gul Darr had entrusted him with the most important task of his career. He was a special emissary, sent back to his own galaxy to deliver masses of data, a selection of recordings, and Gul Darr's personal report to an individual named Rok Wllon. He also transmitted Gul Darr's request that the data, recordings, and report be presented to an emergency meeting of the Council of Supreme, as well as to Supreme itself, and Rok Wllon had promised that this would be done.

And now URSDwad could do nothing but wait.

Beneath his placid exterior, he was badly frightened. At Gul Darr's side he had walked the surfaces of one decimated world after another and stirred the dust of exterminated populations with his footsteps, and he believed fervently in the crucial importance of his mission. He knew that what was happening to a neighboring galaxy could happen to this one. His species had dedicated itself to the service of the Galactic Synthesis and to Supreme for countless generations, and the fact that his native world was artificial did not mean that he loved it less. From what he had seen in the Lesser Galaxy, it required little imagination for him to envision the population of Primores transformed to rippling dust and Supreme itself left unattended. The thought terrified him.

He had deep misgivings about Rok Wllon. He did not know what his official position was, or how it happened that he had access both to the council and to Supreme itself, but URSDwad feared that Rok Wllon would not faithfully transmit the report Gul Darr had prepared.

And that message must reach Supreme and the council. "Tell them," Gul Darr had said, and URSDwad could not forget the terrible intensity with which he spoke, "tell them that this Unidentified Death Force, this Udef, has got to be checked somewhere, by someone. If it isn't, it'll exterminate all the intelligent life in the universe."

## 2

They were members of the Council of Supreme: seven starkly contrasting and improbable life forms that aptly demonstrated the fecund diversity natural evolution could achieve given unlimited time and millions of worlds upon which to practice its mistakes.

They sat around an enormous circular council table in the vast Hall of Deliberations, each poised on a massive piece of furniture custom designed to accommodate the shape of the councilor who used it. Six of the seven councilors had turned their contrasting and improbable organs of sight on an empty chair. ONE, the First Councilor, was absent.

The privilege of chairing a special meeting belonged by tradition to the councilor who had convoked it. Rok Wllon, the Eighth Councilor, waited irritably for their attention and finally rapped on the table. He began, "ONE sends his greetings—"

THREE, a large ball with an upper hemisphere bristling with eye stalks, inflated its vocal sack with a deafening hiss. "Why couldn't ONE come here and speak for himself?" it demanded. "ONE is always having emergency meetings called that he is too busy to attend."

The question was out of order, the interruption rude, and the declaration untrue. Rok Wllon sniffed indignantly and drew himself up to his full width. THREE muttered something that might or might not have been an apology in its own language but could be construed as one, and Rok Wllon began again.

"ONE sends his greetings from the Lesser Galaxy and asks for our council."

*Now* he had their full attention. Even THREE stopped twitching its eye stems and focused all of them on Rok Wllon, staring. TWO, an enormous head and body completely surrounded by a tangle of telescoping limbs, straightened up abruptly and demanded, "What is Gul Darr doing in the Lesser Galaxy?"

That breach of ethics set THREE's eye stems fluttering, jarred

SEVEN into regurgitating its weekly meal from one stomach to another, and left Rok Wllon breathless. All of the councilors were aware that ONE was Gul Darr, a notoriously eccentric galactic trader. Probably all of them knew TWO as E-Wusk, a less notorious but equally famous trader and an associate of Gul Darr's. But never in Rok Wllon's memory had a councilor had the bad taste to refer to a colleague by his real identity.

E-Wusk muttered an apology for his absent-mindedness and lamely corrected himself. "What's ONE doing in the Lesser Galaxy?"

Rok Wllon waited until the flutter of resentment had subsided. Then he again drew himself up to his full width and struck what he considered a dramatic pose. He was immensely broad when viewed from the front, but unbelievably thin in profile, and when he became excited his eyes enlarged, crowding his single gaping nostril until his breathing became a shrill whistle and the distinctive light blue hue of his epidermis deepened to violet.

"All of us vividly recall the invasion of our galaxy that preceded and in fact brought about our appointments to this council. I don't need to describe to you the seriousness of that invasion—"

"Then don't," THREE muttered.

Rok Wllon ignored it. "—because we all remember it so well. ONE, in his capacity as First Councilor, has attempted to discover the source of the invasion, so that the council can take steps to prevent its happening again."

"Entirely commendable," SEVEN remarked. It was a massive lung in a sluglike body—now largely concealed because, like Rok Wllon, it wore its robes of office to conferences—and its speech was a hoarse wheeze.

"When ONE concluded that the invaders came from the Lesser Galaxy," Rok Wllon continued, "naturally he went there to investigate."

"Naturally," SEVEN wheezed. SEVEN was the council's peacemaker. A neckless uniped, its custom chair swiveled so it could turn its body to direct its single sensory organs, and now it was watching THREE's fidgets uneasily.

"Concluded how?" THREE wanted to know.

"He concluded that someone—or something—had driven the invaders from their own galaxy," Rok Wllon said. "They came to our Galaxy Prime seeking refuge, and by chance they discovered weaknesses in the economic and social relations of our member worlds that they were able to exploit—with results distressingly familiar to all of us."

"I don't believe it," SIX protested. She was a gaunt, angular, nocturnal triped with three looping arms that she impatiently twined and untwined during debate, and the diffused and softly filtered light of the great hall was so painful to her that behind her light shield her three enlarged eyes were constantly tearing. "ONE thought the invaders came from the Greater Galaxy," she said testily. "He told me so himself."

"He told that to all of us," FIVE's metallic voice announced. She was a conical head and a twig of a body surrounded by multifingered tentacles. Her natural voice was almost nonexistent, so she placed an amplifying disc on the table in front of her to make herself heard during conferences. "We discussed it," she continued. "I clearly remember his saying the invaders came from the Greater Galaxy, and if you would like the record searched—"

Rok Wllon controlled his temper, though his whistling inhalations became noticeably higher in pitch. "After the invaders were identified and defeated, many concluded that they had come from the Greater Galaxy. ONE continued to study the problem, and he found evidence that indicated otherwise. So he organized an expedition with three ships and went to the Lesser Galaxy to test his conclusions."

"At whose expense?" THREE demanded. Its special sphere of responsibility was governmental finance.

Rok Wllon did not know what solvency the First Councilor had used. Perhaps Supreme itself had financed the expedition. Supreme was not supposed to make decisions like that, but the previous council had voted Gul Darr unlimited solvency when he was investigating the invaders, and technically he was still doing so. Or perhaps Gul Darr had financed the expedition himself, from the profits of his trading firm.

He made his answer safely evasive. "Supreme knows."

"ONE is commendably generous with his own time and resources," SEVEN wheezed.

"Certainly the council did not finance it," THREE said crossly. "It sounds highly irregular to me. If ONE expects to be reimbursed, I shall have some searching questions for him. Never mind. ONE is in the Lesser Galaxy, testing his conclusions. No one questions ONE's judgment or competence. He is quite the most competent individual I know in everything he undertakes. What I want to know is this: what does he want of us that couldn't wait until our regular meeting, and why couldn't he come and tell us about it himself?"

"ONE concluded that the invaders had fled from something," Rok Wllon said. "Now he has discovered what it was."

Again he had their full attention. All visual organs were focused on him, and no one spoke. "He found *death!*" Rok Wllon announced dramatically.

THREE emitted an angry snort. It had the disconcerting mannerism of protruding a pseudopod from almost anywhere on its rotund body—sometimes with eye stalk intact—and pounding the table with it. Rok Wllon waited uneasily. The flabby fold that encircled the Third Councilor's equator was its vocal sack, and when the sack was fully inflated, THREE won every argument, at least temporarily, because no one else could be heard over its strident bellow.

Now the sack was fully inflated. THREE demanded querulously, "What kind of a discovery is that? Is there a place in the universe where one could not find death? Death is everywhere. It is the predestined end of everything. Surely ONE did not need to travel all the way to the Lesser Galaxy to discover this!"

FIVE had leaned forward alertly. The gestures of her multifingered tentacles were the precise, infinitely patient, superbly gentle but irresistibly powerful movements of a great surgeon, which she was. She also was the council's medical authority. She waited politely until THREE had finished. Then she asked, "What do you mean—he found *death?*"

"He found worlds of death," Rok Wllon said. "Worlds where entire populations died."

FIVE said in a hushed, anxious voice, "Plague? An entire world population wiped out by disease? Even if such a thing were possible, it would be extremely unlikely. Individual resistances vary so widely—"

"He said *worlds!*" THREE snapped.

FIVE's vocal amplifier sputtered a medical specialist's horror at the notion of a plague carelessly diffused from world to world. "How regular were their communications?" she demanded.

"As far as ONE could determine, they had none," Rok Wllon said.

"Preposterous! Plague can't spread across space! There must be a vector. Of course there were communications—smuggled goods or refugees from a plague world, secret illegal landings, failure to impose proper quarantine precautions, all criminally careless and disastrous. There *always* are communications!"

"None of the worlds in question had achieved space travel," Rok Wllon said politely. "And ONE did not say the cause of death was plague. He merely said that he found many worlds of death—worlds where all the larger life forms had died. He sent recordings of his findings. Would you care to view one?"

He had one emplaced and ready for projection. Without waiting for an answer, he activated it. The three-dimensional image filled the center of their circular table with a scene that slowly marched past them as the recorder moved along an urban street. It was an unending procession of weathered and crumbling bones, with this hasty recording their only memorial.

When they'd had ample time for a searching look, Rok Wllon turned off the projection.

"*Worlds?*" FIVE demanded.

"At the time of ONE's message, he had examined and recorded more than fifty," Rok Wllon said. "He found no world where even a single individual of any major life form had survived. Would you like to see more?"

"That skeletal structure—most unusual—could you lend me the recording for study?"

"I'll have copies made for you of all of ONE's recordings. Would anyone else like copies?"

There was no response. Rok Wllon continued, "ONE felt that a cause of death that can move from world to world—aided or unaided —also could move from galaxy to galaxy—aided or unaided. He felt that the situation should be investigated thoroughly."

"I concur as long as the investigators maintain proper precautions," FIVE said. "If they were to return to this galaxy infected—"

"ONE has specifically requested that you recommend medical specialists who will know how to prevent such a catastrophe."

FIVE acknowledged the request with a slight bow. "With pleasure. I'll send you a list today. What is it that the council must decide?"

"ONE reminds us that a proper investigation even of such a small galaxy as the lesser one will require a fleet of ships with capable crews and teams of scientists for each ship."

"How many ships?" THREE demanded.

"As many as the council deems appropriate, of course. ONE suggests a thousand."

THREE winced. "Have you consulted Supreme?"

"Of course. Supreme concurs."

"Did Supreme suggest where the solvency is to come from?" THREE demanded caustically.

SIX bent her gaunt form toward Rok Wllon and for an instant raised her light shield to squint perplexedly at him. "I don't understand."

"What is it you don't understand?" Rok Wllon asked politely.

"How can a plague in the Lesser Galaxy possibly affect us unless someone like ONE goes there and catches it?"

"It is well to learn everything we can about a cause of death that has decimated entire worlds," FIVE said. "May we never have a practical use for the knowledge, but the universe contains many mysteries beyond our understanding, both benign and malignant, and I would much prefer our studying this one in the Lesser Galaxy rather than in our own. What does ONE propose to do?"

"At the date of his report, he had found only words that were long dead," Rok Wllon said. "He first must discover whether the cause of those deaths still exists and kills. If it does, then he will attempt to discover ways to combat it. He points out that there may be many peaceful world populations in its path that are doomed if no one comes to their assistance." Rok Wllon paused. "Surely it is our solemn obligation to do everything we can to succor worlds so threatened, even if they are located in another galaxy."

"Resolved," FIVE said.

"Agreed," SEVEN wheezed.

While allowing proper time for further questions or debate, Rok Wllon reviewed the likely vote. TWO, old E-Wusk, automatically supported any measure favored by his friend Gul Darr, and the absent councilor's vote could be entered in support of his own proposal. Rok Wllon's vote, and FIVE's, brought the total to four, one short of a majority, but he felt certain that SEVEN would join them. The gentle, kindly slug was at pains to please everyone—it wore its robes of office, which dried out its ultra-sensitive epidermis, merely because Rok Wllon favored them, and too frequently it seemed to cast its vote according to which faction would be displeased the least. But in this case there was a cause. SEVEN would not place itself on record against saving a single life, let alone a world population.

That made the vote five to three; but a minority of three was entitled to continuing reports and the privilege of reopening debate. It was called a challenging minority, and a challenging minority on a proposal concerning an expedition to another galaxy simply was not tolerable.

Rok Wllon turned his attention to the doubtful councilors. FOUR was the council's nonentity, a faceless life form with a row of sensory humps located across his shoulders. Now the humps were twitching and jerking as he focused and refocused his organs of sight and hearing to follow the discussion. He rarely spoke, and when he did, because his vocal apparatus was located in his stomach near his brain, all of his pronouncements arrived accompanied by echoes, as though from a great distance. His most trivial remarks were delivered with an excessive profundity of overtones, and Rok Wllon considered most of his remarks trivial. SIX's light shield made a blurred enigma of her reactions. Neither FOUR nor SIX would have the courage to oppose FIVE on a medical question without the active leadership of THREE. THREE would not oppose FIVE on medical grounds, but if it could somehow twist the question so that its own specialty, finance, became involved, it would fight bitterly and carry FOUR and SIX with it.

As the other councilors, one after the other, waived their right to further debate, Rok Wllon decided on a bold move. When his turn finally came, he carefully restated ONE's request: a thousand ships, fully equipped with scientific specialists, crewmen, equipment, and supplies as required, for use in investigating causes of death of inhabitants in the Lesser Galaxy and such related activities as ONE deemed necessary.

Then Rok Wllon moved that the council approve the request to whatever extent Supreme was willing to finance the undertaking.

THREE regarded him with surprise. "What if Supreme refuses?"

"Even the initial expenditure would be substantial," Rok Wllon replied gravely, "and not even ONE knows how long that enormous fleet would have to be maintained, or what reinforcements might be required. If the council were to assume responsibility for such an indeterminate amount of solvency, we might at some future date find ourselves in the embarrassing position of having to revise priorities. I don't mean to intrude into your specialism, but—"

"Never mind," THREE said. "You're entirely correct."

"Supreme is in a much better position than any of us to evaluate the dangers ONE describes in terms of the potential cost of an investigation. Having done so, Supreme can supply solvency from its own reserves for whatever portion of ONE's request it considers essential."

THREE beamed its approval. "An excellent suggestion. I concur."

A moment later, Rok Wllon's motion carried by unanimous vote.

Rok Wllon adjourned the meeting, and the councilors moved toward their private transmitters: THREE performing a series of bounces that it controlled with startling accuracy; SEVEN, the uniped, moving in soaring hops; SIX swinging along briskly on her three legs; FOUR, a biped only as far as knees and elbows, where each limb divided into three functioning parts, rocking toward his transmitter in long strides; FIVE flowing toward hers, one tentacle carrying her amplifying disc.

TWO, old E-Wusk, waddled majestically on his multitude of limbs. Suddenly his laughter boomed out. "Ho! Ho! Ho! Any time this council deals with a crisis that quickly, it isn't much of a crisis!"

Rok Wllon, who was a true biped, had to hurry to overtake him. "Could I speak with you privately?" he asked.

The old trader stopped and regarded him irritably. He lived for business, and he knew very well that the Eighth Councilor wouldn't be calling as a customer. "When?" he demanded.

"As soon as possible. It's extremely important."

"Come to my office," E-Wusk said resignedly.

"Within the time unit," Rok Wllon agreed and hurried toward his own transmitter.

He sternly repressed any temptation to relax, to indulge himself in self-congratulations. Admittedly he had performed an all but impossible task and done it brilliantly; but his day's work was only beginning.

3

A councilor's official residence was as covert as his identity, which made it an excellent place for concealing guilty secrets. Rok Wllon's secret was a small room whose walls were lined with full-length mirrors acquired during governmental service on worlds where the inhabitants worshiped at such shrines to vanity.

Before he removed his councilor's robes, he stepped into his mirror room to view himself. It disturbed him that the other councilors, except for SEVEN, refused to wear them. He had argued that robes would vest their deliberations with a badly needed panoply of dignity in addition to reminding them of their considerable responsibilities; and they had replied that an official apparel was ridiculous for an ultra-secret organization that met privately and whose members were known only to themselves.

Traditions, Rok Wllon thought gloomily, meant nothing in these modern times. Formerly a councilor attending a meeting had to undergo an elaborate procedure of identification that had been maintained for centuries to protect the integrity of the council and the personal safety of its members. It was Gul Darr who had suggested that the system be modernized into something more efficient and less unpleasant, and this was done.

Rok Wllon regretted the change. Passage through the long, dimly, red lit tunnel, with its stifling atmosphere and tingling identity probes, had been time-consuming and thoroughly unpleasant, but he had considered it a purefying experience, a sacrifice properly required of one honored with high office. Under the new system, the identity certification of a Councilor of Supreme was no more a distinctive experience than stepping through a public transmitter.

Gul Darr had even gone so far as to propose replacing the vast Hall of Deliberations with a smaller and more comfortable room, since no one used their meeting place except the eight-member council. Fortunately the others felt that tradition should not be disregarded completely.

And of course a councilor's robes could not be worn in public. Rok Wllon removed his regretfully and stepped through his private transmitter to E-Wusk's business office.

The old trader already was settled in his favorite corner in a tangle of limbs, with his clerks crowded around him. They seemed to be simultaneously shouting details of the trading transactions that had accumulated during E-Wusk's absence, and E-Wusk was absorbing all of it and enjoying himself immensely.

A jerk of a telescoping limb directed Rok Wllon to make himself comfortable in whatever style of furniture he fancied among the assorted shapes and styles scattered about the room for the use of customers. A sweep of another limb sent the clerks scurrying away. E-Wusk heaved a sigh and composed himself for whatever boredom Rok Wllon proposed to inflict upon him.

Rok Wllon moved a chair close to E-Wusk and seated himself. "Have you ever heard of a world named Montura?" he asked.

E-Wusk meditated for a moment, felt out a question on his referencer, harrumped twice, and then answered, "No. If I have had dealings with that world, I don't remember it and I have no record of it."

"It's located in the Greater Galaxy," Rok Wllon said.

E-Wusk waved a limb impatiently. "Profitable trade with worlds of the Greater Galaxy is theoretically possible, assuming that the merchandise exchanged has a high enough value per volume unit. But I never have attempted to trade there, and I know of no one who has. I have heard rumors, of course. All my life I have heard rumors of trade with the Greater and the Lesser Galaxies. But never has any reliable person shown me a sample coming from such trade."

"Gul Darr is engaged upon an extremely important mission," Rok Wllon said. "He needs your assistance."

"He has it whenever he asks for it."

"We must establish a trading mission on Montura. It must be done in such a way that the natives of Montura will regard us with esteem. No one is better qualified to achieve this than yourself."

E-Wusk waved the compliment aside. "If Gul Darr requests that I go to the Greater Galaxy, I will do it."

"I request it, since I am acting for Gul Darr in his absence. I have asked Supreme how we can best assist Gul Darr, and Supreme answered that we must establish a trading mission on the world of Montura."

E-Wusk delivered himself of a massive, rippling shrug. "I don't understand how that will assist Gul Darr, but maybe that's because I don't understand what Gul Darr is trying to do. If he needs a trading mission on Montura, I'll take one there. I'll leave tomorrow."

"You should have a staff."

"Of course." E-Wusk shrugged again. "Trading with an unfamiliar world can be complicated, and when the unfamiliar world is in an unfamiliar galaxy, the complications become positively exhilarating. I'll take the best staff available. I'll also take partners to assist me. Gul Ceyh is exceptionally useful in matters of this kind. So are Gul Kahn and Gul Meszk. They will be eager to assist Gul Darr in a time of need."

"A trading mission with three master traders in addition to yourself should achieve instant and overwhelming success," Rok Wllon observed.

"Of course. But what, precisely, are we to do? I have learned from experience that those assisting Gul Darr are tokens in a game for which only he knows the objective. I don't mind being manipulated by Gul Darr, but it is difficult to know what to do when one doesn't know why one is doing it."

"Gul Darr can be overly secretive," Rok Wllon agreed. "In this case, though, Supreme is the player. Supreme says we can best assist Gul Darr by developing friendly relations with the natives of Montura and obtaining their assistance. I asked how this might be done, and Supreme replied that Montura is a trading center. From this I deduce that a trading mission is the best means of establishing friendly relations with the natives."

E-Wusk tossed a trio of limbs impatiently. "Supreme explains even less than Gul Darr does. I can trade anywhere, but I still don't understand how this will help Gul Darr. What sort of assistance does he require from Montura's natives?"

"As you said, Supreme explains less than Gul Darr does."

"I'm willing to help Gul Darr whenever and wherever he requires it, but I'm a trader, and only a trader. I wouldn't know how to go about obtaining assistance in anything but trade."

"Agreed," Rok Wllon said soothingly. "I am entrusting the trading mission to you. Once you have prepared the way, I'll find another individual with different capabilities and experience to obtain the natives' assistance."

"That is satisfactory," E-Wusk said. "Now if you'll excuse me—I must complete a few parcels of unfinished business if I'm to leave tomorrow."

"The matter is not quite that urgent," Rok Wllon said, still being soothing. "I have at least one extended personal errand of my own to perform. You can prepare yourself at leisure and still reach Montura before I do."

"Will Gul Darr come to Montura?"

"That is not known. He is on a long and difficult and perhaps dangerous mission of his own."

"I hope he does," E-Wusk said. "He always knows what to do, and when he's away, no one else seems to. Anyway—" The enormous body shook with laughter. "Ho! Ho! Ho! Adventuring with Gul Darr is rare sport. Very well. I will see the others, and we will prepare to go trading at Montura whenever you are ready for us."

Rok Wllon took leave of him and transmitted to his unofficial residence, a modest apartment where he was known simply as Rok Wllon. Both the council meeting and his interview with E-Wusk had taken less time than he'd anticipated, and he was early. He indulged in a vinegar bath, soaking luxuriously while he savored his success and congratulated himself on his efficiency. Gul Darr should be pleased. So should Supreme, if Supreme possessed such an emotion —sometimes Rok Wllon was uncertain about that.

He knew that Gul Darr possessed far too many emotions, not to mention irrational biases. For one, Gul Darr fervently disliked Rok Wllon. This did not disturb Rok Wllon, who disliked Gul Darr with equal fervor. He considered the First Councilor's personal ethics to be abominable, but he did not hold Gul Darr responsible for that. The First Councilor came from the planet Earth, where all personal ethics were abominable.

But Rok Wllon could not deny Gul Darr's competence, and he was well aware that competence, in crisis situations, had to be placed above personal ethics. He deplored the necessity, but he conceded it.

He felt enormously pleased that Gul Darr, too, was able to put aside his personal feelings when a crisis demanded it. Gul Darr did not like Rok Wllon, but he did respect his abilities, and when a delicate and highly responsible task had to be undertaken, it was to Rok Wllon, the Eighth Councilor, that Gul Darr sent his special emissary. Not to his old friend E-Wusk, the Second Councilor, who was the galaxy's leading authority on trade and commerce and a blundering idiot in everything else, but to Rok Wllon, whom he disliked.

And Rok Wllon had performed in a manner that fully justified the confidence placed in him. Now he had a greater responsibility: to carry out the suggestions Supreme had entrusted to him and to him alone.

But first he had Gul Darr's emissary to deal with.

ursDwad arrived precisely at the agreed time sequence, which pleased Rok Wllon. Whatever else could be said of Gul Darr, he trained his assistants properly. Rok Wllon received ursDwad without ceremony but with the politeness due a colleague's assistant, got him seated, and moved to his desk.

"Gul Darr," he announced with a pompous flourish, "will be pleased to know that I have been able to persuade the council to grant his request. The thousand ships are authorized, complete with crews and scientific personnel."

"Equipment and supplies?" ursDwad asked.

"Naturally those are included. The approval depends upon the amount of solvency Supreme is willing to furnish, but I am confident that Gul Darr will receive everything he has asked for."

"Gul Darr will be most gratified," ursDwad remarked politely.

"Further, I have presented all of his data and recordings to Supreme and asked Supreme for recommendations. This was Gul Darr's suggestion, but I would have done so in any case before presenting his request to the council, as Gul Darr is well aware. Supreme confirms the necessity for a thorough investigation of this—this *Udef*. When I asked for recommendations as to how Gul Darr might be assisted in this investigation, Supreme suggested that we establish a mission on the world of Montura."

ursDwad echoed blankly, "Montura?"

Rok Wllon activated a projection of the triple galactic system. "Here is our Galaxy Prime, which Gul Darr for reasons of his own calls the Milky Way. Here is the Lesser Galaxy, where Gul Darr at this moment is investigating death worlds. And here is the location of Montura, close to the center of what we commonly call the Greater Galaxy."

ursDwad was regarding the projection blankly.

"As Gul Darr is well aware," Rok Wllon continued, "Supreme rarely explains. I asked how Gul Darr's investigation might be assisted, and Supreme said, 'Send a mission to the world of Montura in the Greater Galaxy. Establish friendly relations with the natives and secure their assistance.' Obviously Supreme considers that the natives of Montura are in some way capable of helping Gul Darr. Supreme describes Montura as a trading center, so the most effective method of establishing ourselves there quickly would be with a trading mission. I have asked E-Wusk to take charge of such a mission, and he has agreed. He will take three master traders with him if they are willing."

He paused. ursDwad had abandoned the projection and now was regarding Rok Wllon blankly.

"That should insure the instant success of the trading mission," Rok Wllon went on. "There may be general problems of relations with the Monturan natives that have nothing to do with trade. Gul Darr will be aware that E-Wusk's talents are not the proper type for dealing with such problems. I have suggested to Supreme that Gul Darr's former assistant, Gula Schlu, would be an excellent choice to handle this responsibility, and Supreme has concurred. Do you remember Gula Schlu?"

ursDwad remembered her. His blank expression had changed to one of astonishment.

"I always thought Gula Schlu's abilities were not given their proper scope by Gul Darr. If she is willing, it will be interesting to see how she manages without his restrictive influence." Again he delivered himself of a pompous flourish. "In accordance with Supreme's suggestion, we will establish a mission on Montura. E-Wusk will supervise the trading, and Gula Schlu, if she is willing, will be in charge of all other matters. And because Supreme obviously considers this mission to be of crucial importance to the problem Gul Darr is investigating, I will direct it myself—perhaps in person. And I suggest that when Gul Darr has learned whatever he thinks he needs to know from his explorations in the Lesser Galaxy, he should come to Montura and join my staff."

ursDwad inclined politely. "I will convey your invitation."

"Do you plan to wait and return with Gul Darr's fleet? I will ask Supreme for a solvency authorization today, but assembling it will take some time."

"I will wait and return with it."

"I expect to leave immediately to visit Gula Schlu and invite her assistance. Since you are going to remain here, I will entrust you with the assemblage of Gul Darr's fleet. Come at this time tomorrow, and I will have the solvency clearance. I'll also have some recommendations for scientific personnel."

"Thank you." ursDwad hesitated. Then he asked, "Did you present Gul Darr's message to the council as it was written?"

"I rephrased it in a manner more suitable to the council's mood," Rok Wllon said glibly. "But of course I presented it. Why else would the council approve Gul Darr's request?"

ursDwad departed, and Rok Wllon went immediately to his official residence, where he seated himself at the communications console and opened his personal inditer, the direct communications link to Supreme with which each councilor was equipped. He first requisitioned, in accordance with the council's action, unlimited solvency for the specific purpose of equipping Gul Darr's thousand-ship expedition to the Lesser Galaxy.

Supreme's assent came instantly.

Rok Wllon then drafted a statement, revised it, revised it a second time, and finally, when it seemed satisfactory, indited it: "Concerning your recommended mission to the world of Montura in the Greater Galaxy: I have invited TWO, E-Wusk, to assume personal responsibility for establishing a trading mission on Montura. I will invite Gula Schlu, who previously has acted as an agent of Supreme, to assume responsibility for friendly relations with the Monturan natives. I will head this mission myself. Have you any other suggestions as to actions that might be taken either here or on Montura to ensure its success?"

"Establish friendly relations and secure the assistance of the Monturan natives," Supreme answered.

"Have you any suggestions as to how we should proceed?"

"Montura is a trading center."

Since these were the answers Rok Wllon had obtained previously, it seemed obvious that Supreme had nothing to add; and it seemed even to Rok Wllon that Supreme was providing a rather sketchy basis for a critically important mission. He persisted, "Is there any special product or equipment that would be useful?"

Supreme answered negatively.

"Is there any known individual, or any individual with a specialized skill, who might be useful?"

"A specialist in diseases or conditions of the epidermis might be of assistance," Supreme answered.

Rok Wllon regarded the statement perplexedly. He knew that no clarification would be forthcoming, no matter how he rephrased the question. Supreme almost never explained itself.

He had one final question, but he hesitated to ask it. He'd felt no obligation to retail Gul Darr's silly exaggerations to the council. The other councilors would have ridiculed him for repeating such nonsense.

But Gul Darr had made a statement in a written report, and he felt that Supreme should be informed, if for no other reason than to make it aware of Gul Darr's mental instability. Again he framed his question carefully before he indited it.

"Gul Darr states that the death force he is seeking to identify is a threat to the larger life forms throughout the triple galactic system.

He also says that if it is not neutralized, it may destroy all the intelligent life in the universe. Is this possible?"

Supreme answered at once, and Rok Wllon sat for a long time staring at the single indited word his console had spat into his lap.

"Affirmative."

# 4

On the spaceship's viewing screen, a dead world.

But not necessarily a world without life. Much of this world's beauty had survived, and a full measure of its ugliness, and both were delineated in the impersonal scrutiny of the viewing screen.

The telescopic eye moved in random twitches—glimpsing, focusing briefly, treating grotesque horrors and pastoral serenity with the same hurried impartiality. It zoomed in on an urban street, and before the viewers had fully comprehended the revolting detail spread before them by the screen's relentless magnification, it was showing them velvety rural pastures fenced with neatly pruned hedges from which yellow fruit hung, mouth-watering in the urgency of its bulging ripeness.

The street had been lined with orderly ranks of graceful, spiraling towers that stood serenely amidst parklike clumps of scarlet and purple vegetation. Broad-leaved ground cover half concealed the scattered dead that lay in its colorful embrace, but those who had died on the wide thoroughfare were starkly silhouetted against its polished white surface. These were gathered in massive clusters, as though stricken while on parade, and they lay molding and decaying beneath dark, rippling clouds of bloated crawling and flying insectlike life that clung obscenely to the rotting corpses and gorged.

The eye twitched again and picked out a rural dwelling and its satellite buildings. The inhabitants lay dead on a flowering carpet of heaving, maroon-colored grass, surrounded by strange animals or something like animals. The heaving grass posed its own monstrous question mark. The minds of those watching at first could not grasp the fact that with so much death entwined in it the grass still lived and responded to winds that still blew.

Occasionally the viewing screen framed an awesome beauty that reminded Jan Darzek of another beautiful world, called Earth by its inhabitants, from which he had been too long absent. The differences were haunting similarities; the similarities, tantalizing differences.

The inhabitants of this world—those who lay on their faces—could have been mistaken for humans except when the highest magnification was used, but the farm animals were like nothing on Earth, from any perspective.

Darzek murmured to himself, "But in a world where England is finished and dead, I do not wish to live."

Thus a poet of another time and place and of a severely limited viewpoint. What said the bard whose *world* had ceased to exist? This world's poets, whether they had sung melodiously, or cackled, or hissed, or shouted—this world's poets were silenced forever, and their very language had been crushed out of existence. When the ultimate catastrophe struck a world that had not achieved space travel and an incipient level of space colonization, no one escaped. *No one.* Tedious eons of evolution had achieved this high civilization, piling with infinite patience one sand grain of progress onto another, until there was soaring architecture, and conscientious husbandry, and expertly woven and dyed fabrics that now rotted with their dead owners, and glittering machines that waited in silence for the touch of a hand now lifeless.

The stars had been its destination, and one tiny, primitive artificial satellite remained in orbit, chirping a coded, solar-powered transmission of scientific information that long since had lost its urgency. All of this splendid achievement and bright aspiration had been halted with the suddenness of a thunderclap on the clear, untroubled morning of a promising spring day. There remained only a dead world and a word—the word taken from a plaque on the satellite and tentatively rendered in the familiar alphabet as Balubda: a dead world's name, abstracted from its orbiting tombstone.

It could not be. Any planetary expert, of whatever scientific persuasion, would argue that a local world-wide catastrophe that exterminated all of the larger life forms was impossible, and at Darzek's elbow several of them were. In such an advanced civilization there had to be mines, subterranean constructions, interior rooms, aseptic environments, perhaps even experimental space capsules where someone would survive. Darzek ignored them. There was no sign of any survivor, and for the moment his thoughts were on poetry.

He believed in the universality of poetic feeling. Regardless of what the scientists might think, poets would welcome and embrace the idea of the instantaneous death of a world. They would believe, with the Earth poet, that in a universe where the world of Balubda was finished and dead, they did not wish to live.

The viewer had picked out a high mountain slope, where a scattering of heavily clothed adults and children lay dead in the snow along with a small herd of the strange animals. They were herdsmen and boys, or herdswomen and girls, or herdspeople.

"I'll take those," a voice said.

Darzek nodded his assent. These corpses seemed undamaged by the rampaging insects, probably because of the low temperature at the high altitude. Perhaps the cold also inhibited bacterial activity, though no knowledgeable scientist would have been willing to guess in advance what might inhibit the organisms of a strange world.

The ship's captain snapped an order. Darzek kept his eyes on the viewing screen, knowing that no further instructions from him would be necessary. He was accustomed to having his plans carried out automatically, just as his casual nod of assent was obeyed implicitly. He was Gul Darr, galactic trader of considerable notoriety, importance, and wealth, who frequently was entrusted with sensitive governmental missions. Further, he owned the ship. No one present was aware of the fact that he also was ONE, the First Member of the Council of Supreme, which *was* the galactic government.

Formerly he had been private detective Jan Darzek, citizen of the United States of the planet Earth, but that was long ago and in another galaxy. Besides, on the planet Earth, private detective Jan Darzek was considered officially dead.

The captain threw on maximum magnification and began the touchy job of putting down a transmitter frame by point transmission. When he succeeded, the pathologists aboard would transmit down to the planet, select their specimens for study, and transmit themselves and the specimens to a sealed laboratory compartment already prepared for them. There, in conditions of meticulous sterility and stringent quarantine, they would attempt to determine the cause of death. Whether or not they succeeded, they probably were doomed to a lengthy confinement. No risk could be taken of carrying a plague of this virulence to another world—or another galaxy.

The pathologists seemed cheerfully indifferent to the danger implicit in the removal of specimens from a death world. There were five of them, experienced professionals from as many worlds, and they brilliantly epitomized a galaxy's diversity of life forms and talents. They were making jokes at the captain's expense because he had miscalculated his first point transmission and smashed a transmitter frame, and they expressed their glee with waving tentacles, or modulating pseudopods, or flapping ears, or curling noses, or ruffled scales. The captain, himself a multilimbed Kaglogg, was good-naturedly preparing for his second attempt.

There was nothing further for Darzek to do, and he refused on principle to encumber an expert with unneeded assistance. He turned, signaled with a jerk of his head, and stepped through the interior communications transmitter to his own compartment. URS-Gworl, who in the absence of URSDwad served as his chief assistant, turned at once and followed him. He had been watching the screen intently and could not have seen Darzek's signal unless he possessed organs of vision in his protruding spinal column. As far as Darzek knew he didn't, but with a random selection of galactic life forms, anything was possible.

Darzek seated himself in an easy chair of his own design, waved URSGworl to another, and leaned back to contemplate a large model of the triple galactic system that filled the center of the compartment. He had begun the search with two questions: *how* and *why*.

This world of Balubda would be the hundred and forty-third they had examined and the first where they had found victims in a condition that made autopsies feasible. Even now Darzek had no idea how wide a swath the Unidentified Death Force had cut through this Small Magellanic Cloud, called the Lesser Galaxy by his colleagues. Their search had been a straight-line pursuit, and they traveled in leaps and inspected only those habitable worlds near their base course.

They found no signs of warfare, either chemical or nuclear; no indication of the use of weapons of any kind; no destruction except to the living; no evidence of natural catastrophe. As they moved along their line of search they traced the dead through a spectrum of stages from crumbling bones to corpses in ever lessening degrees of decomposition.

Two questions remained: *how* and *why*.

Darzek said suddenly, "What about phychic violence?"

URSGworl stared at him. "A psychic weapon? But that's—"

"Nothing," Darzek said firmly, "is impossible. Are the teams ready? I want to go the moment the scientists have finished."

URSGworl went to inspect the teams, leaving Darzek to his meditations.

He had no expectations concerning this, their first complete scientific study of the victims. He was incapable of believing that a moving catastrophe of such magnitude could have its cause delineated by anything as simple as a pathologist's scalpel. The destroyed worlds must number in the thousands.

Had it been done—was it being done—deliberately? He asked himself what rapacious conqueror's blood lust would require that many worlds to satiate it. There were no signs of looting, no indications of a terrible victory horribly exploited. The dead lay where they had fallen, their bodies molested only by vermin. Their valuables were untouched; their abandoned dwellings and buildings, as far as a casual search could determine, were undisturbed.

Darzek postulated a technologically advanced but morally degenerate life form on a rampage, destroying one world population after another from space with some kind of death ray, unaffected by the horrors it created because it struck from afar and left without a backward glance in search of its next victim. But it seemed to him that even this kind of conqueror would return eventually, either to loot the planet or to claim it as his own. Darzek failed utterly in his attempt to posit a villain who would wreak this measure of merciless destruction for no reason but the pleasure he derived from it.

"How?" he asked himself. "And why?"

A signal light flashed. URSGworl's flat voice announced, "There is extensive brain damage in all the specimens. They found no indication of disease. They don't think disease could have caused the brain damage, but they won't certify that. Of course they refuse to comment on anything but the medical evidence."

"It's a wise expert that restricts his expert opinions to matters he's expert in," Darzek observed. "Have they got as much as they think they'll get? Then let's go down."

First they searched an urban area, carrying their humming recorders along streets and through buildings, pausing to touch or investigate closely only items of unusual interest. Darzak found no indication anywhere of anything but panicky flight. An entire population had fled from buildings to die in the open. Mothers had snatched up young children, and because of that brief delay, mothers with young children lay nearest the exits. There had been no attempt to save property. There had been no looting, and only vermin had touched the bodies after they fell.

There was no clue anywhere as to what they had been fleeing from.

The teams scattered for wide-ranging investigations all across the day side of the planet. Then, after passing through three decontamination chambers and discarding a layer of protective clothing in each, they returned to their compartments. The scientists considered these precautions sufficient for the search teams. They had merely moved among the dead; they hadn't dissected them.

Darzek retired to his own compartment to face a perilous decision. If he pursued this death force with reasonable caution, he might never come close enough to learn what he had to know. If he pursued it energetically, he would be in grave danger of overtaking it. The problem was to come close enough to observe and study without joining the victims. Only in that way could they hope to discover a means of combating it.

URSGworl burst in on him, eyes staring, face pink with excitement. "The death force!" he gasped.

Darzek bounded through the transmitter. In the control room, the duty watch was gathered about the navigational screens gazing awesomely at a myriad of pinpoints that seemed to be converging on them.

"A fleet of ships," Darzek said instantly. "An enormous fleet. No wonder it cuts a wide swath."

He sounded the general alarm and alerted his other ship, setting both captains to plotting a complicated transmission escape course. He asked the communications technicians to prepare message beacons to warn URSDwad and, eventually, their own galaxy. The entire Milky Way Galaxy did not possess such a thing as a space warship, so they had no weapon except flight, and no armament except fervent prayers to any receptive gods that the converging fleet lacked the technology to track them through an intricate series of transmitting leaps.

Moments before they made their first leap, a message arrived. It was from URSDwad. In his haste to overtake them he had overshot their position and had to return. The ships converging on them were Darzek's own thousand-ship fleet.

While Darzek's captain, now promoted to grand admiral, was briefing the newly arrived captains and working out search formations, and his scientists were organizing schools so their newly arrived colleagues could review the little that had been learned and the much that they needed to know, Darzek took URSDwad to his compartment for a complete report.

He listened in silence until URSDwad mentioned the world of Montura. "Is it the capital of the Greater Galaxy?" he asked.

"Supreme described it as a trading center. I tried to learn something about it, but the public referencers on Primores don't list it, and when I applied directly to Supreme, the answer was, 'A trading center of the Greater Galaxy.'"

"No doubt it's an important communications center. What does Rok Wllon propose to do about it?"

"He has asked E-Wusk to take charge of a trading mission to

Montura. And because there might be problems that have nothing to do with trade, he intends to invite Gula Schlu to join E-Wusk."

Darzek stared at him. Then he burst into laughter. "She's been home long enough to become thoroughly bored. She just might do it."

URsDwad hesitated and then added apologetically, "Rok Wllon thought her abilities were not given their proper scope in your service."

Darzek laughed again. "Wait until he finds out what scope her activities will have in his service! I'm sorry I won't be there to see it!"

"Rok Wllon intends to go to Montura himself and supervise E-Wusk and Gula Schlu and any other specialists Supreme might recommend. He has invited you to come to Montura and join his staff when you have completed your explorations."

"The conceited ass! But what the devil has Montura to do with our Udef, if anything? My inclination is to study a thing where it is, not where it isn't. I think we'll save Montura as a last resort."

Darzek approved the search formation the captains recommended, and they translated it into navigational instructions: a line of search, with 800 ships; a reserve line, with 150; and—far in the rear—a base line of 50 widespread ships that would serve as rear guard, receive and file reports from all ships of the fleet, and in the event of overwhelming catastrophe be distant enough to survive and preserve the expedition's records. The ships would rotate between the three lines in order to give crews and scientists some respite from the tension that would increase steadily as they overtook the Udef.

Then came the tedious process of moving ships into position, testing communications, jockeying to establish the maximum practical distance between ships. Finally all was ready. Darzek's captain announced, "First transmission!"

The throb was barely perceptible. Darzek recorded the leap on his model of the Lesser Galaxy, moving their position ahead by a pinprick. They came out of transmission with another throb, and the captain's voice sounded again. "We have an inhabited planet on the screen." He paused and then corrected himself. "It *was* inhabited."

A thousand ships could not begin to explore a galaxy adequately; the 800 ships of Darzek's line of search did not even span the swath of destruction. The captains had laid out a zigzag course designed to probe its outer dimensions, and as a result they failed to gain on the Udef. The ill-fated inhabitants of the world of Balubda remained the most recently murdered that they had found.

Darzek's tediously compiled record of destroyed worlds suddenly acquired a thousand additions in a single day—highly urbanized and industrialized civilizations, worlds of pastoral nomads, agricultural worlds, even worlds where no intelligent life form had gained ascendancy. All were victims of identical orgies of slaughter.

They finished a leg of their zigzag course, pivoted, and started off anew. Immediately there was a startling discovery: vandalism. A world of small agricultural communities lay devastated as though by a rampaging army. Darzek led a ground search himself, pondering the fact that this society's apparently low-grade technology had produced a magnificent cloth of spun glass—of which every windowpane in the village had been punched to shreds—and a system of broadcast electrical power that was still functioning. Interiors and exteriors of buildings were smashed; fragments of broken household goods lay in the streets where they had been flung. Items of obvious value had been hurled about with the same careless indifference accorded worthless trivia. It made no sense until the pathologists filed their reports.

Then Darzek understood: these victims were physiologically much less susceptible than other life forms they had autopsied. The death force worked slowly enough on their brains so that they had time to go insane before they died. In their tormented delirium they ravished their own property until they dropped dead.

They found a blood world. Darzek had seen blood in many colors, but on this particular world its vivid redness, even when dried, seemed singularly apt. Here most of the victims had died inside, and the interiors of their dwellings were drenched with blood. It seemed to Darzek that no horde of rampaging barbarians had ever indulged a blood lust so viciously, but the pathologists quickly exorcised that fantasy.

This life form wore its brain in a tough membrane sack, a near evolutionary goof probably made necessary by the fact that the brain continued to grow throughout the creature's life. A nonflexible brain case, such as a skull, would have resulted in death at an early age or an overbalancing cranial edifice that would have immobilized the creature. Evolution's answer had been the expandable membrane, and it had worked—until the Udef struck. These brains had literally exploded, ripping the membrane case asunder and splattering the surroundings with blood and cellular matter.

And still they did not gain on the Udef. Darzek discarded the zigzag course in favor of a straight-line search, and he labored to keep

his inventory up to date as from the entire front of their advance came reports of new horrors.
On world after world after world.

They measured their progress in the freshness of the dead they encountered, but this provided a fantastically complex and uncertain method of calculation. Putrefaction worked at different rates on different worlds, with fluctuations affected by a multitude of factors, including the types of microorganisms and the drastic variations in the cellular structures they fed on. But Darzek felt confident that they were coming closer. Definitely, they were coming much closer.

He had long since lost track of time. He slept when tired, and then only in fitful naps while data were being compiled, and his dreams were of freshly dead civilizations: of walled and castellated cities defenseless against a menace from above; of graceful villas and crystal-windowed palaces from which the inhabitants had fled to die in gardens of iridescent, hauntingly perfumed blooms; of dead piled high among massive, neolithiclike structures of piled rock; of lonely dead scattered about fragile, solitary wind-swept farmhouses. When the significant discovery finally happened, he had no personal awareness of whether it had taken months to achieve, or weeks, or only days.

They had completed another transmitting leap, and his own ship jockeyed toward the nearest habitable world. As the viewer began its searching telescopic probe, those watching uttered a unison cry of amazement.

The nearest habitable world was inhabited.

Its flourishing civilization was still flourishing. Its inhabitants went methodically about their business of living; their machines functioned; their world was untouched.

While the scientists watched and marveled, Darzek began to monitor reports from ships nearby. These constituted a tedious inventory of uninhabited worlds until a ship broke in excitedly to report another intact civilization. It was dictating a description, and Darzek was meditating the problem of whether they should backtrack in search of the Udef or remain there and let it overtake them, when the voice transmission became a shattering scream that went on, and on, until it lapsed into a silence more wracked with torment than the sound.

Before the scream had ended, Darzek sent out the prearranged order that scattered the fleet. Then he ordered his own ship to investigate. They found a silent ship orbiting a world so newly dead that it seemed to be still dying. The victims lay in the open about their dome-shaped conclaves, their liquid life substance still oozing from body orifices.

Everyone aboard the ship was dead. Several crew members had leaped into space in a vain effort to flee their tormentor, and their exploded bodies slowly orbited the orbiting ship. From his own ship, Darzek formed an emergency crew to operate the death ship. He placed half of his scientific contingent aboard and told it to study the ship and its dead crew meticulously and compile every scrap of information it could. Then he ordered the death ship to the base line.

Next he summoned ten of his ships and told each captain to find himself a planet with an intact civilization and place his ship in orbit at the extreme distance from which his viewer could effectively penetrate cloud cover. Darzek returned his own ship to the untouched world already discovered and did the same.

The attacked ship had been in close orbit, and he was gambling that a ship in remote orbit would be overlooked by the Udef, at least some of the time. Whatever the risk, so desperate was the need for the evidence of trained eyewitnesses that he had to take it.

They watched and waited.

The face of a doomed world filled their viewing screens, and Darzek's urge to do something, to rescue someone, was so fierce that he felt physical pain. To put down a transmitter frame, to quickly load his ship with passengers . . . no time to persuade them, of course, couldn't communicate anyway, have to kidnap them, but at least there would be a few survivors . . . assuming that Darzek's ship survived. It was a world of magnificent builders. The towers, even when seen from space, were breath-taking. If they acted at once, perhaps—

But would the handful their ship could accommodate want to be saved? *In a world where England is finished and dead, I do not wish to live.* They would have to reshape their lives, and their first task would be to somehow cope with a world of corpses. *Think,* Darzek rasped at himself. What can be done to save a world, or any part of it, with the Udef about to strike?

The captain said hoarsely, "It's here!" The off-duty watches sprang to their posts. A battery of viewers had been set up, some fixed on preselected targets while others supplied random glimpses of a world in its death throes. From every habitation the populace was erupting, limbs threshing in agony, to collapse in widening puddles of ooze. Darzek experienced instantaneous revulsion and had to force himself to continue to watch until the last inhabitant they could find alive performed a final, agonized twitch and expired.

Then he wrenched himself from the viewing screens, too stunned and horrified to think. Not until the scientists began their discussion did he realize that he had seen nothing at all.

"What was it?" he demanded.

No one answered.

Instruments and observers had maintained a constant surveillance of a world and its surrounding space. Readings and impressions were compared. Nowhere in this solar system had there been a trace of any invader except themselves, and yet a civilization had been murdered before their eyes and instruments.

A world had died.

Nothing had killed it.

Dumbly they sat around a conference table with the full record spread before them, and they watched, in projected recordings, the civilization die a second time. Finally Darzek asked, "Is it possible that the Udef could be invisible to us?"

"To us, yes," a scientist answered grimly. "But not to our instruments."

"If there's a limit to our sensory capacities, there's also a limit to the sensory capacities of your instruments," Darzek retorted.

They rebuilt the instruments. They observed, rebuilt again, observed, rebuilt. They watched the death agonies of twenty more worlds, losing three more crews in the process, and the evidence of their senses and of their instruments remained the same.

Twenty more worlds had died.

Nothing did it.

In one respect they had advanced their knowledge. Darzek now knew that it was incorrect to say that the entire populations of these worlds died simultaneously. Even individuals that were struck at the same time died at varying rates, and the Udef followed definite, traceable, highly varied patterns. Sometimes it moved in a broad spiral that gradually enveloped the entire planet, but more often it took a continent at a time. On the twenty-one worlds, fully a dozen distinctive movements could be traced through the death agonies of the victims.

ursDwad observed thoughtfully, "Perhaps they know on Montura."

"If Rok Wllon finds anything at all that could possibly be of use to us, he'll let us know," Darzek said. "He won't bother with a courier —he'll bring it himself so he can gloat about how brilliant he's been."

"You could send me to Montura," URsDwad said. "Supreme did say that the natives of Montura could help us."

"If it comes to that, we'll go together," Darzek said. "But only as a last resort. First we'll make every effort to find the answer here."

They designed and built more instruments, they adjusted and readjusted them, they invented tests and conducted experiments with the death throes of one civilization after another in the background, they lost seven more crews, and they detected nothing at all.

The worlds died.

Nothing did it.

## 5

Miss Effie Schlupe, Gula Schlu to her galactic colleagues, had been rewarded with a small governmental sinecure when she retired to Earth. She was appointed director of the secret certification study group that the galactic government maintained there. The group needed no direction. The studying was done by experienced, expertly disguised aliens, who also wrote the group's reports. Miss Schlupe's contribution was her annual recommendation that Earth be certified eligible for membership in the Galactic Synthesis, which was ignored.

Now it was 1995, and she had celebrated her seventieth birthday in the same bored fashion that made her sixty-ninth birthday unmemorable. She sat alone in her health food store, rocking, knitting, and looking forward to her five-thirty closing time, when she would lock her front door and unlock her alley door. Her evening customers, who bought her illegal beers and wines, were far more congenial than those who called during regular business hours. She was tempted to lock her front door permanently, but her back-door activities needed some kind of cover, and it amused her to be dispensing illegal alcoholic beverages under the aegis of a health food store.

This day was as uneventful as any other. Old Mr. Forlanni stopped by for his daily cocktail of blended prune, papaya, and cucumber juices. Mr. Forlanni declared, to anyone willing to listen, that Miss Schlupe's prune, papaya, and cucumber cocktail was the best to be had in the entire Greater New York area. "It would even make a woman feel like a new man," he would say, chuckling.

But the testimonial of an elderly man addicted to a daily prune, papaya, and cucumber juice cocktail was not one likely to bring a rush of business. Miss Schlupe kept to herself the fact that the chief invigorating ingredient in that monotonous slush of vitamins was the generous shot of hard cider with which she surreptitiously laced every serving.

After Mr. Forlanni departed, smacking his lips, young Mrs. Jadfro stopped in to shop for a birthday present for her sister. Mrs. Jadfro was a health food fanatic; her sister was not. Their annual exchange of birthday gifts represented a continuing campaign of attrition in which Mrs. Jadfro attempted to convert her sister to the doctrine of sanity in eating, and her sister tried to corrupt Mrs. Jadfro with her own degenerate brand of hedonism—if it tastes good, it's good for you. This year, after much soul-searching contemplation, Mrs. Jadfro decided that the alfalfa tea represented too drastic a step toward sanity for her sister, and she selected a blend of mints and rose hips instead.

Then came little Sandra Halmer, age four. Sandra was not so much a customer as a charity case. Miss Schlupe had unwisely stocked some health food candy that did not sell. Even as a gift, no one wanted more than one sampling of a Vita-Carob-Sesame-Honey-Energy-Drop. She tried giving pieces to the children of customers, but it resulted only in her having her floor spattered with secretly discarded Vita-Carob-Sesame-Honey-Energy-Drops. No one would eat them except little Sandra. Miss Schlupe was tempted to present her with the entire stock and have done with it, but she feared that the resultant digestive cataclysm might get her sued. Also, she enjoyed watching people enjoy themselves. Sandra was restricted to a daily ration of one Vita-Carob-Sesame-Honey-Energy-Drop, which she sucked ecstatically.

A shadow fell across the window while Sandra was consuming the last of her energy drop. A face peered in at Miss Schlupe. She calmly returned the stare, and the stranger shifted his gaze to the tidy boxes of herb teas, and the rows of vitamin phials and bottles of juice extracts with which Miss Schlupe's small display window was ornamented.

But only for a moment. The stranger moved on, which in no way surprised Miss Schlupe. She maintained a window display because she had to do something with the vacant space behind the front window, but she didn't expect it to attract customers. Visiting a health food store, she thought, was not the result of visual stimulation, but of gastronomic martyrdom.

Fifteen minutes later, the same shadow returned. Miss Schlupe was occupied with her third cash customer of the day, a Mrs. Conling, who for reasons best known to herself had decided to double her husband's vitamin $B_1$ and $E_3$ intakes. Again the stranger contemplated the window arrangement briefly and then moved on.

Mrs. Conling left. A few minutes later the stranger's face was back at the window. This time he opened the door and came inside.

It now was obvious to Miss Schlupe that he had been waiting until he could confront her without a witness. She greeted him with a welcoming smile. Already she had sent three would-be holdup men to the hospital and routed a fourth in such panic that he accidentally shot himself on the way out the door. She was the galaxy's only qualified proponent and practitioner of a system of self-defense she called *juriptzu,* which was her own special blend of judo and mayhem. If the stranger's objective was her day's receipts, which thus far totaled $5.63, she would welcome the diversion.

While he looked about him, evidently satisfying himself that she was alone, she studied him. He was an entirely ordinary-looking middle-aged fat man, probably too heavy for her to flip without breaking a display case. His clothing looked new but not especially distinctive. The most noticeable thing about his facial expression was his total lack of one. His face looked wooden; perhaps he meant to give an impression of innocence.

Finally he turned to her. "Good afternoon, Gula Schlu," he said politely.

Miss Schlupe dropped her knitting. No one on Earth, not even the three alien members of her certification group, knew that this had been her name in galactic society. "Who are you?" she exclaimed.

Her caller seemed pleased. "Don't you recognize me, Gula Schlu?"

"Smith!" she exclaimed. "Rok Wllon! You got yourself a new disguise!"

The face took on expression and formed a synthetic smile, a notable achievement for the artificial epidermis of a wholly unhuman shape.

"Indeed, yes. How do you like it?"

"Much better than the old one. That disguise made you look like a dead fish. This one is more like a live wart hog. Is it really you?"

It was indeed the alien calling himself Smith who on a fateful day years before had paid Jan Darzek a million dollars for unspecified services. When Miss Schlupe had last seen him, he had become a member of the Council of Supreme and supervisor of all the certification study groups in the galaxy. Technically he had been her superior for years, but she hadn't heard from him since she left Primores.

"What are you doing here?" she demanded. "A member of the Council of Supreme shouldn't be slumming on Earth."

He hushed her. Even on Earth, where only Miss Schlupe and the three aliens had any notion of what it signified, a councilor did not want his status mentioned aloud.

"Gul Darr has a critically important job for you," he said.

"Just a moment."

She hung her *CLOSED—BACK SOON* sign in the front door and locked it. Then she led Rok Wllon to her back room and waved him to a chair.

She remained standing and regarded him with suspicion. She did not like the Eighth Councilor. She'd always resented his smug moral superiority, and she suspected that he could be as devious as anyone when he thought he could get away with it. With his synthetic face he could have got away with a great deal if she hadn't known his fatal weakness. He could not tell a direct lie.

She said, "Did Mr. Darzek send a letter?"

"No, but—"

"Did he specifically ask for me?"

"Well, no. He is in another galaxy. Supreme asked for you."

"That transistor-clogged brain doesn't know I exist."

"But it does!"

"Did Supreme ask for me by name?"

"Well, no. I suggested you, and Supreme concurred."

Miss Schlupe slowly backed into a chair and sat down. "Supreme," she announced firmly, "is nothing but a muddled super-adding machine trying to make intelligent beings behave like numbers. I hope you haven't been contributing a muddle of your own to this."

"I have only come to convey Supreme's invitation," Rok Wllon said, wounded dignity ringing in every word.

"What's Mr. Darzek doing?"

"He's on an important mission."

"To another galaxy, you said. What does this job I'm offered have to do with his mission?"

"Supreme says it is critical to it."

"Does Mr. Darzek know you're offering the job to me?"

"Of course. I sent word to him with URsDwad."

"Exactly what is Mr. Darzek's important mission?"

"He is attempting to determine the cause of death of world populations in the Lesser Galaxy."

"Where is that?"

"You call it the Small Magellanic Cloud."

"I don't believe a word of it. You make it sound as if Mr. Darzek is running a bureau of vital statistics. Determine the cause of death— phooey! That isn't like Mr. Darzek at all."

"Gul Darr said," Rok Wllon announced, keeping his pseudo eyes fixed on hers, "that if we are unable to solve the problem, all the intelligent life in the universe will be exterminated."

"*That* sounds like him!"

"Supreme has concurred. And I have recordings to show you."

"All right. I'll see your recordings. For weeks the headlines have been looking like last month's newspaper, which may mean that I'm ready for another fling at galactic intrigue. Tell me about this critically important job."

Rok Wllon drew himself up pompously. "There's a world called Montura."

"Never heard of it. Where is it?"

Rok Wllon's description of the world of Montura made no impression on Miss Schlupe, but E-Wusk referred to their destination as Montura Mart, and *that* sounded interesting.

She met E-Wusk on a strange world called Ffladon. It would have been the gateway to the galaxy if she had been coming instead of going. Because it was a world without transmitters, its transfer stations were literally that—orbiting stations where goods and passengers arriving from space had to transfer to chemical rockets for the descent to the planet.

"They say it's against their religion to travel without passing over the good earth that their God gave to them," E-Wusk remarked sourly. "That explains why they won't use transmitters on the surface, but why in the name of their God or anyone else's won't they use them between the plant and the transfer stations?"

"They insist on passing through the good air their God gave them," Miss Schlupe suggested.

Rok Wllon had remained on Earth, pursuing some mysterious mission of his own, and after her solitary journey to the edge of the galaxy she had greeted E-Wusk with more pleasure than she'd thought possible. Any familiar face, even a large, distinguishedly ugly one that beamed at her out of an untidy tangle of telescoping limbs, seemed a thing of beauty.

He greeted her with the same measure of affection and asked about Gul Darr, which surprised her. E-Wusk should have been in regular contact with Darzek—they both were members of the Council of Supreme—while she hadn't seen him for years.

"He's been absent from recent council meetings," E-Wusk said. "He is sorely missed."

"Rok Wllon says he's on a dangerous mission to the Lesser Galaxy," Miss Schlupe said.

"So he told the council." E-Wusk flapped a cluster of limbs and uttered his booming laugh. "But of course. All of Gul Darr's missions are dangerous. Otherwise, he would not undertake them. Gul Darr thrives on danger."

"He'll thrive on it once too often," Miss Schlupe said darkly.

E-Wusk laughed again. "Gul Darr's life is dedicated to the quest of avoiding death by old age. Oh, ho! Ho! He is doomed to failure. Gul Darr is indestructible. Does he plan to join us on Montura?"

"I have no idea. All I know about this business is what Rok Wllon condescended to tell me. Our mission is critically important. All the intelligent life in the universe is threatened. Supreme says Gul Darr can be assisted by cozying up to the natives of this world called Montura. What do you know?"

E-Wusk was regarding her perplexedly. "All the intelligent life —did Rok Wllon really say that?"

"He said Gul Darr said that. Did you see those recordings Gul Darr took? A lot of intelligent life has been wiped out already."

"Rok Wllon did not tell the council that Gul Darr said that."

"He never tells more than suits his purpose," Miss Schlupe said. "He cannot tell a lie, but he can be exceedingly stingy with the truth. What sort of place is Montura?"

E-Wusk's shrug was a massive heave of his entangled body. "I know little about it. The traders there, not being of our galaxy, will be uncivilized and require constant watching, but I anticipate no problems. Trade is trade, wherever it is practiced. I have sent Gul Ceyh and Gul Kahn and Gul Meszk on ahead. They should be well established by the time we arrive."

"What are the natives like?"

"The natives of Montura? I have no information about that. They must be a shrewd species to be able to make their world such an important trading center. I'm told that traders from hundreds and hundreds of worlds center their businesses there."

"What I can't understand is how all those worlds get along without a galactic government."

E-Wusk shrugged again. "Obviously they have trading agreements and a means of enforcing them. Violations probably mean banishment from the mart, and for a trader or a world dependent on trade, that's the worst fate imaginable. The only legitimate functions of civilized government are the regularization of trade and the exchange of solvency, and the mart will provide those."

"But these worlds aren't civilized," Miss Schlupe pointed out impishly.

"Probably they are becoming civilized. Trade has a civilizing effect on worlds." He rubbed his limbs together in pairs. "A vast new market like this is a tremendous challenge. A right guess can net a fortune. A wrong guess can be catastrophic. But what a fascinating challenge it is!"

"How do they handle solvency exchanges?"

"They don't," E-Wusk said gloomily. "That's the problem with doing business with the uncivilized. Every transaction is by barter. It results in some exceedingly complicated exchanges, sometimes involving large numbers of traders. It also means that successful trading requires two correct guesses: what will be in demand on Montura, and what to bring back from Montura that can be profitably traded in this galaxy. Of course in our initial contacts we will merely study the mart and test demand with samples. But I'm forgetting. Rok Wllon said you would not concern yourself with trade."

"Right. While you make a big splash in the trading community, I'm supposed to butter up the natives and win their cooperation. What that amounts to is keeping you traders from messing up a promising friendship by unscrupulously fleecing those innocent, uncivilized Monturans."

E-Wusk quivered with laughter.

"Actually, I haven't the faintest idea of what I'm supposed to do," Miss Schlupe said. "No doubt it'll become perfectly clear when we reach Montura. I hope. Pack up your samples, and let's get started."

## 6

At first glance, the world of Montura reminded Miss Schlupe of the planet Saturn. It had rings.

The rings were artificial satellites, huge orbiting bins where goods brought to Montura Mart could be stored until traded. E-Wusk was impressed. Miss Schlupe thought it no more than an ingenious exercise in technological obsolescence.

"Not so!" E-Wusk said. "What would be true of a world in our galaxy doesn't apply to Montura. We have a galactic government and excellent communications. If I want a shipload of a certain kind of grain from a certain world, I can send a message and buy it. Or I can ask for bids and make counteroffers or negotiate. Once I buy it, I have, by the law of trade, three terms in which to arrange shipment. I can resell the grain—including whatever time remains of those three terms—and storage or shipment becomes the new owner's responsibility. Or I can order the grain shipped to any world that might constitute a market, either to complete a prearranged trade or on speculation. It would be most uneconomical to take goods to one centrally located world, and sell or trade them to someone who must then take them somewhere else. The cost of transport would be prohibitive.

"But in this galaxy, which has no central government, no solvency standard for monetary measurement, and no galaxy-wide enforceable law of trade, a central place to bring goods and trade them for something else becomes highly practical. Probably it's a necessity."

Miss Schlupe remained skeptical. "I thought the satellites would be survivors of a time when chemical rockets were still in use. Why have them, except to save the time and trouble and expense of moving everything down to the planet and then moving it back to space again?"

"Chemical rockets *are* still in use," E-Wusk said. "Look—there goes one. So they don't have space-to-surface transmitters. Even if they did, the satellites still would save them time and effort and expense. It's much easier to shift freight compartments in space than under Montura's gravity standard, whatever that is."

They parked their ship in a berth at a large transfer station and rode a chemical shuttle rocket down to the planet. Seen from space, Montura was a beautiful world—but most worlds were beautiful when distance blurred their blemishes. As they slanted in for a landing, the beauty faded into wasteland and became an enormous plateau that was pitted and eroded like a decaying lunar landscape. Montura Mart lay in a wide, barren valley that bisected the edge of the plateau. Turning her head to keep it in view as they roared in, Miss Schlupe saw a building the size of a city. A vast, domed structure stood at the center, and protruding from it were a multiplicity of long, multistoried wings, each of them terminating in a pair of lofty, circular towers. The landing field surrounded the mart, and several monstrous freighters were parked there, but most of the ships were sleek shuttle craft like the one they arrived in, built for hauling passengers and light freight between the mart and the satellites.

They staggered forth with a throng of fellow passengers—traders all, Miss Schlupe assumed—and so inured was she to the variety of life forms in her own galaxy that even the more monstrous of these did not seem worth a second glance. In time the most active curiosity could be overwhelmed and stultified by nature's unrestrained virtuosity.

Gul Ceyh was waiting for them. His eyesight was reputed to be faulty—he had no eyes in his head, but each of his eleven arms terminated in an eye instead of a hand—but he recognized Miss Schlupe instantly and greeted her like the old acquaintance she was. He made the necessary arrangements about their luggage and found places for them in a crawling ground conveyance that eventually deposited them at one of the pairs of towers.

"This is the twelfth segment," Gul Ceyh said as he escorted them inside. "The mart is divided into fifty parts, each with a wing and towers. They're all identical, and you'll certainly get lost if you forget your number. Twelve is *kuror* in the most common mart language. Twelfth segment is *kurog twanlaft*."

The traders had taken a complete floor at the top of one of the towers. When E-Wusk discovered that the only access to it was by transmitter from the lobby on the ground floor, he sputtered indignantly.

"Agreed," Miss Schlupe said. "If the clods have transmitters, why make us take that stupid ride down from the transfer stations?

Maybe they have a part-time god that lets them use transmitters on the surface only."

"The members of the gesardl are said to have space-to-surface transmitters," Gul Ceyh said gloomily. "We commoners have to use rockets."

They waited in line to use the lobby transmitter, just as one waited for an elevator on Earth. Finally their turn came, and they stepped through to their floor. They emerged in a large circular room without windows. Bands of light crisscrossed the ceiling, and much of the floor was honeycombed with variously sized waist-high cubicles.

"This," Gul Ceyh announced pompously, "is the Prime Common. We took the name Prime from our Galaxy Prime—though of course no one here calls our galaxy that. But we have to identify ourselves. Most traders use the names of their worlds."

"What are those things?" Miss Schlupe asked, indicating the cubicles.

"The common is a workroom. An office. All of the larger trading establishments have one. The cubicles are for the traders and undertraders to work in."

Eleven enormous, self-contained apartments opened off the common, each with its own lounge that featured a dramatic expanse of curving windows overlooking what would have been spectacular vistas if the surrounding country had offered anything except an utterly barren landscape. Miss Schlupe caught only one glimpse of color as she moved from apartment to apartment—a patch of purple ornamenting a distant hilltop. The strange vegetation seemed to make the surrounding barrenness more depressing. Gul Ceyh offered her a room in the apartment the traders were sharing or her choice among the unoccupied apartments. She finally selected an apartment with windows overlooking the mart.

She wandered about trying the doors, which shot back into the wall at a touch, and marveling at the strangely shaped lavatory furnishings that apparently were designed to meet the functional requirements of every conceivable life form. The furnishings of another small room were even more bewildering and only vaguely identifiable as kitchen equipment. She would have to have lessons before she touched anything. The walls, which looked like neither wood nor metal, gave forth solid thuds when she thumped on them.

The furnishings were both spartan and impoverished: a few rolled-up mats, a few hassocklike stools. Probably the tenants were expected to supply their own, and these had been left behind by their predecessors. She selected one of the apartment's rooms for herself.

By then her luggage had arrived, and she piled it in one corner, unrolled a sleeping mat, and tried, without success, to call the place home.

She found the traders in one of the common room's larger cubicles, moodily gathered about an upholstered hump that could have been intended as a conference table. Gul Meszk and Gul Kahn, the other master traders E-Wusk had sent on ahead of him, had joined E-Wusk and Gul Ceyh. They greeted Miss Schlupe and moved a hassock into position for her.

"Why the gloom?" she asked brightly. "Don't tell me you expert traders have lost your shirts already!"

The common English expression emerged strangely in galactic speech. All of them turned to stare at her: Gul Meszk, a furry hoofed quadruped with spike-tipped horns and an extra pair of small limbs that functioned as hands and arms; Gul Kahn, who had neither arms nor mouth but instead possessed a generous supply of arm-length fingers and a shaggy beard of long, independently activated filaments that he dipped into nutritive liquids for his nourishment; Gul Ceyh, who placed two of his eye-tipped arms in her hand so that the eyes could look up at her perplexedly; and E-Wusk, who had piled himself into a tangled mound of limbs in the most remote corner of the cubicle.

Gul Meszk left off absently preening his fur to remark, "Shirts? We wear no shirts!" Which was perfectly true. None of them did.

Miss Schlupe was looking concernedly at E-Wusk. For a moment she feared that he was ill, but he was merely quivering with rage and humiliation. Each of the other three traders also was, in his highly individual alien fashion, seething with indignation.

"What *is* going on here?" she demanded.

They told her, talking in turn about the indignities the mart had inflicted upon them, and when Miss Schlupe could no longer keep her face straight, she exploded into laughter.

In their own galaxy, these pompous traders were personages of distinction and overwhelming business importance. At Montura Mart they were nonentities of the lowest order. Traders from outside the galaxy who touched down at the mart tended to be adventurers in search of quick profits or speculators attempting to salvage something from rash ventures gone awry elsewhere. Even among nonentities they were looked down upon.

If this weren't problem enough, they had arrived at the mart with nothing to trade. The astute Greater Galaxy traders refused to accept a sample as evidence of a good's quality and availability a galaxy away. A trader's status at the mart depended entirely on the quantity and value of what he had in docked ships or satellite storage, registered and available for exchange, and—ultimately—how quickly he could dispose of what he received in trade and bring in new goods to replace it.

Fortunately Gul Ceyh had included a few measures of Dwanlunk crystals with his samples. These luminous, veined pebbles from the world of Dwanle had the charm of novelty and were valued highly enough to bring them a very tentative marginal status as traders and a short-term lease on their accommodations. If they did not establish a respectable volume of trade, and quickly, they would be summarily evicted.

E-Wusk looked stonily at Miss Schlupe, who had managed to stop laughing and was wiping her eyes. "Our mission is jeopardized!" he hissed.

"Nonsense! Maybe we don't have status, but we're established here and ready to start doing business. It shouldn't take you long to stand these minor-league traders on whatever they use for ears. Who decides what constitutes a respectable volume of trade?"

"The gesardl," Gul Ceyh said.

"No. Our own gurgesard," Gul Meszk said.

Montura Mart was owned by fifty proprietors—individuals, or trading companies, or worlds. Each of these elite entities was known as a gesard. Collectively they were the gesardl, the ruling council or board of governors of the mart.

Each gesard held absolute ownership of a pie-shaped wedge of the enormous circular arena, the central market area where goods were displayed. Its ownership extended to the multistoried structure that fronted on the arena and included the corresponding wing and towers of the fifty that extended from the main building. The gesard naturally utilized the most choice space for itself, not only in the arena, but also in the common rooms facing it. Space it did not need was assigned to gurgesardl. Custom or law limited each gesard to ten gurgesardl.

Outsiders, such as themselves, were called kaskirdl. Gul Meszk bitterly described the function and status of a kaskird, and when he finished Miss Schlupe said thoughtfully, "Then we're janitors."

Gul Meszk cocked his head at her inquiringly.

"Janitors," she said again. "Sweepers up of others' leavings."

"Janitors," Gul Meszk agreed.

The sweepers up were expected to be humbly grateful for that privilege. In order to achieve the lowly status of kaskird, an outsider had to make the rounds of the five hundred gurgesardl, importuning each in turn with a glowing verbal portrait of the business he expected to transact. If a gurgesard chanced to believe him, at least in part, and happened to have a bit of display space or a common that wasn't in use, and further was in a suitably generous mood or pleased with the applicant's humility, he might grant the outsider a short-term lease, during which time he could function as a sublicensee of the gurgesard.

In return for this lavish favor, the gurgesard took an incredible 10/10 per cent of every transaction—ten per cent of everything the kaskird sold, and another ten per cent of everything he received in exchange. The gurgesard of course paid the giant share of this extorted tribute to his gesard, and it required very little calculation to establish that the fifty members of the gesardl ranked high among the wealthiest institutions in three galaxies. The fiendish ingenuity with which the gesardl's trading monopoly was fashioned awed E-Wusk and his colleagues into morbid attitudes of unworthiness.

"What are the Monturan natives like?" Miss Schlupe asked.

A moment of meditative silence followed. Then Gul Kahn remarked that one encountered a dazzling diversity of life forms at the mart, many of them exceedingly strange; but they hadn't thought to inquire which, if any, were native to the world of Montura.

"Which type dominates the gesardl?" Miss Schlupe asked.

As lowly kaskirdl, the traders had not been honored with attendance at a meeting of the gesardl. They could not say definitely whether they'd even see one of them.

"All right," Miss Schlupe said. "I'll figure it out myself. What language do these characters speak?"

"A multitude of languages," Gul Meszk said mournfully. "There are interpreters available, of course, but few of them speak the languages of our galaxy. This is one reason we progress so slowly. One has to search interminably for an interpreter before every discussion of business."

"So why not hire one of these interpreters?" Miss Schlupe wanted to know.

That hadn't occurred to them.

She left them to a complicated argument about products with a high value per volume unit. She had a problem of her own to meditate.

Before she could take steps to establish favorable relations with the natives of Montura, she would have to find out who they were.

Also, she wanted to see this fabulous Montura Mart for herself.

## 7

In the first-floor lobby, Miss Schlupe was delighted to discover a bank of transmitters she had overlooked before. She spent some time attempting to master the destination board before she used one, with the result that she finally reached the mart's arena on her nineteenth attempt.

She stepped from the transmitter, took another step, and then she halted, staring, while those behind were forced to bump and crowd around her. It was the culmination of her long lifetime of delight in humble spectacles: the epitome of every county fair she had ever seen inflated to galactic proportions. One improbable exhibit after another was crowded side by side along wide aisles that converged on the distant center of the arena, where an enormous column blossomed at the top into a vast mushroom that supported the rose tinted, translucent dome.

The unending mass of traders that thronged the aisles seemed to be oozing in all directions, in defiance either of scientific principles or the dynamics of jammed public places, and every individual struggling in that mass looked as though it had escaped from one of the fair's sideshows.

Miss Schlupe pushed her way into an aisle and began her own oozing as quickly as the uncertain and contradictory crowd movements permitted, pausing when she could not move at all to study the wild tableaux of unlikely goods and even less likely traders. She was enjoying herself immensely. Strange creatures conducted unintelligible arguments, underscoring their points with dramatic outpourings of sound, movement, odors—occasionally even colors. The goods that were the subjects of these exchanges sometimes looked exquisite and priceless and at other times, in other locations, looked like garbage. The aisles were wide, but displays of merchandise overflowed into them: containers, cartons, bundles, bales, jugs, crocks, kegs, and boxes were stacked about the booths and shelves and display tables, sometimes constricting the aisles almost to the point of impassability, but no one seemed to mind. Miss Schlupe escaped into a side aisle, a mere crack between displays, and slowly made her way forward to another main aisle that proved to be more crowded than the one she had abandoned.

She began to speculate as to what the things on display were used for. These enormous, hideously veined, fetid-smelling leaves; they couldn't possibly have an ornamental value, but neither could she imagine anyone eating them. At one booth a slobbering tentacle placed a sample in her hand: a small green stone with a colorful pattern of red and white spots. She thanked the giver with as much sincerity as she could manage in a conversation with a being that had no visible head. Then she noticed that others who received this bounty were munching on it with evident pleasure. She slipped away as quickly as the crowd permitted. She didn't want to be guilty of a breach of ethics or perhaps even a legal transgression, but her resolution of the day was not to eat rocks. The only teeth she possessed were her own, and the nearest competent source for human bridgework was a galaxy away.

There were live animals on display, some of them cunning furry or feathery creatures that looked as though they would make wonderfully cuddly pets. Miss Schlupe would have been hesitant to inquire about them even if she'd known the language. She feared that they were going to be eaten.

There were acres of grains, of every conceivable size and shape and color, exhibited in pots, urns, crocks, bins, barrels, and chests, or heaped haphazardly on trays. There were variously sized and shaped vials of liquids, of a dazzling variety of colors and viscosities, and the traders gathered around these containers in deeply religious attitudes to taste a specimen, or sniff it, or inhale it, or meditatively rub it between appendages, or pour it in a congealed, slowly puddling glob from one container to another.

There were strangely shaped ingots of unlikely metals, some feather light, some so heavy that Miss Schlupe, attempting to pick up a small display cube, at first thought it fastened down. There were metals as hard as diamonds, and metals so soft that the sample was squeezed out of shape by anyone examining it. She saw what looked like precious gems worth fortunes on Earth casually displayed in quantities comparable to bushels or barrels; and she saw something resembling a rusty tin can reposing on velvety cloth in a display case—so precious an object that prospective customers could not be permitted to touch or even breathe on it.

The people—she could think of no other collective noun for intelligent beings—the people were far stranger than the merchandise, and she became increasingly apprehensive as she considered the likelihood that the natives of Montura might be one of the more repulsive types. Could she develop an attitude of friendship in beings whose very appearance made her want to vomit?

In all of her experience with the nonhumans of her own galaxy, she had never before encountered them in such variety or such overpowering numbers. They overloaded and overwhelmed her senses—sight, hearing, and smell. There was no escape. The mass oozing toward the exits moved as slowly as the mass oozing toward the central column. Suddenly she felt exhausted, and she gravely feared she was going to be sick. She looked about for a place to sit down, but there was none. She was forced to stagger along with the crowd until she could walk no further, and then she settled herself onto a conveniently placed bale that stood in a crevice between two booths. She buried her face in her hands, which enabled her to conceal the fact that she was holding her nose.

Immediately she felt better. She remained seated, resting her aching feet and marveling at the strange shapes of feet and/or footwear that moved past her. When her dizziness finally passed, she raised her eyes to the translucent dome and studied the peculiar patterns formed by the nonsymmetrical spidery framework woven through it.

Now she was close enough to the center of the arena to see that the enormous central column had a spiraling row of oval windows, and at the top, where it widened into the mushroom, a double row of windows completely surrounded it. She wondered whether the mart's customers ascended to the top to enjoy a spectacular bird's-eye view of the arena.

She was diverted by someone pawing at her arm. A tall, gaunt, segmented individual, with a dozen stick legs that converged in a basketball-shaped body, stood over her and unleashed a violent, head-spinning onslaught of unintelligible speech.

Miss Schlupe responded politely in English, "Did someone step on your—if you'll excuse the expression—feet?"

The apparition articulated further, with increasing loudness, until Miss Schlupe began to wonder if she were being held accountable for her ancestry. She answered in both small- and large-talk, the two forms of common speech of her own galaxy, and got no response except another unintelligible outpouring.

Her verbal assailant finally stalked away—stalk being a strikingly apt figure of speech, she thought. Her feet continued to ache. She relaxed again and turned her attention to the dome and the intriguing column. Abruptly her assailant towered over her again. This time he brought reinforcements in the form of an individual the size and general shape of a grocery cart minus its wheels. The new entrant sputtered a different flavor of unintelligibility, and it dawned on Miss Schlupe that the previous onslaught was being interpreted for her. She patiently listened to a variety of intonations, delivered in rapid succession. During each pause she said politely, in English, "Boo! You can't scare me."

The interpreter left and returned with another, a banana-shaped body on skids with a prune for a head, who subjected her to another series of unintelligible intonations. Then the second interpreter fetched a third, who on the fourth try managed to ask, "Is this your language?" It spoke large-talk, the most complicated Galactic Prime dialect, in a stilted but highly precise accent.

Miss Schlupe fervently claimed the language as her own.

The third interpreter, who was as massive as a two-legged elephant, made a movement that could have been either a graceful bow or an attempt to assuage an awkwardly placed itch. "This," the interpreter said, indicating the segmented character who had started the altercation, "this says you are sitting on his quaq-sister."

Miss Schlupe leaped to her feet and backed away in horror. The bale she had been sitting on put out a few tentative, telescoping legs, humped itself once or twice, and scurried away beside her segmented brother. Or perhaps he was a quaq-brother. Miss Schlupe's profuse apologies, in every language her acute embarrassment could inspire, went ignored.

The interpreter, apparently satisfied with this successful resolution of a delicate problem, bowed, or responded again to the same itch, and started away. Miss Schlupe leaped after him.

"Just a moment," she called in large-talk. "I want to hire you. Obviously my need for an interpreter is more desperate than I realized."

An expression of perplexity suffused the mammoth face. The interpreter said, "You want to hire—but it could not be done! I am a djard!"

As they drifted with the crowd, Miss Schlupe attempted to unravel the meaning of djard and finally made it out as something between an apprentice or trainee and an indentured servant. Obviously the thing could not be done. A gesard, or gurgesard, or even a kaskird, would not go to all the trouble and expense of finding a djard with linguistic capabilities, or training one, and bringing him to Montura Mart, only to have him hire himself out to someone else. His boss probably brought him there because he needed his own interpreter.

"Do you know of any interpreter I could hire?" she asked. "I would pay well."

"But why not bring a djard of your own here to interpret for you?" mini-elephant asked perplexedly.

"None of my kind has been here before," Miss Schlupe explained. "None of us knows the languages spoken here. I'd like to learn them, but I have no one to teach me."

He halted and faced her, meditating her problem with engaging concern. "Perhaps the kloa would be willing to help you."

"Is that another kind of djard?"

"The kloa have no djardz. Or perhaps they do, but they are very numerous, and they are always willing to be helpful. I'll take you to them.

He led her into a narrow side aisle. Miss Schlupe kept closely on his oversized heels, attempting at the same time to express her gratitude and negotiate a path through the overflow of merchandise and avoid entanglements with surrealistic zoological specimens that barred her path or were attempting to pass in the opposite direction.

They reached a main aisle and turned toward one of the posh gesard headquarters that faced onto the arena. The djard led her inside. At the front of the enormous common room was a lavish display of products. Beyond it were double rows of cubicles in the manner of her own common except that these cubicles were large, well-furnished offices. At most of the desks, perched on tall stools, were thick-bodied creatures a meter or so tall that made Miss Schlupe think of large insects with football heads. Their fellows were scurrying about in all directions: multilegged, multiarmed little monsters with taut, hairless, scaly skin showing wherever their plasticlike clothing did not cover.

The djard intercepted one of them for a brief conversation. Then he motioned to Miss Schlupe and moved on, and they passed through the common with her following on his heels. Suddenly he turned aside, and with his massive form out of the way she was able to see for the first time what loomed ahead of her. She came to a rigid halt, staring.

It was a mountain: a massive piece of rock, milky white with rainbow threads, like uniquely colored white quartz. The shape was oddly irregular, with ripples, bulges, and hollows, and as she dazedly began to stumble toward it she became aware that it neither rested on the floor nor stopped at the high ceiling. It stood in a deep pit, and the upper stories had been cut away to make room for it, or framed around it, so that this immense chunk of rock extended from its subterranean base to the top of the building. Each of the floors of this multistoried kloa headquarters had a balustrated opening around the rock.

But it was neither the unexpectedness of encountering a stone mountain in the center of a building nor its lovely color that halted her and drew her hypnotically forward. It was the lights.

The thing was lighted from within. Lights winked on here and there, briefly or steadily illuminating a minute portion of its surface. Sometimes these pinpoints enlarged and intensified until the brightness seemed blinding. More often they merely winked and faded. Occasionally several lights merged and a large area suddenly became illuminated with a dazzling flash. Sometimes ripples of light moved rapidly across the surface. Twice some interior eruption of light set the entire looming mountain ablaze. At other times the whole surface lapsed into darkness. Then the tiny flashes, the ripples of illumination, the flaring and the fading, begain again.

She wrenched herself away and hurried after the djard. "What's that?" she exclaimed, clutching at him.

"The kloatraz," he answered blandly.

One of the strange, scurrying creatures was approaching them purposefully. The djard greeted it, they spoke a few words, and then the djard turned to Miss Schlupe.

"This is Arluklo. He may be able to help you."

Miss Schlupe studied the creature doubtfully. "He's a—a kloa?"

"He is Arlu*klo*. He is a *klo*. He is one of the *kloa*." The djard's oversized face was expressionless, but this did not lessen the scowl of disapproval in its voice.

"I see. And—does it speak my language?"

The djard's patience was being taxed severely. "Why don't you ask it?" he demanded.

Miss Schlupe turned to the squatting klo. When not in motion, its many legs sagged to a crouch and its head sank toward the floor. She began, "Do you speak—"

Her eye caught an abrupt movement. The djard was hurrying away. Perhaps he resorted to flight to avoid her next stupid question. Her embarrassment was intensified by the fact that she had to hurl her thanks after him.

She tried again. "Do you speak—do you understand my speech?"

"Very well, yes." The creature had a thin, piping voice.

"I would like to engage an interpreter who can assist my trading group when needed and who would be able to teach me one of the languages in common use here!"

"That was my understanding."

"Are you able to do it?"

"I have permission," the klo piped noncommittally.

Reflecting on her experience with the djard, Miss Schlupe thought an expression of gratitude might be in order. She said, "I would like to thank your employer personally for extending the permission."

"I have informed it that you thank it personally," Arluklo said.

She decided not to try to figure that out. Arluklo invited her to his own cubicle, and she followed meekly, and seated herself on a normal-sized hassock while the klo climbed, spider fashion, onto a stool that brought his head to the level of hers.

His speech was flawless. He had mastered perfectly the full, richly complicated range of large-talk, in which Miss Schlupe, still rusty from want of practice, occasionally found herself floundering. After a brief discussion they made arrangements to meet daily, and then Miss Schlupe circled the arena until she found the kurog twanlaft, the twelfth segment. She returned to the Prime Common by way of two pairs of transmitters.

The traders were still in conference, and the atmosphere was one of deepening gloom. Miss Schlupe entered the cubicle triumphantly, seated herself, and announced, "I've found an interpreter. He'll be available whenever we need him, and he's going to teach me one of the mart's languages."

They turned on her in astonishment. "How did you manage it so quickly?" Gul Ceyh asked.

"It was simple," Miss Schlupe said. "If you need an interpreter and language teacher, this is what you do: You go down to the arena and sit on someone's quaq-sister. Eventually a quaq-brother will show up to complain about this unnatural act, and when you don't understand him he'll bring one interpreter after another until he finds one who speaks your language and can ask you to kindly remove your person from the quaq-sister. You try to hire him, but he's in bondage as a djard, so he introduces you to one of the kloa, who will have a remarkable mastery of large-talk, and——"

"One of the kloa!" Gul Ceyh exclaimed.

"Right. Collectively, they are the kloa; individually they are each and every one of them a klo. If you confuse that point, it reflects unfavorably on your intelligence. My teacher is Arluklo, and his boss generously gave him permission——"

She broke off. Gul Meszk, Gul Ceyh, and Gul Kahn were staring at her in mingled horror and consternation. "Now what's wrong?" Miss Schlupe demanded.

"You couldn't!" Gul Ceyh exclaimed, disapproval dripping from each intonation. "Not with one of the kloa!"

"I could," Miss Schlupe said firmly. "I did. I think he'll make an excellent teacher. Beggars can't be choosers, as we say on Earth. Any port in a storm, and not being able to communicate is a storm, believe me. Strike when the iron is hot. Don't look your gift horse in the mouth. What's wrong with the kloa?"

"They're slaves!"

"That may not do much for them socially, but it doesn't mean they can't be good teachers. So what?"

"No one has anything to do with them except in the way of business," Gul Meszk said.

"Shame on no one. When I go to Arluklo's cubicle for a language lesson, who's to know we aren't transacting business? And what does it matter, anyway? I doubt that Arluklo is any more a slave than that djard who couldn't give me lessons because his boss wouldn't let him."

"Did you see the kloatraz?" Gul Ceyh asked.

"It's not easily overlooked. What is it?"

"It's a computer," Gul Ceyh said. "It's a computer built on an entirely new and totally unknown—to us, anyway—principle."

"It certainly looked new and totally unknown to me. What about it?"

"Kloatraz," Gul Ceyh said. "That means 'kloa master.' That's what the kloa are slaves to. The computer owns them."

"Both parties have my sympathy, but unless you have a list of socially approved language teachers, I'm going to continue my lessons." She changed the subject. "How's the planning coming?"

Gul Kahn said sourly, "We can't discover a way to transport products this far and trade at a profit."

"It's the factor of double transportation costs," Gul Meszk said, with a rumbling sigh. "It makes the distributive unit expense so high that we'll take a loss on every shipment, coming and going. It can't be done. If we had sources and markets in this galaxy—"

"Find some," Miss Schlupe suggested.

"There's no universal solvency," Gul Ceyh said, adding another voice of doom.

"There's no solution," Gul Meszk said. "It can't be done."

"A fine attitude for the shrewdest and most experienced traders of our galaxy," Miss Schlupe said scornfully. "E-Wusk—"

The old trader looked an entanglement of despondence himself.

"When you've finished here, I'd like to talk with you," Miss Schlupe told him.

E-Wusk assented with a gloomy flip of a pair of limbs, and Miss Schlupe turned away, muttering to herself. "I wonder if there's a galactic proverb about too many cooks. Or too many pessimists. It amounts to the same thing."

## 8

After the traders had finished their meeting, E-Wusk came to Miss Schlupe's apartment. She showed him to a corner of her lounge where he could spread himself out comfortably. When he'd got his limbs arranged to his complete satisfaction, she sternly pointed a finger at him.

"E-Wusk—you've forgotten why we're here."

"We're here to trade!" he protested. "Supreme itself recommended it."

"Wrong. We're here to establish ourselves. Trade is just one of the ways we're to do it."

"But we're here to establish ourselves by trading," he said, still protesting. "Why else would traders be sent here if not to trade?"

"Did Supreme say you were to come to Montura Mart and get rich?"

He twitched his limbs perplexedly. "No, but—"

"If you lose solvency, whose solvency is it?"

"Mine, of course. And Gul Ceyh's. The two of us arranged the financing, and we're to operate as partners. The others came to help out. Once we're established, they'll return to Galaxy Prime to make purchases for us and dispose of what we acquire in trade."

"That's what I suspected," Miss Schlupe said grimly. "Trust Rok Wllon to ball up a project. He should have explained this matter of solvency when he handed the job to you. You're on a critically important mission for Supreme. If you lose solvency, it isn't your solvency, it's Supreme's. Supreme doesn't care about profits or losses. What Supreme wants us to do is establish friendly relations with the Monturan natives."

"In that case, why a trader?" E-Wusk asked bewilderedly.

"Because this is a trading center, and trade is our excuse for being here."

E-Wusk ruminated for a long time, twitching his limbs in sequence. Finally he asked, "What am I to do?"

"Tell your fellow traders they've convinced you we can't operate here. Send them home with thanks, and tell them you'll stay just long enough to liquidate."

"But how can we establish ourselves in a trading center without trading?"

She said desperately, "E-Wusk—you aren't listening. Of course we'll trade. We'll do the most trading you've ever handled in your life. *But we don't have to make a profit.* Transportation costs don't matter. Value per volume unit doesn't matter. If you close every transaction at a loss and squander billions in solvency, that doesn't matter. The important thing is to build a huge volume of business quickly, so we'll have instant status as important traders. Find out what's in demand here and bring in a fleet of it. Trade for whatever you can get. Transport that back to our galaxy and sell it at a loss, or just dump it in space, and bring in another load. You'll be doing an enormous volume of trade, your gurgesard and his gesard will be making large profits on your business, you'll have instantaneous fame as the best trader on Montura, and as a result we'll be solidly established here—and *that's* what matters. Understand?"

"Supreme would pay for the losses?" E-Wusk asked doubtfully.

"Of course. Look at it from Supreme's point of view. With the fate of this galaxy, and ours, and maybe the universe, depending on our acquiring status here as quickly as possible, what does a little solvency matter?"

E-Wusk heaved a fluttering sigh. "I did not understand it that way, but when you explain things they become clear to me. I must develop a huge volume of trade and pretend to be making a profit. Then my gurgesard and my gesard will make profits, and we will earn the respect of the mart."

"Now you have it."

E-Wusk heaved another sigh. "Is that how Gul Darr would have proceeded?"

"That's exactly how he would have procceeded."

"Then I'll do it."

"Good. Mind you—when I said solvency doesn't matter, I didn't mean that you can operate stupidly. If you brought in goods no one wanted and tried to give them away, you'd be thought a laughing-stock instead of an astute trader. You'll have to nose around and find out what's in demand and send for a lot of it."

E-Wusk gathered his limbs together and pushed himself upright. "I'll go tell the others. I'll send orders back with them for the first shipments."

"Send for some of your own people to help out. We don't need four traders here. We need one trader and about a hundred djardz. *That* will impress people. Get yourself some djardz."

"I will," E-Wusk promised.

Gul Ceyh, Gul Meszk, and Gul Kahn left for their home galaxy the next day. They carried with them E-Wusk's confidential correspondence—supposedly aimed at liquidating the Montura Mart operation, but actually requisitioning a massive shipment of goods and a hundred assistants.

Miss Schlupe persuaded E-Wusk to come with her to Arluklo for language lessons. The old trader made a promising beginning, but once he'd mastered numbers and weights and measures and some basic terminology, he lost interest. He devoted his time to a study of mart procedures and a complicated analysis of fluctuations in product demand. Arluklo helped him by providing translations of the gesardl's daily tariff sheets.

With Arluklo's expert assistance and by dint of some strenuous study, Miss Schlupe quickly achieved a fumbling competence in one of the mart languages. To give practical effect to her lessons, they took regular turns around the arena together, and she soon was able to recognize and classify the most numerous life forms among the mart's population. She began to make friends among the traders, especially those who had daily duty at the same places, and she gradually acquired a vocabulary of the more common mart products. As her fluency improved, she delighted in wandering about the arena looking for strangers who understood the language she was learning. One day during a conversation with a pleasant-looking monster who supervised a display of something that looked like putrefied fruit, she chanced to mention the column at the center of the arena.

"That's where the gesardl meets," the monster said.

She asked Arluklo about it. "Is that the gesardl's headquarters?"

"Not the headquarters," Arluklo said. "There would not be room for a headquarters there. Headquarters are on a lower level, beneath the arena."

"I suppose keeping track of all the mart transactions would require an enormous staff," Miss Schlupe conceded. "What's the column used for?"

"The gesardl meets there. At the top."

"That's what the trader said. Then there must be a"—she fumbled for a word, failed to find one, and switched to her own large-talk—"a lounge up there."

"A meeting place," Arluklo said.

"A private meeting place?"

"Only the gesardl and those they invite can enter."

Miss Schlupe, her curiosity sharpened, went to have a closer look at the column. There was a large open space about it laced with entangled lines of traffic because all the main aisles converged there. Miss Schlupe joined one of them that seemed to circle the column and trickle off into aisles on the other side. As she passed the column, she walked as closely to it as possible and was able to manage several quick glances through the lower windows.

It was a hollow cylinder five or six meters in diameter. Inside, at the center, stood a much smaller column, probably the dome's structural support. Around the smaller column spiraled a narrow, open staircase.

Twice Miss Schlupe circled back for another look, her curiosity increasing with each glimpse of the interior. Circling back a third time, she approached the column from another angle and found herself passing a door. It resembled the doors in her apartment. She slowed to a stop, glanced about her, and then pressed the release plate. The door slid open. She entered quickly and closed it behind her.

She was in a circular room, empty except for the central column and its staircase. She peered through the oval windows to see whether her action had outraged anyone, and then she resolutely began to climb. The stairs rose through a circular opening, and she found herself at the second level. She continued to climb—third level, fourth level, fifth level. Each was a small, circular empty room like the one at the bottom.

She was reluctant to climb higher. The stairs had no handrail, and a misstep could have resulted in a nasty fall. Obviously the gesardl didn't climb the stairs to reach its meeting place. It would have a transmitter frame in its meeting room or at one of the top levels, and the danger of an outsider climbing the stairs to eavesdrop—the look up was as dizzying as the look down—certainly was minimal.

She climbed down again and prowled thoughtfully about the bottom room before she left. Her exit was as unnoticed as her entrance had been. Excitedly she hurried off to find E-Wusk.

Without bothering to explain herself, she led the reluctant trader down to see the column. "Look!" she said dramatically, opening the door for him. "You don't have to curry favor with a gurgesard for the use of a centimeter of arena display space. Just see the gesardl and rent this. Central location, best in the mart. All the main aisles lead directly to it."

E-Wusk regarded the small room with skepticism. He seemed instinctively distrustful of any enclosed space that lacked a corner for him to sit in. "If one set up displays, there would be no room for customers," he objected.

"It'd be a bit crowded," Miss Schlupe admitted. "Still—what about small items? Couldn't they be displayed on the wall, both inside and out? Customers could circle around and look at them."

"Perhaps. But would it be wise to approach the gesardl directly? My gurgesard surely would object, and all the other gurgesardl would support him."

"I see. It'd mean going over his head and disregarding the proper chain of command, and all that sort of thing. We don't want the reputation of being shoddy politicians, and if you do try to approach the gesardl through your gurgesard, he'll probably grab the place himself. It's a shame. Such a beautiful location. There's got to be some use for the dratted place."

Miss Schlupe had a more pressing problem to worry about. E-Wusk's first shipments arrived, along with his assistants, and Prime Common soon was bustling with trading activity. In the bundle of cargo manifests was a message for Miss Schlupe from Rok Wllon. He had encountered difficulties in locating the kind of specialist Supreme thought they needed to favorably influence the Monturan natives, but he hoped for success at an early date. He asked for a progress report.

She had no progress to report, because she still did not know which of these outlandish life forms was native to the world of Montura. Arluklo, questioned on this subject, said none of them were, but she was reluctant to believe him.

As her linguistic ability progressed from discussions of things to discussions of ideas, they frequently had communication problems. The phrase "native to Montura" seemed clear enough, but she had to think it in English and say it in large-talk, and the thought's destination was Arluklo's native language, whatever that was, and his reply traveled the same route in reverse. What, really, had she asked, and what had he answered?

At this stage it seemed unwise to be too conspicuously interested in Montura's natives, and she hesitated to question Arluklo at length. Instead, she began to make casual inquiries among her rapidly enlarging circle of acquaintants in the arena, and she soon concluded that any Monturan natives lurking among the variegated life forms thronging the mart were there anonymously. No one knew anything about them.

She began to ask questions about the world of Montura. Were there cities she could visit? No one knew. No one remembered seeing a city or any other kind of native habitation on the brief rocket descent from a transfer station. No one had heard of any Monturan city except the mart.

Finally she borrowed one of E-Wusk's space freighters and persuaded its captain to feign mechanical difficulties and obtain permission from the port authorities to perform test maneuvers. While he simulated the maneuvers, Miss Schlupe busied herself with the ship's viewing screen.

"Is it possible to send a message to Supreme?" she asked E-Wusk when she returned to the mart.

"Certainly. What sort of message?"

"A message concerning the problem of establishing favorable relations with the Monturan natives. There aren't any Monturan natives."

"Of course there are. Supreme said——"

"Precisely what *did* Supreme say? Do you know? All I know is what Rok Wllon said Supreme said."

"Rok Wllon said 'natives,'" E-Wusk ruminated. "So I would assume that Supreme said 'natives.'"

"In which case one would expect to find some kind of local population on this planet, whether that population evolved here or migrated sometime in the remote past."

"One would think so," E-Wusk agreed, eying her perplexedly.

"Well, there isn't any. There are no cities, no roads, no buildings, no farms, no factories. Except for Montura Mart, this dratted world is uninhabited. In a few hours one can't look at every square meter of a world's surface, but I did a careful general survey, and I scrutinized every promising area in detail, and you know how much detail you can see with a viewing screen. If the key to saving the universe is the help we're going to get from the Monturan natives, the universe is in serious trouble. There aren't any Monturan natives."

"Perhaps when Supreme said 'natives' it was referring to the population at the mart. Perhaps it meant to say 'Monturan residents.'"

"That's the only possible explanation," Miss Schlupe said. "So what we've got to do is impress the mart's population. We want them to think we Galaxy Prime creatures are the best traders, and the most congenial hosts, and the most friendly, the most brilliant, the most reliable, the most likable creatures in the universe. It's not a small order. How does one go about absolutely overwhelming an entire community of aliens?"

"Surely by developing a huge volume of trade—"

"That's only the foot in the door. That was before we knew we had to impress the entire mart population. To bring this thing off properly, we'll have to do something really spectacular."

"What?" E-Wusk asked.

"I don't know," Miss Schlupe said. "I'm fresh out of spectaculars. But give me a little time, and I'll think of something."

## 9

The United States Congress devoted a portion of the summer of 1995 to its annual debate concerning the medical profession. Once again the doctors were accused of profiteering from their grudging participation in the National Health Plan. The doctors issued the same denials they had voiced in 1994 and previous years, claiming that they hadn't but fully deserved to.

Doctor Malina Darr read the stories wistfully. She didn't know whether the medical profession was profiteering, but she was fervently aware that she was not. As a dermatologist, her patients were covered by the National Health Plan only when referred to her by other doctors. The general practitioners of her town of Colliston regarded dermatology as a fad contrived by cosmeticians to extract money from their patients. They could be tolerant of fads, but they were determined to extract their patients' money themselves.

The bank had just delivered itself of a final-notice-before-foreclosure concerning her mortgage. Earlier that week the Midwest Medical Foundation, which had loaned the funds that partly financed her medical education, pointed out in exasperation that all the other doctors of her class had long since paid off their obligations in full. Her financial distress was doubly painful because she knew it was undeserved. She was the best-read, the most up-to-date and comprehensively educated medical specialist in her district—because her lack of patients left her almost unlimited time for study.

The only thing that had kept her even precariously afloat was the advice of syndicated columnists. These nectareous personalities polluted the television channels for hours each day, dispensing homilies, home recipes, and hokum to pathetic viewers who sought capsuled solutions to unsolvable problems. Fortunately for Doctor Malina Darr, not all of the columnists were quacks, and several were highly competent. Every time one of them was asked a medical question by a teenager with a devastated complexion, or a youth with a vanishing hairline, the answer brought a few scarred or balding young people to her door.

She was earning perhaps seventy per cent of what she had to have to live on, and the massive indebtedness that haunted her was increasing daily because of interest and penalties. She studied, she went weekends to a nearby medical center to treat charity patients without pay so she would not forget how to practice her profession, and she watched every approaching pedestrian in the hope that he might be drawn to her door. Very few were.

She had grown up viewing life with eager optimism, and life had responded by giving her everything she'd ever wanted: a loving and loved husband whom she'd met in medical school; two charming, beautiful, intelligent children; a future of unbounded brightness to look forward to.

And then life had taken much of it away. Her husband had been murdered in a robbery attempt by a krelliol addict who wasn't aware that an intern dermatologist wouldn't be carrying that drug. She was left with her two children and the debts her husband had incurred for his medical education. At horrendous sacrifice and probably permanent damage to her physical and mental well-being, she returned to medical school and completed her own training. Everyone had told her it couldn't be done, but she had done it. Everyone had told her she couldn't move into a strange community and establish a successful medical practice, but she'd been determined to do that, too.

Now, two years later, she was on the verge of bankruptcy and striving heroically to avoid the unavoidable. She could not remain where she was; she lacked the resources to go elsewhere.

On this dreary day of wind-driven rain, her future looked as dismal as the weather; but she would continue to fight, for two excellent reasons. Brian, age nine, was so like his father in appearance and manners that she spoiled him outrageously. Maia, a year younger, was as badly spoiled as her brother because Malina scrupulously avoided favoring one child over the other. Because of the rain, they were playing indoors, and Malina occasionally heard them shushing each other so as not to disturb Mother's nonexistent patients.

She was looking out at the depressing downpour and thinking about the rusted eaves troughs and the three leaks in the roof when the telephone rang. A flat, precise voice informed her that Mr. Smith would like an appointment.

"One moment, please," she responded. She waited an appropriate interval to feign examination of her blank appointment book before she answered. "I have an opening this afternoon at three," she said. "Would that be convenient?"

"That will be satisfactory," the voice said. "I shall come at three. Thank you."

She hung up with a sigh, wondering which of the syndicated columnists had mentioned falling hair that day. She wished this anonymous Mr. Smith no ill fortune, but neither would she experience excessive regret if he had an advanced case of Stoyer's alopecia and needed a course of hormone injections.

But when Mr. Smith arrived, at precisely three o'clock, it was immediately obvious that his affliction was not related to falling hair. He was totally bald. His epidermis, however, had fascinating peculiarities of hue and texture that defied instantaneous diagnosis. He was an ordinary-looking middle-aged man, extremely broad framed and somewhat overweight. His clothing, which was expensive and stylish, somehow contrived to look shabby on him. He walked awkwardly, with a slight shuffle. He had no obvious racial characteristics, and there was no trace of any kind of accent in his speech.

He settled himself on the edge of the chair she indicated, and she took a record card and said, with pen poised, "A few preliminary questions, Mr. Smith. Your birth date?"

"I do not come to consult with you for medical reasons, Doctor Darr." His pronunciation was so wonderfully precise that it sounded odd. "That is, I do," he went on, "but not concerning myself. I am calling on you as an agent. I wish to engage your services."

Silently she sighed her farewell to the consultation fee. She had been counting on that. Now the children would have soup again for supper. "What sort of services?" she asked politely.

"Medical services, of course. I understand that you are a—a dermatologist?"

"That is correct." She noticed, now, that there was something exceedingly odd about his eyes.

"You are a specialist in conditions affecting the skin?"

"Of the physiology and pathology of the skin, yes," she answered mechanically.

"Would this include defects present at birth?"

"Congenital defects. Of course."

His eyes were fixed searchingly on her face, and they now seemed more than merely odd. They were remarkable. "Inherited defects?" he persisted.

She studied him for a moment, puzzled because she could not say *why* his eyes were remarkable. She never had encountered such an expressionless physiognomy. She could read no emotion there at all. Even his vague attitude of puzzlement was apparent in his voice but not in his face. "Inherited defects, congenital defects, or defects," she said, smiling.

"Those are the services I wish to engage."

"May I ask who is to be treated?"

He gestured vaguely. "A group of people in need of your services. The project will require that you leave your—your community—for an extended period of time. There possibly would be some danger involved, but I would consider it minimal. We would of course pay all of your expenses in addition to the established fee or stipend."

"Am I to understand that this position requires traveling?" she asked.

"Indeed yes. Of course."

"Extended traveling?"

"Very extended traveling."

She felt curious without being the least interested. She said, intending it as a joke, "I suppose this concerns the medical problems of some tribe of Indians in the upper Amazon Valley."

He considered this gravely; his eyes—his remarkable eyes—remained fixed on her face. "If these Indians have skin problems, then the cases may have something in common."

She no longer felt curious. Since no fee could possibly result from this conversation, she felt that her time could be spent more profitably in thinking about which kind of dehydrated soup to have for supper.

She got to her feet. "I appreciate your consideration, but I couldn't leave my children."

"Your—children?" She thought she saw a flicker of astonishment distort his blank look. His voice sounded tense with consternation, as though children constituted a transgression of natural law. "You have children?"

"Two," she said, smiling again. "Ages nine and eight."

She continued to stand; he remained perched on the edge of his chair. He ruminated slowly, "You couldn't leave your children. You couldn't leave—but, in that case—" He paused, almost visibly grappling with his perplexity. "In that case—do you mean you would have to take them with you?"

She shook her head. "I mean that I couldn't go. They're healthy youngsters, but I'm not about to plunk them down in a jungle somewhere."

"Jungle?" Again he paused to grapple with his perplexity. "Jungle?

There is no jungle!" The flat voice actually took on tones of indignation.

"Wherever it is. I prefer to bring my children up in close proximity to civilization." She had discovered what was remarkable about his eyes. They did not blink. They did not blink now. They had been fixed on her unblinkingly since he arrived.

But his momentary indignation had passed, or he had managed to contain it. When he spoke again, his voice was expressionless. "That will pose no difficulty. The civilization there is better than here. Far better. Immeasurably better."

"Is it a city?"

"A large city, yes. A very modern city. What you call crime does not exist. But with regard to your taking your children, I should have to reflect—I probably should consult—I don't know if I could permit it. If we were to increase the established fee, would you consider not taking them?"

"There is no fee, of any conceivable size, that would persuade me to undertake extended traveling if my children could not come along," she said firmly. She paused. "You keep talking about an established fee or stipend. What is it?"

"One million dollars."

She glared down at him furiously, wondering whether he were a cloddish practical joker or a mental case. "I'll believe that when I see it," she snapped. "Good afternoon, Mister Anonymous Smith."

Awkwardly he pushed himself erect. His face remained expressionless, his eyes unblinking. "Good afternoon, Gula Darr."

*"What did you call me?"*

It had sounded like a rank insult, but his attitude was one of complete innocence. "Gula—excuse me, *Doctor* Darr."

He nodded absently, turned, shuffled out. She did not know whether to laugh or weep. She hadn't collected a fee that week—the few patients she'd treated hadn't paid her—and Brian's tenth birthday was Monday. She had no notion at all of how to manage the party he so dearly wanted, or even a present. But that couldn't be helped.

She would fight. She would fight to the end, even though she knew the end would not be long in coming.

She awoke the next morning with a painful headache. "Physician, heal thyself," she murmured and went off to soak in a hot bath. Brian came pounding at the bathroom door.

"There's a truck here, Mama."

She roused herself. The headache continued to pound mercilessly. "What sort of truck?"

"A truck with boxes. The man wants to know where to put them."

She sat up with a splash. "We aren't expecting any boxes. We don't want them."

"Maybe it's my birthday present," Brian said hopefully.

It didn't seem remotely possible. There were distant relatives, but they'd never remembered a birthday before. It would be nothing less than a miracle if they suddenly did so at this moment of dire need.

"Does the man want money?" she asked.

"He just wants to know where to put the boxes."

Was it possible that she'd ordered medical supplies and forgotten about it? She sank back into the tub and pressed both hands against her forehead. "Make sure he has the right address," she called. "Ask him to check. Ask him to make sure the boxes say 'Darr' and '147 Main' on them. If they do, he can leave them inside the front door."

Brian did not return. "Wrong address," she concluded and abandoned herself to her headache. When finally she left the tub it still was raging unabated.

She dressed herself and unsteadily started down the stairs, hands again pressed against her forehead. On the landing she collided with Brian and Maia. They were staring down into the living room, both of them tense with excitement.

The living room was full of boxes.

"There wasn't room inside the door," Brian explained.

A narrow aisle had been left along one wall. Malina edged through it sideways to the hallway, edged past more boxes, and dashed through the front door and down the walk to the street, waving wildly. The truck was two block away and gathering speed.

She returned to the house. "Didn't he want anything signed?" she asked Brian incredulously.

Brian shook his head. He picked up a box and shook it. Nothing rattled. "What are they?" he asked.

"I haven't the faintest idea," she said.

The boxes were a meter long and perhaps a third of that high and deep. Each box had her name and address neatly stenciled on it. She lifted one; it was lighter than she had expected, though she could not have said what she had expected, or why. She ripped a flap open, tearing the tape that sealed the box. She could see nothing inside except an inner wrapping or padding of newspaper. She ripped open the other flap and tore aside the paper.

The box was full of money.

She went again to the front door and looked out dazedly. She did not know what she expected to see that hadn't been there before—the truck driver returning in rage, accompanied by the police, perhaps. She saw no one except her next-door neighbor, a dour, elderly woman who disliked children. Probably the neighbor had witnessed that remarkable parade of boxes into the house  She still was watching the place suspiciously.

Malina returned to the living room and opened another box. Moncy. She ignored the excited questions flung at her by the children—she hardly heard them. She was thinking of the peculiar Mr. Anonymous Smith with the remarkable unblinking eyes. "A million dollars," he had told her. And she had replied, "I'll believe that when I see it."

Without counting or even attempting to estimate the amount of money in each box, or the total number of boxes, she had a feeling of certitude that she was seeing the million dollars. She opened another box. Money.

She went to the telephone and called her attorney.

Hours later, at the bank, the contents of the last box had been counted and recounted. The bank president himself certified the grand total, treating her with a deferential respect she never before had experienced in such an institution. She received it with a wan smile, thinking of the previous week's conversation with one of his vice-presidents concerning her mortgage.

He handed her a receipt. It read, "ONE MILLION & No/100 Dollars."

Her attorney was talking rapidly, explaining that she would incur no liability in leaving the money on deposit, since that represented the fulfillment of her responsibility to safeguard it properly. As long as she was able to return the money on demand, any commitment the mysterious Mr. Smith thought she had made could be passed off as a misunderstanding.

"Anyway," he said reassuringly, "when you told him you would believe the offer only when you saw the money, you in no way implied that you would accept it—just that you wouldn't consider it bona fide until he demonstrated his ability to pay the sum offered, which is perfectly understandable. You now have no obligation whatsoever except to fully consider his offer and return the money if you decide not to accept. I'd suggest that you take a cashier's check for the million, made out to yourself. When he calls again, you can terminate this funny business by endorsing the check over to him.

"Thank you," Malina said. "I'll consider that."

While watching a million dollars being counted, she'd had a vision —a dream of debts paid, of a fresh start in building a medical practice with adequate financial backing, of trust funds for her children's futures, of a life style in which there could be an occasional luxury without the prior sacrifice of a necessity. She wondered how much of her life Mr. Smith was expecting to buy for his million dollars. Surely not all of it, but probably much more than she'd be willing to bargain away, even for one million.

But perhaps she could take less money and have the commitment defined in a way that would permit her to accept it. Or perhaps not, but it would cost her nothing to ask. It had occurred to her that in their future negotiations, the anonymous Mr. Smith would be at a slight disadvantage.

She already had the million dollars.

## 10

There are names that have their own peculiar magic and evoke exotic visions and scents and sounds. For Malina Darr, *Montura Mart* did none of these. It was not even enigmatic. It seemed every bit as prosaic as the name of the Crossway Mart, where she occasionally bought potatoes and onions.

But the experience was enigmatic enough, from the moment the mysterious Mr. Smith presented himself at her office until she and her children looked out onto the depressingly barren surface of the world of Montura.

Several times her suspicions were aroused, but Smith glibly explained, or she performed her own glib rationalization—as when Smith suggested that she should take clothing for herself and the children for the entire three years of her commitment, and she wondered what kind of a large, highly civilized city did not sell clothing; or when she quizzed him about the school her children would be attending and he doubted that there was one. But she could understand that the clothing available in a foreign city might not be comfortable or the proper sizes for her children; and she could understand that the schools would be conducted in a different language and teach unfamiliar subjects at far different levels of accomplishment for their ages. In the end she convinced herself that she could take textbooks along and tutor the children herself, if the need arose.

She terminated her practice, sold her house, paid off all of her debts, and—without realizing that she was being prophetic—reflected wryly that she had severed every Earthly tie. The job Smith described sounded both interesting and challenging. She was committed for only three years, including travel time, and when she returned she could take up her life again, blissfully free from financial worries. Her children would have the broadening experience of travel as well as life in a foreign place, and they could hardly contain their excitement.

They turned their backs on the inhospitable town of Colliston and traveled, by way of public transmitting terminals, to Nashville, Tennessee, where Smith registered them at a motel next to an enormous shopping center. There they were outfitted for their trip—not only with clothing for three years, but with everything else Malina could think of assisted by Smith's prompting: enormous stocks of preserved foods, toys, books, every kind of sundry. Smith also ordered a complete medical office for her, including books, instruments, and an entire pharmacy of medicines and supplies. When Smith also insisted that they have complete medical and dental examinations, Malina began to think that their highly civilized destination must be something out of the Middle Ages.

"Won't we be able to buy *anything* there?" she demanded.

Smith glibly explained. Foreign products might take some getting used to, and in the meantime—and again Malina glibly rationalized. Smith paid for everything, and he rented a suite of rooms just to use for sorting and packing. He even brought in professionals to help Malina cross-organize her purchases so that there were a number of self-contained units and she would not find that the entire supply of some item had been stowed at the bottom of a cargo hold.

Finally they were ready. Their luggage and the shipping containers were hauled away by truck. They made their own departure at 2:00 A.M. in a taxi, carrying only light hand luggage. Malina felt deeply apprehensive about the hour. She wondered if it had been deliberately chosen to avoid witnesses—she could envision a newspaper story that ended, "They were last seen getting out of a taxi at the intersection of—"

But it was too late to turn back, and she could not abandon her dream of financial independence. The taxi snorted away, and Malina led her sleepy children up the walk to the door Smith held open for them. It was a stately old house in an eminently respectable neighborhood, but they saw very little of either. Smith led them down the stairs to the basement and through an oddly designed transmitter frame that looked nothing like those used in the public transmitter terminals.

And then, in a spaceship parked in orbit somewhere beyond Pluto, they learned the truth.

They traveled, and even with the miracle of enormous transmitting leaps through space, space was so vast that the journey seemed interminable. Smith, who now preferred to be called Rok Wllon, did his best to keep them occupied. They had a language to learn, something called small-talk, which was alleged to be the galactic civilization's version of Basic English. It was formidably complicated with pronunciation peculiarities, and its alphabet, Malina thought, would have made Egyptian hieroglyphics seem a model of simplicity and logic.

To Malina's embarrassment, Brian and Maia took to it delightedly. It was a game, and they quickly became able to mug elaborate conversations with Rok Wllon, who was astonished at this precocity in immature humans. Malina's natural pride in her children was tempered by her mortification at finding herself the group's slow learner.

Small-talk proved to be a kind of linguistic shorthand for large-talk, a vast panorama of linguistic horrors. They labored on; presumably the spaceship traveled, but in an enclosed, windowless, completely self-contained five-room compartment, they were unaware of that. The only proof that they were in space came from their compartment's low gravity. The children were able to make soaring leaps about their playroom, and once Brian collided with the ceiling and gave himself a worrisome concussion.

At an early stage of their journey, their compartment, and the freight compartments containing their belongings, were transferred from Rok Wllon's private ship to a public space liner. They remained in their compartment during the exchange, experiencing only a bit of tilting and a jolt or two, while Rok Wllon engaged in a project that intermittently occupied him throughout their voyage: explaining space travel to Brian. The spaceship of course was a hollow hulk except for operation and service sections. The essential paraphernalia of old-fashioned ships and airliners on Earth—doors, corridors, stairs, elevators—weren't needed, so passenger and freight compartments could be intermixed and taken aboard as they were engaged to be hooked up to power and ventilation connections. The tons of freight that might be stacked above their compartment didn't matter in space, and however deeply their compartment was buried, they were only a step from the passenger lounge—or, when in port, the transfer station—by transmitter. That much was clear enough.

But Brian's questions focused on a blunt "What makes it go?" variously expressed, and Rok Wllon's attempts to answer this became increasingly amusing because obviously he did not know, any more than the average traveler on Earth could have explained matter transmission or a jet engine.

Brian understood transmitters. At least, he accepted them. The Universal Transmitting Company had opened for business in the year of his birth. It now had terminals in every city and town on Earth, and local trans networks laced every populated area. And their spaceship, Rok Wllon assured Brian, operated on a modification of the same transmitting principle utilized in Earth's transmitters.

"But what makes it go?" Brian persisted.

"When we went to Nashville," Rok Wllon said, "you walked into a transmitter frame in Colliston and came out of a receiving frame in Nashville. Now supposing, instead of you moving *through* the frame in Colliston, you stepped into it and sat down, and the frame transmitted itself. Then the transmitter frame that was in Colliston would be in Nashville, and you'd step out of it there."

"That's just like walking through it, except I'd waste time sitting down," Brian said.

"But space is so large," Rok Wllon said desperately, "that you can't travel from world to world in one transmission. The transmission begins to diffuse."

"You mean space won't warp that much?" Brian asked. Malina wondered what he had been reading.

"Something like that," Rok Wllon agreed stiffly. "So the only way we can transmit through space is through transmitting leaps, and since it wouldn't be possible to have receiving stations placed in space at the end of every leap, the transmitter, which is the spaceship, has to transmit itself without a receiver. Understand?"

Brian seemed to ponder this; actually, he was thinking of another way to ask, "What makes it go?"

Every ship carrying passengers had a passenger lounge, instantly accessible by transmitter, but Rok Wllon did not think they were ready for the experience of mingling with their fellow galactic citizens. He kept them at their studies. Much later, when he felt that they had their languages under control and had learned how to behave in public places, he permitted them to tour the transfer stations at worlds where the ship called.

These artificial satellites featured something like a restaurant, where travelers could eat while having a fantastic view of the wheeling, star-studded sky through a transparent dome. Malina and the children ordered food by pressing buttons—having learned in advance which buttons would bring them food most closely approximating their own—and their dinners arrived by way of transmitters built into the table. When Malina had her first taste of the galactic civilization's cuisine, she felt profoundly grateful for Rok Wllon's thoughtfulness in insisting that they bring an enormous stock of canned goods with them.

The three of them dawdled over the rubbery concoctions, pretending to eat while they admired the revolving sky and tried not to gawk at their fellow diners. Each passing monster challenged the evidence of Malina's senses and set the children to giggling.

"Hush!" Malina said. "You look just as funny to them."

"Do we smell as bad?" Maia whispered.

"Probably. Stop holding your nose. See—none of them are doing that."

"Most of them don't have noses," Maia complained.

One life form was an expanding and contracting puddle of tissue with an astonishingly loud voice. Another was approximately human in appearance except for double pairs of arms and legs and a wholly unconscionable number of facial features. There was an enormous starfish topped with an oversized head that made it look like an octopus, and when it was ready to leave each arm sprouted a multiplicity of tiny legs, and it scurried away.

During an unexpected lull in the seething babble of incomprehensible conversations, a large, featureless ball of wrinkled, hairless flesh suddenly began to sing. The composition was complex and utterly unearthly, but it seemed pleasantly musical for all that, and when finally the song concluded, Malina felt like applauding. Later she described it enthusiastically to Rok Wllon, and he informed her that she'd been listening to the creature's digestive processes.

When they had become somewhat acclimated to the strange sights and sounds and smells of the transfer stations, Rok Wllon took them down for a brief visit to the world of Ffladon. A precipitous mountain range made the land mass a vast desert crisscrossed with oases along vast river systems. They behaved like the bewildered tourists they were, staring at the multilegged inhabitants—who very politely ignored them—and sightseeing from a taxi, which was an uncomfortable cart pulled by a spidery-legged, tailless crocodile that paused frequently to steal mouthfuls of leaves from a plant that looked like vulcanized spinach.

At Ffladon they changed ships again, this time from the public space liner to a private ship, because there was no intergalactic space service. The last leg of their journey was long and uninterrupted, for there were no transfer station stops in the Greater Galaxy, but they came finally to the depressingly barren world of Montura.

At the Montura Mart landing field they were greeted by a bulky, multilimbed apparition whom Rok Wllon introduced as E-Wusk. E-Wusk regarded Malina with intense curiosity and exclaimed, "Gula —Darr?" when Rok Wllon introduced her. Then he concentrated his attention on Brian and Maia, making faces at them—an impressive performance because he had so much face to work with—and lashing his telescoping limbs in antics that instantly convulsed them.

They went at once to the Prime Common, the Galaxy Prime headquarters in one of the fifty pairs of towers that rose around the edge of the mart. Many creatures of E-Wusk's species were at work in the cubicles that filled the room.

"For the present I'll put you in Gula Schlu's apartment," E-Wusk said. "She has several vacant rooms."

They selected a room for themselves, a simple task because all of the bare, windowless rooms looked alike. After a look at the mart building from the curving lounge windows, Malina obtained the use of some ingeniously stacked boxes to store their belongings in and left the children to unpack the hand luggage. She went to join the others. Now that she finally had arrived, she was eager to get to work.

E-Wusk had arranged himself in a corner of one of the larger cubicles. Rok Wllon was perched on the edge of a hassock, evidently perturbed about something. "What is Gula Schlu's business?" he was demanding.

E-Wusk twined and untwined limbs, square himself away, paused to ruminate for a moment. Malina quietly seated herself on the opposite side of the cubicle and watched with fascinated amusement. Obviously whatever the mysterious Gula Schlu was involved in would be a long and complicated story.

"I cautioned her against it," E-Wusk said finally. "She claims she is following Supreme's orders and also that it will strengthen our position here. I'm already the largest trader at the mart by volume, but she claims—"

"What is her business?" Rok Wllon interrupted.

E-Wusk again squared himself away and paused to ruminate. Malina had the embarrassed sensation of having inadvertently walked in on a family quarrel.

"The mart has a central column that supports the arena's dome," E-Wusk said. "There are tiny rooms inside, one atop the other. Gula Schlu—"

"What *is* her business?" Rok Wllon demanded.

"That's what I'm telling you!" E-Wusk protested.

Rok Wllon bounced impatiently on his hassock. Malina had a side view of him, which disconcerted her. Her training in anatomy led her to believe that such a thin body couldn't possibly contain the necessary vital organs.

"Gula Schlu suggested that I take over this column as a place to display my samples," E-Wusk said. "She said the location was the best in the arena, which is true, but I rejected her advice for a number of excellent reasons. For one, the rooms were too small. If samples were displayed, there'd be no room for the customers. For another, it would have involved disregarding the established mart organization, and the other traders—"

"You rejected her suggestion for a number of excellent reasons," Rok Wllon said dryly.

"True enough. But if you already know about it, why are you asking me?"

"I don't know about it!" Rok Wllon shouted. He subsided resignedly, leaned back on his hassock, and said, "Please continue."

"Gula Schlu, entirely against my advice, petitioned the gesardl—that's the governing body—and obtained permission and opened her own business in that central column." E-Wusk waved a cluster of limbs wearily. "I implored that she should not. I gravely feared—and fear—that she will disgrace herself and destroy our mission. She said it couldn't possibly disgrace her, it could only make her notorious." He waved his limbs again, this time mournfully. "She said she'd achieve status quickly and get acquainted with a lot of important people, and her notoriety wouldn't matter as long as she was successful. I must admit that she is tremendously successful, though I don't understand what she is doing. She certainly has become notorious. She's the best-known person at the mart, and she knows everyone of importance. It remains to be seen whether she will disgrace herself."

Rok Wllon exploded again. *What is her business?*

Brian and Maia had joined them. They tiptoed in with exaggerated care and took places beside Malina on her hassock, and they watched the progress of the discussion with open mouths, staring first at E-Wusk and then at Rok Wllon.

"I told you I don't understand her business," E-Wusk said. "It makes no sense at all to me. Montura Mart is a strange, primitive place, with outlandish goods, and abominable tastes, and infantile business practices. The traders here have never heard of the regularized solvency that makes civilization possible. As far as I'm concerned, the tested methods are best, but what we have to contend with here at the mart—"

Rok Wllon seemed about to explode again. E-Wusk broke off and said hastily, "I don't know anything about Gula Schlu's business. Here she comes now. Why don't you ask her about it?"

The most remarkable creature Malina had seen since she left Earth had just stepped from the transmitter. It was a woman, small, gray-haired, looking spry and briskly alert in spite of being elderly. She had a lovely smile on her face, and in a crinkly dress she would have looked like a generalization of everyone's favorite maiden aunt. She was wearing blue jeans and a flannel shirt.

And she was human. Malina looked, disbelieved, and then looked again.

She sprang to her feet. The children climbed onto the hassock and added their stares to hers. After the long, weary, bewildering succession of monsters, each more unlikely than the one that preceded it, suddenly here was a fellow human being.

At the same moment the woman saw them. She exclaimed, in English, "Good God!" Then she turned on Rok Wllon. "Smith, this time you've blown a gasket for sure. Is *this* your precious specialist?"

Before he could answer, she hurried over to Malina. "Excuse me. I'm Effie Schlupe. Miss Effie Schlupe. In high galactic society they call me Gula Schlu. I should have waited on Earth to see what Smith was up to. Every time he acts on his own initiative, he puts his foot into it."

Rok Wllon spoke stuffily in large-talk. "The project was ordered by Supreme. I proposed Doctor Darr as the required specialist, and Supreme concurred. I hardly thought it necessary to consult you, or Gul Darr either."

"Lord save us!" Miss Schlupe gasped. "Gul Darr—Doctor Darr—is *that* why you chose her? Because her name is the same as that pseudonym Mr. Darzek uses? Smith, you blew *all* your gaskets on that one, and so did Supreme!"

"It seemed to me," Rok Wllon said defensively, still speaking large-talk, "that the job required certain qualities that you Earthlings are lavishly endowed with—qualities, I remind you, that disqualify you for membership in the Synthesis, though I concede their usefulness in uncivilized crises. Since you and Gul Darr utilize those qualities so effectively, I suggested to Supreme that perhaps a relative, especially one with the proper specialist qualifications—"

"You idiot! Darr isn't Mr. Darzek's name on Earth, and she couldn't possibly be a relative!" Miss Schlupe turned to Malina. "Are these your kids? Why'd you bring them?"

Malina said uncertainly, "Mr. Smith—Rok Wllon—assured me they'd be safer here than at home." She asked anxiously, "Won't they?"

"They will as far as I know. But I don't know how far I know, and neither does Smith. He's never been here before. Smith—"

"The name," Rok Wllon said stuffily, "is Rok Wllon."

"Your name is anything I want to call you, and right now it's mud.

Didn't you get my message? Your specialist isn't needed. There aren't any natives on Montura. I passed the word to Supreme and asked Supreme to forward it to you."

Rok Wllon said angrily, "Supreme specifically recommended a skin specialist. My choice was Doctor Darr, and Supreme approved it, and Doctor Darr accepted. Do you presume to question Supreme's instructions when Gul Darr himself has said all the intelligent life in the universe is threatened? This is a crisis beyond our comprehension!"

"It's certainly beyond yours," Miss Schlupe said. "Sit down and be quiet." She plunked herself onto a vacant hassock and asked Malina, "You're a medical doctor?"

Malina seated herself again. The children remained standing. They were still staring at Miss Schlupe. "I'm a dermatologist," Malina said.

"And your name actually is Darr?"

"It was my husband's name," Malina said. "I adopted it. I'm a widow."

"What did Smith tell you your job would be?"

"He didn't. He just said he had an important job for a dermatologist, and he wanted to engage my services at the usual fee or stipend. I asked him what the usual fee was, and he said a million dollars, and—"

She broke off confusedly. Miss Schlupe had been seized by a convulsion of laughter. "What's so funny?" Malina asked.

"I'll tell you later. Go on."

"I told him I'd believe that when I saw the million, and the next day—"

"A truck delivered the million dollars," Miss Schlupe said, wiping her eyes. "In small used bills, wrapped in newspapers and packed into a roomful of cardboard cartons with your name stenciled on each one."

"How do you know?"

"Because my boss was hired in precisely the same way. Jan Darzek. A private detective. He's the one that established the usual fee. He thought the job offer was a joke."

"So did I!"

"So he said he'd do it for a million dollars, just to go along with the gag. A million in small, used bills. And darned if Smith didn't deliver the million. He goofs things up dreadfully, but he certainly comes through where money is concerned."

"Was there anything wrong with the money?"

"Perfectly good U.S. currency. This is the silliest thing Smith has ever done. He chose you because he thought you were related to Mr. Darzek, whose galactic name is Gul Darr."

Rok Wllon, who was listening sulkily, muttered something inaudible.

"As for why he wanted a dermatologist," Miss Schlupe went on, "we'd better find out right now if he goofed that up, too." She turned to him. "Smith, let's have the lowdown. We're all in this together. Exactly what did Supreme say this skin specialist was supposed to do?"

Rok Wllon drew himself up defensively. "Supreme didn't say exactly. Supreme rarely does. I asked if there was any individual with a specialized skill that might be useful in establishing friendly relations with the Monturan natives and securing their assistance, and Supreme said a specialist in diseases or conditions of the epidermis might be useful."

"As far as we've been able to find out, these sensitive-skinned natives don't exist," Miss Schlupe said. "That's probably why the mart was established here—there weren't any native inhabitants around to object. Never mind. I'm glad you goofed. It'll be nice having a few humans to talk with. After they've rested up from their trip, maybe Dr. Darr can help me with my business."

"Are you sure the children will be safe here?" Malina asked.

"I don't know what could happen to them. If crime exists here I've never heard it mentioned. There aren't even any streets for them to get run over in."

"Gula Schlu!" Rok Wllon's tones were icy. He crossed the cubicle with one large stride and stood over Miss Schlupe. "Gula Schlu, I insist on knowing. What is this 'business'?"

"Oh, that," Miss Schlupe waved a hand indifferently. "It just seemed to me that there must be some quicker way of getting to know people and being known. E-Wusk could operate here for years and never get acquainted with anyone but the big traders, and most of the time it's the little people who know what's going on in the world. So I got permission to use that central column in the arena. It's an ideal location. All I had to do was remodel a few windows—"

"What kind of business, Gula Schlu!"

Miss Schlupe turned to Malina. "As soon as you see the arena, you'll know why I thought of it. It's just a lot of county fairs jammed together under one roof. There was only one thing lacking—refreshment stands. Each life form needs its own special kinds of nourishment, so no one ever thought of trying to sell food for immediate consumption at a place like this. But I checked all the foods available here and found some pretty good prepared meats and a lot of interesting vegetables. And there are some fascinating grains—you should see the rolls I can make, though I had the devil's own time finding a yeast that would work. There's a wonderful computer over in the Kloa Common, and I told it the available foods, and it had information on the food requirements of all the life forms here, and it came up with three formulas that meet the needs of every life form on Montura except one. So I leased the column and the space I needed to prepare the food, and I got permission to harvest a crop of wild fruit that no one had ever found a use for. It looks a little like apples, except for the purple color and the size—some are as large as basketballs. I had to build a portable mill to process them. When I finally got everything together, the result was absolutely delicious, if I do say so myself, and the business has been a smash success. Of course I had to invent money, because all the trade here is done by barter, and you can't measure the value of a refreshment stand snack in shiploads of things. It took some working out, but I did it, and I'm making tremendous profits. And I know everyone at the mart, and if there's ever anything here that needs finding out, I'm the one that can do it." She turned to Rok Wllon. "Isn't that why we're here?" she asked defensively. "To establish ourselves so we can find out things that will help Mr. Darzek?"

"Gula Schlu!" Rok Wllon thundered. "What *are* you selling?"

Miss Schlupe answered, in a small voice, "Cider and submarine sandwiches."

## 11

"If Mr. Darzek were here," Miss Schlupe said, "he'd know what to do. He always does."

They were moving slowly along an aisle of the arena: Malina and the children, Miss Schlupe, and her scurrying little friend Arluklo. Rok Wllon sourly followed behind them. Malina was engaged in a difficult mental adjustment. She had gradually conditioned herself to meet most alien life forms face to face without wincing. Now, suddenly confronted with an incredible variety of them, she had to regard them as prospective patients.

She was wearing full-length slacks and a long-sleeved sweater, and she had dressed Brian and Maia similarly, on Miss Schlupe's recommendation. "Most of them are nice people," Miss Schlupe had said. "They're cooperative, and helpful, and friendly, and they'd make lovely next-door neighbors wherever you lived. But some of them are actually *slimy,* and in that crowded arena you keep bumping into them. And some of them are like sandpaper. I lost all the skin off an elbow one day when one of them brushed past me. Since then I've worn nothing but long sleeves and long pants. I wish I'd left the dresses home and brought something more practical. What I'll do when these jeans wear out I don't know."

Maia was asking Arluklo questions in large-talk. "Who eats those ugly-smelling leaves?"

"I don't know of anyone who does," Arluklo answered politely. "They are used to make perfume."

Maia turned to her mother and demanded, in English, "Does he mean someone *likes* that smell?"

Malina answered vaguely and returned to the task of considering alien life forms as patients. The longer she thought about it, the more alarming the prospect seemed. This creature with the strange hat that turned out to be ears that enfolded its knobby head: the epidermis was a deep shade of blue, which in humans would have called for instantaneous emergency procedures. Blue probably was its normal condition, but how could she know? Faced with utterly strange physiologies and pathologies, what could she possibly use as clues to normality or abnormality?

The idea of treating one strange life form had not disturbed her, but when she learned that Supreme had used the word "native" to mean everyone in residence at Montura Mart—

"I can't do it," she said. "Every life form would be its own separate lifetime study, and there must be hundreds of them."

"Thousands," Miss Schlupe said carefully. "Don't worry about it. Rok Wllon brought you here—let it be his problem. If only Mr. Darzek—"

Brian dashed up with something small, furry, and squirming and thrust it into Malina's hand. Instinctively she squealed, which set him howling with laughter. A sinister-looking, multiple-legged creature had fought its way through the crowd on Brian's heels, and it now faced her menacingly.

"Buy it!" Brian commanded.

"Buy me one, too!" Maia pleaded. She had been too timid to abduct an animal for herself, and her eyes fervently coveted Brian's.

Malina called over the head of the outraged owner, "Miss Schlupe —would it be possible to buy two of them?"

Miss Schlupe, after one attempt at conversation, referred the problem to Arluklo. The little klo seemed capable of translating any combination of grunts, hisses, clacks, squeals, or other noises into meaningful expression. An outpouring of sputters and whistles followed, after which Arluklo politely informed them that the animals were not for sale. The furry creature was returned to the offended owner, Brian was reprimanded for taking it without permission, and they moved on with the children in tears.

But in that wonderland they quickly were taken with a new passion, a flying snake, though they knew their mother's probable reaction and did not ask for one. When they were out of hearing, Miss Schlupe, who had been quietly talking with Arluklo, informed Malina that the small furry animal was considered a gourmet delicacy on more than a hundred worlds. The cuddly little creature Brian had surrendered so tearfully was in fact its owner's lunch.

The products displayed were sometimes as puzzling to Malina as her prospective patients. Mounds of golden grain proved to be fertilizer; a pulpy, sweet-smelling, delicious-looking fruit turned out to be an insectlike life form that gourmets preferred to eat alive. Precious stones looked like water-soaked charcoal; piles of gleaming diamonds were identified as a by-product of the stomachs of a domestic animal—when ground to powder, they made a popular food seasoner. Not all of the odors were unpleasant. Brian and Maia reveled in some of them, as well as the sights and touches and sounds, and even, when Malina did not intercept samples quickly enough, tastes.

Again she attempted to concentrate on her future patients. For a short time she found herself walking behind a creature whose back displayed what would have been an alarming case of psoriasis in a human. She abandoned him for one whose excessively hairy shoulders displayed unmistakable signs of incipient baldness and then turned her attention to a massive skin cancer until Miss Schlupe, after consulting Arluklo, informed her that it was the creature's organ of hearing.

"Mama!"

Brian and Maia dashed up to her waving enormous, translucent, multicolored leaves on long, flexible stems. There was no outraged merchant in pursuit, but Malina tracked the leaves to their source and asked Arluklo to interpret for her.

But the leaves had been freely given. The proprietor of the display, a strange little hairless creature with a double tail, had been delighted with Brian and Maia. They reminded him of a pet he'd owned as a child.

"Keeping them out of mischief is going to be a problem," Malina said worriedly.

"Oh, they'll be all right," Miss Schlupe said. "That long trip and all —no wonder they're in high spirits. I felt like jumping around a bit when I finally got here."

"I don't think I've seen any children since we arrived. Aren't there any?"

The question was referred to Arluklo. He answered that there were many small adults at the mart but no children that he knew of. Apparently there was no explanation except the possible fact that most traders visited the mart for short periods and didn't bother to bring their families.

"I'd hoped the children would have someone to play with," Malina said.

"Never mind," Miss Shlupe said cheerfully. "If all else fails, Arluklo will find a klo or two who won't mind playing with them. They're happy to oblige with almost anything, and they're just the right size "

"They need a place to play, too," Malina said. "Is there any kind of park nearby? If there are no children here, and no schools, and no playgrounds, they'll have nothing at all to occupy them."

Miss Schlupe snapped her fingers. "I know where there's a sort of park. You can see some of it from one of the Prime Common apartments. I'll ask for permission for you to use it."

As they approached the central column the crowd thickened, and they began to encounter happy monsters drifting along while munching Miss Schlupe's submarine sandwiches or sipping the foaming purple cider. Rok Wllon glared at them resentfully, and Miss Schlupe told him, with a grin, "A fair without a refreshment stand is unthinkable."

They edged through a side aisle and turned back, and Miss Schlupe described to Malina the frenzied maneuvers she'd had to perform to get her business launched. Her greatest achievement had been in persuading the gesardl, the mart's obtuse governing body, to let her have her own transmitters and the use of some air vehicles.

"Can you imagine having to bring every crate of sandwiches and every keg of cider in through the arena?" she asked, gesturing at the crowd of customers surrounding the central column. "I told the gesardl—no transmitters, no business. The wild orchards were a worse problem. They're scattered over half a continent, and the fruit ripens at different times, depending on the latitude and the altitude. I had to invent a portable cider mill, and some gesardl employees move it and my work force from orchard to orchard as the fruit ripens. I'm just barely keeping ahead of the demand, so I may have to import some cider or the juice to make it with. There are only three air vehicles on the entire world of Montura, two transports and a little passenger flyer, and they're mine whenever I want them. No one else has any use for them—though of course the gesardl sticks me with a stiff rental for the aircraft and a chauffeur."

Rok Wllon was stalking along behind them and listening in an attitude of thundering disapproval. Miss Schlupe spoke to him defiantly. "I know everyone of importance at the mart. The gesardl gives me anything I want. Why shouldn't it? I have the most profitable operation in the arena, and I'm paying fifty per cent of the profits as rent. It's a graft, but we aren't here to make money. We're supposed to get the friendly assistance of the natives for Mr. Darzek. Well—I'm ready to deliver it any time he wants it."

Rok Wllon had no comment.

When they left the arena, they looked in briefly on the assembly-line operation by which multi-armed assistants were putting submarine sandwiches together. Miss Schlupe's greatest worry had been the possible mix-up of the different kinds of sandwiches, which easily could have poisoned some of her customers. "So I sell them by number and color," she said. "A sign over each sales window lists the ingredients in each kind of sandwich, in the most common mart languages. And each sandwich comes in a numbered paper bag with its own distinctive color. I had to invent the bags. I also invented paper mugs for the cider. There's no room in that refreshment stand for washing dishes."

She picked up a bundle of sandwiches and a crock of cider for lunch. "Number two is the closest to human food," she said, displaying a blue bag with a vivid black hieroglyph on it. "If you close your eyes and hold your nose a bit, you'll swear one of these meats is salami." The cider, unfortunately, had to be drunk warm. She hadn't yet solved the refrigeration problem.

They returned to their apartment to eat their lunch, and the children consumed sandwiches and cider delightedly. Malina found the roll strange-tasting but delicious and the meat passable. The vegetables had a savory tang for which a taste might be cultivated, and the cider was delightful—full-bodied, strong-flavored, and sweet.

When Brian and Maia had eaten to the point of immobility, Malina was able to persuade them to take naps. She went herself to corner Rok Wllon in the Prime Common.

"It's time we had a talk," she said. "I need to know what I'm supposed to be doing."

"But we've only just arrived," Rok Wllon protested.

"We arrived yesterday, and today I'm ready to work. Where's that group of people with skin problems?"

"There's no hurry," Rok Wllon assured her. "We agreed on three years, didn't we? We must of course study the mart population carefully, and then perhaps we will consult Supreme again."

He slipped away almost furtively and joined E-Wusk in his cubicle. Malina determinedly returned to the apartment and conferred with Miss Schlupe. Miss Schlupe dispatched one of E-Wusk's assistants as her escort, and they went by transmitter to the lower level where Miss Schlupe's bakery was located—Miss Schlupe had work and storage rooms scattered all over the mart, wherever space had been available—and from the bakery Malina went by Miss Schlupe's private transmitter to the refreshment stand at the center of the arena.

On the column's second level she found what she wanted—a place where she could sit undisturbed, and observe these outlandish life forms soon to be her patients, and meditate. An employee, another model of E-Wusk, brought a hassock for her, and she placed it in a vacant space by a window.

Around and past her flowed the frenzy of Miss Schlupe's refreshment business. The cider was piped from an upper level down to the spigots where her sales people drew foaming mugs on order. Crates of sandwiches were suspended from the lower-level ceiling, where they could be replaced from the stairs without disrupting the flow of business below: numbers one, two, and three; jagged line with a twitch at each end, ink blot with a stroke across it, square with one side missing; colors red, blue, and yellow. Miss Schlupe was a genius.

And though Malina possessed neither Miss Schlupe's lively imagination nor her gall, she asked herself, as she looked down on her unsuspecting prospective patients, "If she could do it, why can't I?"

The milling crowd around the sales windows was much too complex to grasp as an entity. She concentrated on individuals, watching one edge forward patiently, hover briefly at a window while he made his purchase, turn away nibbling or munching or chomping or rasping or grinding a sandwich; or, from another appendage, sipping or slurping or sucking or lapping or absorbing a mug of cider. One life form bought only cider, at least a dozen mugs carefully held side by side in its three enormous disc-tipped arms; and as it turned away from the window it passed its mouth over the liquid and inhaled it. Then it fastidiously deposited the paper mugs in a waste container and went burping off.

Miss Schlupe arrived, bringing Brian and Maia, and asked her if she was making any progress.

"As I understand it," Malina said, "the idea is to favorably impress these monsters. Do favors for them. Scratch them when they have an itch. That sort of thing. The only thing I can think of for a doctor to do is—doctor. Has the mart ever had an epidemic?"

"Arluklo would know. Just go over to the Kloa Common and ask for him."

Miss Schlupe had offered the children jobs. Their payment would be in the fibrous tokens that were the money she had invented. At the moment it wouldn't buy anything except cider and sandwiches, but she confidently expected it to become a common medium of exchange at the mart. "A lot of traders are going to get the idea that a tidy profit can be made in the arena from small sales for personal use or immediate consumption."

Brian and Maia were put to work filling sandwich crates for the sales force, and Malina, after seeing them safely occupied, avoided the crowded arena by transmitting back to the bakery. From there she walked to the arena and located the Kloa Common by the simple expedient of following several kloa who were scurrying along ahead of her.

She drifted through the common, asking each klo she met for Arluklo and receiving unintelligible replies. Then she saw the looming, creamy whiteness and the flashing lights, and she moved hypnotically toward it.

The kloatraz. Staring at it, she had an inspiration. If this marvelous computer knew enough about the mart life forms to help Miss Schlupe plan their sandwiches, why couldn't it help Malina treat them medically?

Arluklo approached her, indistinguishable from his fellow kloa until he called her Gula Darr in large-talk. She asked him for the favor of some information, and with his usual studious politeness he escorted her to a cubicle, got her seated, and scrambled onto a high stool to face her.

She asked, "Does the mart have a chief medical officer?"

She had to rephrase the question twice. Finally the klo answered, "One of the gesardl is charged with medical responsibilities."

"Is this member of the gesardl a doctor?"

"No. He maintains a consultant who is a—a health scientist."

"Does the mart have a hospital?"

Again she had to rephrase the question. Arluklo answered, "No."

"How are the sick cared for?"

"There is no care for the sick," Arluklo said. "There is medical care for the healthy, so there will be no sick."

"Who provides that care? The mart's health scientist?"

"Each common has its own health procedures established by its own health scientists."

"I see. Does the kloatraz have medical information about the various life forms at the mart?"

"Very little," Arluklo answered.

"Since it had dietary information Gula Schlu could use in planning the food she sells, I thought perhaps—"

"But that is commercial information!" Arluklo exclaimed.

"Commercial? I don't understand."

"The kloatraz has complete information concerning products each life form trades or accepts in trade."

"And a life form would be likely to trade for food it is able to eat. Of course. But what about the medicines each life form trades for?"

"Few medicines are traded at the mart," Arluklo said.

And that, Malina thought, probably means that each life form tends to develop its medicines on its home planet. In any case, the kloatraz would be of no help to her. She asked, "Does every common have a *resident* health scientist?"

"I think not," Arluklo said. "I could inquire."

"Please do. As you know, I am the health scientist for the Prime Common. I was thinking of establishing a health clinic, where I would offer free consultations to life forms that do not have their own health scientist in residence. Is there a need for such a clinic?"

"I could inquire," Arluklo said.

"Please do. Has the mart ever had an epidemic?"

Arluklo did not know what the term meant. His ignorance raised questions that had never occurred to her: Was it possible that universal diseases were non-existent or extremely rare—at least in the Greater Galaxy? There couldn't be an epidemic at Montura Mart if no disease was capable of afflicting more than one or a very few life forms.

She reminded Arluklo to inquire as to the possible need for a clinic and took her leave of him, pausing for another look at the kloatraz on her way out.

When she returned to the Prime Common, she asked E-Wusk for a place to work. He presented her with an unused cubicle, where she seated herself on a hassock too small for her, at a desk too low for her, and could think of nothing to do.

Apparently Supreme had information that indicated some kind of dermatological crisis at Montura Mart. Otherwise, why pay a million dollars for a dermatologist? And Supreme was wrong. Not only was there nothing for a dermatologist to do, there was no need for any kind of doctor.

Later she told Miss Schlupe what she had learned, and Miss Schlupe said, again, "If only Mr. Darzek were here—"

Malina went to her bedroom and found Brian and Maia having a joyful battle with their sleeping mats. The room was a mess. She immediately arranged with Miss Schlupe for the use of one of the vacant rooms as a play and school room, but she knew it was not enough. She simply had to find a place where they could run off their surplus energy.

The next morning the gesardl imparted its grudging permission for them to use the park.

"Except that it isn't really a park," Miss Schlupe said, pointing to the patch of purple visible from the lounge of an apartment across the common from theirs. "It's just a freakish place where things grow. I've flown over it several times, visiting my cider mill, and I don't remember ever seeing anyone using it."

"Is it safe?"

"Perfectly safe. I made a point of asking about that. You can go this afternoon."

"Do you want to come with us?"

Miss Schlupe shook her head. "I've seen parks on too many worlds. They make me homesick. Grass that isn't anything like grass, trees that aren't, and never a decent picnic table to be had. No, thank you. You'll find it interesting, though, and the kids should have a good romp. I'll stay here and catch up on my work."

After an afternoon of looking after Brian and Maia, Malina thought ruefully, Miss Schlupe probably had a great deal of work to catch up on. She turned down Miss Schlupe's offer of a picnic supper of cider and sandwiches. "I don't want to spend the entire afternoon there," she said. "There's no point in overdoing things on the first outing."

After a lunch prepared from their stock of canned goods and much appreciated by Miss Schlupe, they went down and boarded a strange little oblong flying saucer of a craft that the gesardl chauffeur had waiting for them in the landing field just outside their tower. They took off, and the ride made Brian's day long before they got to the park.

Against the setting of a barren Monturan landscape, the park was as much an anomaly as the mart. It was the only place in sight where anything grew. They were in the air only a few minutes, and then the flyer settled gently beside a low mound that marked the park's boundary.

The children scrambled out excitedly. Shimmering purple vegetation covered the ground everywhere and grew thickly on the mound, making it a mass of fluffy softness. At the mound's outside base, the growth came to an abrupt end; on the other side the park stretched before them, rising steeply to the crest of a hill, with a scattering of trees or something that resembled trees.

Their chauffeur made himself comfortable on the flyer's seats, coiled his hair about his face, retracted arms and legs, and instantly fell asleep. Malina followed her whooping children into the park. Brian turned a series of sommersaults and then came to his feet and stood staring down at the purple ground cover.

"Is that stuff *grass?*"

"It's what the world of Montura has instead of grass," Malina said. She smiled and reached out to smooth his ruffled blond hair.

"Are we the first human children to see it?" Maia asked. She had heard Miss Schlupe remark that they were the first human children to leave their solar system and also the first to leave their galaxy, and such distinctions had impressed her.

"The first to see it and the first to walk on it," Malina said.

Maia smiled and tested the springy softness with the toe of her shoe.

"Look at the funny leaves," Brian said, staring upward.

"They're pretty," Maia said. "A pretty yellow."

"Our leaves turn yellow in the fall," Brian said. "Is it fall here?"

"Probably not," Malina told him. "And it probably isn't correct to call them leaves, or to call these plants trees."

"What do the Monturans call them?" Maia wanted to know.

"There aren't any Monturans. But someone else, someone at the mart, may have named them."

Maia tumbled to the ground and rolled gleefully. "It feels scrumptious," she panted, stroking the purple fuzziness. "It's pretty, too. Everything is pretty."

"Beautiful, dear," Malina suggested.

"The things that are the most pretty are beautiful," Maia conceded.

"Indeed they are," Malina said. She was puzzling over the abrupt end of the growth at the park's boundary, as though a line had been drawn. Beyond it was the same hideous, eroded wasteland they had seen around the mart. Within the park, miraculously, was fertile ground and lush vegetation. It was as stunningly unreal as a cool oasis in a hot desert.

They walked to the top of the slope, and then they turned back and raced downhill toward the flyer.

"Do we have to leave now?" Maia asked plaintively, when they had reached it.

"Of course not. But I've had exercise enough. You two run and play, and I'll read my book."

Cheering, they started off. She called them back and said, "Remember, now—you're guests here. This park belongs to someone, and you must be respectful of his property. It would embarrass the entire Prime Common if the gesardl thought you guilty of bad manners."

They listened politely, but she knew their minds were on the unsupervised romp they were about to have. It would be almost literally the first time in months that they had been out from under their mother's thumb, and she could understand their impatience.

Brian edged away. Maia, effecting a more dignified departure, sniffed deeply and announced, "Everything smells nice."

Malina seated herself on the mound that marked the boundary of the park. She caressed the purple softness and remarked, "It *is* fragrant, isn't it? Run and play, but don't go far, and come back at once when I call."

Whooping deliriously, they raced back up the slope. Malina looked after them and worried. They desperately needed to be on their own occasionally, and the park was perfectly safe. She had walked to the top of the slope so she could look the place over and satisfy herself that there was no danger. But it was a strange world, and she worried.

With a sigh she opened her book, Shakespeare, and wondered if this world of Montura also was a stage.

The chauffeur, still stretched out in the flyer, was shaking the little craft with his snores. Malina felt drowsy herself, and she had to force herself to concentrate. Perhaps she did doze off; when next she thought of the children, they were nowhere to be seen. She called to them several times and succeeded only in awakening the chauffeur, who glared at her resentfully. Resignedly she got to her feet and went to look for them.

* * *

When Brian and Maia reached the top of the slope, they paused to look back at the two motionless figures below, sleeping chauffeur and reading mother. Brian said scornfully, "Grownups never have any fun." He turned his attention to the treelike plants, which grew sparsely on the side of the hill they had just climbed but stood in thick clusters on the reverse slope. "Look at those funny old leaves," he said.

The plants were tall, with glossy, smooth surfaces on the trunks and branches, and from the branches hung long, spearlike clusters of bright yellow. Brian leaped at them, but the lowest were beyond his reach. He went to the trunk and examined it, obviously intent on climbing.

"Don't," Maia said. "You'll get us in trouble."

"For picking a leaf off a tree?" Brian asked scornfully. He leaped again, without success, and then he ran down the other side of the hill, dodging among the plants and shouting gaily, while Maia called after him to wait for her. At the bottom of the slope was a small stream. Brian leaped across it almost successfully.

He shook the water from one foot. "Come on!" he called.

Maia held back. "Mother said not to go too far."

"You're scared!" Brian called mockingly. He chanted, "Scaredy! Scaredy!"

His taunts had no effect except to make her back away stubbornly, so he leaped back again, wetting his other foot. "Let's follow it," he said. "Maybe it'll get narrower."

"Mother said—"

"We haven't gone far. She's just over the hill."

They set off gaily to follow the stream. At intervals Brian leaped to the far side and back again, getting both feet thoroughly soaked because the rippling water gradually became wider.

"We're going the wrong way," Maia said finally.

"Why don't you just wade across?" Brian asked.

He slipped off one of his shoes and stripped the wet sock from his foot. Maia watched him doubtfully. As he dipped a cautious toe into the cold water, the gravel stirred and a mottled, grotesque head broke the surface. A bloated body telescoped out of the gravel, and the creature began hunching toward them.

"Keep back!" Brian called protectively to Maia. "It might bite. What a funny-looking fish!"

"Strange-looking," Maia said, adopting her mother's corrective tone.

"It's a strange-looking fish. We'd better start back."

"Let's go the other way and see if the water gets narrower."

"There's another fish!" Maia exclaimed. "It has two heads!"

Brian bent close to the water to study this monstrosity. "Naw," he said disgustedly. "It's just got two big eyes. Anyway—"

The second creature swished closer as he spoke, and he paused to stare at it. Whether eyes or heads, the thing clearly was strange beyond his powers of description. He abandoned it with a shrug.

"Wish we could wade."

"Better not," Maia said. "Those things might bite."

"I'm not afraid of them. We haven't had any real fun since—"

"Look!" Maia gasped.

On the far side of the stream, something was moving slowly among the treelike plants.

"It's a monkey!" Brian exclaimed. "A big white monkey. Or a white chim—chim—" He hesitated. "Do we have white monkeys on Earth?"

"I don't know," Maia said. "What's it doing?"

The creature moved purposely from plant to plant, and sometimes it slowly circled a trunk, its head hunched forward as though to scrutinize it. So intent was it upon this action that without seeming to notice them it passed within a dozen meters of where they stood staring at it speechlessly from the other side of the stream. It was as tall as an adult human, and its bulky shapelessness at first seemed to be covered with white fur. When the creature came closer, this fur looked more like a closely cropped fuzz on a skin that hung loosely or lay in awkward folds.

Brian suppressed a chuckle and whispered, "Maybe it's just looking for a tree to climb."

Impulsively he reached into the stream and fished a round stone from the bottom.

"Don't!" Maia pleaded, but the stone already was in the air. It fell harmlessly some distance from the creature, which stopped short and looked about it. It turned a blank, pinkish masklike face in their direction, but only for an instant. Then it resumed its scrutiny of a plant.

"It's scared of us," Brian chuckled.

He found another, larger stone and hurled it with all of his strength before Maia, pulling futilely at his sweater, could stop him. They both watched breathlessly as the missile traced a high arc and headed downward. It was descending safely behind the creature when the strange figure swerved abruptly, turned back, and was stuck squarely on the head. It toppled without a sound.

"You hit it!" Maia whispered awesomely.

"I meant to hit it," Brian said, affecting heroic indifference.

"Is it dead?"

"Naw. A little stone like that wouldn't kill anything. It's just knocked out."

"It'll be plenty mad when it wakes up," Maia said. "We better go."

"I'm not afraid of any ol' monkey. Maybe it's just pretending so we'll go away."

He fished another stone from the water and threw it at the still form on the opposite bank. The stone struck nearby, but the creature did not move. Before Brian could repeat the experiment, their mother's voice floated down to them.

"Brian! Maia!"

Brian hurriedly pulled on his wet sock and shoe, and then he caught up with the running Maia and passed her. Halfway up the hill, he turned and waited.

He said soberly, "I guess we better not say anything about the monkey."

"I guess not," Maia agreed.

Minutes later, the little flyer floated skyward for the brief return journey to the mart. As it cleared the hill, both children risked cautious downward glances to see if the monkey was still there. Even though the clustering yellow vegetation of the strange plants partially concealed it, the white form stood out starkly against the purple ground cover.

So did the forms of the two monkeys who bent over it.

12

After she'd seen the children off to bed, Malina went to the common room. At any hour of the day or night some of E-Wusk's assistants could be found at work there, fussing with records or interviewing customers. E-Wusk was alone in the cubicle he used for an office, his limbs drawn up in meditation, but he unfolded himself courteously when she approached.

"How was your expedition?" he asked.

"A huge success," she told him. "For once they tired themselves out. They haven't been so quiet in weeks. They even lost their appetites, but that could be the result of overdoing the sandwiches and cider. Anyway, they went to bed without an argument for the first time since we left Earth. Where is Gula Schlu?"

"I couldn't say. I haven't seen her since morning."

"We were supposed to have a conference this evening with Arluklo."

"No doubt her business has detained her," E-Wusk said. "It seems to be a remarkably complicated business. She tried to explain it to me, but I told her I'd rather not know. Oh, ho! Ho!" His laughter seemed to reverberate inside him, and he sounded like a grotesque parody of a Santa Claus. "If I knew how to run her business, she'd soon have me working for her. Oh, ho! Ho! I know Gula Schlu too well!"

Malina agreed that Gula Schlu was exceedingly capable. She tried to question E-Wusk about the practice of medicine in general, and dermatology in particular, on his native world and other worlds he had experienced, but the old trader was interested in diseases only when he could sell a shipload of something or other as a remedy. Malina left him, finally, and went looking for Miss Schlupe.

At the manufacturing headquarters, all was bustling activity. Because the arena never closed, Miss Schlupe's assembly lines rolled all twenty-six hours of the Monturan day. Miss Schlupe was not there. Using the transmitter, Malina stepped through to Miss Schlupe's office on the third level above the column refreshment stand. It contained only the transmitter frame, a circular hassocklike desk, and an equally large hassock used for a chair. Malina climbed one flight and found an unattended storeroom jammed with crates of sandwiches and cider kegs. On the two levels below the office were centered the frenzied activity of keeping the sales personnel on the ground level supplied. No one had seen Gula Schlu recently.

By way of Miss Schlupe's transmitters, Malina visited the bakery —also in full operation—and the main storage rooms. No one had seen Miss Schlupe.

She went down to the arena. Subtle shifts in the kinds of life forms encountered there could be noted as the planet revolved. Now night was at hand. Only the dimmest of indirect lighting was used, and a preponderance of large-eyed nocturnals could be found among those thronging the aisles. Even in the dim light, more of them seemed afflicted with serious problems of the epidermis than the daylight traders. If Malina had encountered such cases on Earth, she would have hospitalized the lot of them in isolation.

At the Kloa Common, the mention of Arluklo's name brought unintelligible commentary but no Arluklo. Again there was no sign of Miss Schlupe. Malina watched the kloatraz for a time, marveling at the intriguing display of lights. Then she attempted to cross the arena to the refreshment stand, but after edging along a crowded aisle for a short distance, she turned back. She slipped into a side aisle, found her way back to the kurog twanlaft, and made the double transmitter trip to the Prime Common.

Miss Schlupe hurried toward her as she stepped from the transmitter. "Thank God! Where have you been?"

"I was looking for you," Malina said. "I thought our appointment —why, what's wrong?"

"Where are the children?"

"In bed," Malina said. Then the tidal wave of alarm enveloped her. She gasped, "Aren't they?"

Miss Schlupe gravely shook her head.

Figures loomed in the background: E-Wusk, Rok Wllon, a group of strange life forms. "We thought they were with you," Miss Schlupe said.

"I put them to bed before I left," Malina said. "They wouldn't—"

Miss Schlupe's worried expression told her that they would and had. Malina dashed to her apartment. The pallets lay as she had left them, robes tucked in at their sides and feet because the temperature dropped noticeably at night. The comfortable cocoons contained no children.

Numbly she turned to Miss Schlupe, who had followed her into the room. The others filled the passageway behind her: E-Wusk, Rok Wllon, some of the strangers.

"We've got ourselves one whopper of a problem," Miss Schlupe said in English. "These unsavory-looking characters are secretaries of the gesardl, and they claim your children murdered a native in the park today."

*"Murdered?"*

E-Wusk and Rok Wllon were displaying stark consternation. The strangers showed no emotion at all but kept their multiple pairs of eyes fixed steadily on Malina. "It's impossible!" she protested. "It can't be!"

"It certainly sounded that way on two counts when I first heard about it," Miss Schlupe said. "Murdered, and native. But it seems that there are natives, though I still haven't been able to find out where they keep themselves. That park is a kind of botanical research station, and your children were seen to throw stones at one of the native scientists. He was hit and killed."

Malina started to say, "They wouldn't—"

The multiple pairs of eyes remained fixed on her. Dimly she took in other features—double pairs of arms and legs. There should have been two noses and two mouths, but she saw none at all. Double pairs of eyes stared at her out of oversized blank faces.

What mother knew her own children? She could not imagine Brian and Maia deliberately injuring anyone or anything, or even making a threatening gesture; but the native probably looked nothing like a fellow human. More than likely its appearance had been monstrous and seemed to threaten them. Could they have been defending themselves?

Maia wouldn't. She would have fled. Brian? Malina could envision him on Earth throwing a stone to frighten away a threatening dog. A thrown stone—a gesture. Even if the story were true, surely he had meant no more than that. But why had they run away? If Brian had thrown the stone as an act of bravery, he would have bragged about it.

The strange lassitude after the outing suddenly seemed sinister. They knew. They had guilty knowledge of what had happened.

She said aloud, "But where could they have gone? Would they try to leave the building?" It was a frightening thought. Except for the park, there was nothing outside but bleak landscape; and why would they want to return to the park?

Miss Schlupe clapped her hand to her forehead. "My God! We thought they were with you. It never occurred to me that they might run off on their own."

She turned and spoke rapidly to one of the strangers, who left at once. "*Now* they won't be able to leave the mart," Miss Schlupe said grimly. "The next step is to start looking for them."

They hurried toward the transmitter. Looking back, Malina saw most of the congregation of gesardl secretaries following on their heels. E-Wusk was trailing along uncertainly. Rok Wllon was no longer in sight.

"Have you any idea where they'd go?" Miss Schlupe asked.

Malina shook her head. "I suppose there are a million hiding places."

"A billion," Miss Schlupe said grimly. "But I'm hoping they're too young to do improbable things like find a perch on the roof. Even so, we'll need lots of help."

They first visited the bakery and the sandwich assembly rooms. Malina followed on Miss Schlupe's heels; the gesardl secretaries followed Malina. E-Wusk had fallen out, perhaps to confer with Rok Wllon. Miss Schlupe questioned her employees. No one remembered seeing the children that evening, but then—everyone was so busy they easily could have passed through the place unnoticed.

Miss Schlupe spoke orders. Assembly line and bakery were closed, and the employees hurried off to look for the children. "If we run out of submarines tonight," Miss Schlupe said, "so be it."

With the gesardl delegation still marching on Malina's heels, they went next to the Kloa Common. Arluklo had returned. The spidery little klo listened to Miss Schlupe and then scurried away for a consultation. They waited, with the kloatraz winking mockingly in the background. Finally Arluklo came back with an affirmative answer, and while he was delivering it, the kloa began to leave their cubicles and head out into the arena to join the search.

"My people don't know the languages," Miss Schlupe explained. "The kloa do, and they can describe the children and find out whether anyone has seen them. If we don't alert the whole mart, they could walk around in the arena for days without being noticed. Or they could walk through a transmitter and hide in someone's living quarters. And think of all the crates and baskets and containers in the area, not to mention the four storage levels below it. Those kids picked quite a place to get lost in."

She turned and spoke at length to the gesardl secretaries, who listened politely but said nothing. Malina still was hearing crashing reverberations—*your children murdered a native*—and when Miss Schlupe spoke again she didn't respond until the question was repeated.

"Did you have any idea that anything was wrong?" Miss Schlupe asked.

The gesardl secretaries seemed to be leaning forward to catch every word, which disturbed Malina even though she knew they couldn't possibly understand English. "I read a book and let them play by themselves," she said stonily. "Then—afterward—they weren't hungry and they did act strangely, but I thought it was because they'd tired themselves out. It was the first time they'd had a chance to play—"

Miss Schlupe snapped her fingers. "They weren't hungry. By now, maybe they are."

She spoke to the secretaries and dashed away. Malina, the secretaries and Arluklo followed in her wake as she determinedly pushed through the slow-moving arena traffic. Wherever anyone blocked her path, she snapped something that included the word "gesardl" and a way opened miraculously.

At the refreshment stand, none of the workers selling food had seen the children. Neither had those working on the upper levels. Miss Schlupe led her procession up the stairs to her fourth-level office, tiredly flopped onto her enormous hassock chair, and motioned Malina to join her.

"It's almost big enough to lie down on," she said tiredly. "I wish I could."

Arluklo and two gesardl secretaries stood waiting by the stairway opening. The remainder of the secretaries were scattered along three flights of stairs.

Miss Schlupe said, "There's no one in my storage rooms at night. If they managed to find their way there, they could have used the transmitter to come here."

Malina tried to visualize Brian and Maia, in their pajamas, making their way invisibly through the mart to the storage rooms and coolly punching this destination on the transmitter board. She couldn't.

"They would be seen somewhere," she said.

"Maybe they were," Miss Schlupe said. "We haven't asked everyone in the mart. Once they got this far, no one would see them. There wasn't anyone here, and there's no one working above this level."

"You mean—they came here—and climbed—"

*Your children murdered a native.* No, she did not know her own children.

"I mean they could have," Miss Schlupe said. "They're bright kids. I brought them here by transmitter several times. I'm betting they could have managed it themselves. Just a moment."

She went to the stairway opening and shouted down an order. A moment later, two of her employees squeezed past the gesardl secretaries still waiting on the stairs. Miss Schlupe spoke orders in large-talk, and they turned obediently and started to climb.

Then, in the mart language, Miss Schlupe spoke to the gesardl secretaries, and two of them followed the workers. Miss Schlupe returned to the hassock, sat down, and kicked off her shoes. "Whether or not they're up there, it's got to be done," she said.

Malina said uncertainly, "Should I go with them?"

Miss Schlupe shook her head. "It's a long, long climb to the top, and they'll have to check every level and every possible hiding place. If they find them, they'll bring them down. You'd be tiring yourself out to no purpose, and you may be needed somewhere else."

She sighed and retrieved her shoes again. "Got to see how my skeleton staff is keeping up with the demand for sandwiches. Back in a minute."

She disappeared down the stairway. There was only one gesardl secretary in sight. He stood by the stairway keeping his multiple eyes fixed on Malina. The unblinking stare seemed accusatory: *Your children murdered a native.* Arluklo stood beside him, head and legs drooping in the queer way the kloa had when they were motionless. Malina said, in large-talk, "Arluklo, what laws apply to those attending the mart?"

Arluklo straightened up and piped mechanically, "The laws formulated by the gesardl."

She meditated that for a moment and decided she'd asked the wrong question. "If someone attending the mart commits an offense against a citizen of Montura, what laws apply?"

"The laws of Montura," Arluklo answered.

"And—" She faltered and then forced herself to continue. "What distinction do those laws make for minor offenders?"

Arluklo did not understand. She knew no word in large-talk for *minor,* so she had rendered it as *small.* She tried again, rephrasing the thought. "Do the laws make any distinction according to the age of the offender?"

Arluklo answered politely that the laws made no such distinction.

"In other words," Malina began. Again she faltered and had to force herself to continue. "In other words, the punishment is the same no matter how old—or how young—the offender is."

Arluklo quietly agreed.

"And—what distinction is made between causing a victim's death accidentally and causing it intentionally?"

For a moment Arluklo seemed uncertain. He pondered the question.

The gesardl secretary kept his eyes fixed on Malina—all of them.

"There is no distinction in the result," Arluklo said finally, "so there is no distinction."

"And—what punishment do the laws permit for causing death?"

She heard the answer quite distinctly, but she asked the question again, and she was asking it a third time when Miss Schlupe returned. Miss Schlupe, with Arluklo's surprisingly firm assistance, moved her through transmitters and walked her along corridors and finally got her back to the Prime Common and her apartment, where Miss Schlupe rummaged through the medical supplies to find a sedative for her.

Then Malina fell asleep or fainted, and her last conscious awareness was of the stare of the gesardl secretary, who followed her to the very door of her bedroom, and of Arluklo's thin, piping voice and its maddeningly precise reply.

The staring, accusative eyes—*your children murdered a native*—those eyes chased her in a nightmarish, drugged flight through a feverish sleep's endless corridors while she sought over and over to escape the terrifying reverberations of Arluklo's spoken word.

The punishment for causing a death, whether accidentally or intentionally, and whether the offender was a mere child or a mature adult, was death.

## 13

She awoke to aching emptiness in a dimly lit, windowless room, and she lay for a long time staring incredulously at the children's deserted pallets. With full consciousness came panic. Had they been found? Was it morning? What was Miss Schlupe doing?

She sprang to the door and opened it. Her gaze met the multiple eyes of a gesardl secretary. At the end of the corridor there was daylight from the lounge windows. It was morning.

She firmly closed the door in the secretary's face and dressed herself. Then she hurried to the Prime Common.

A few of E-Wusk's assistants were at work, heroically attempting to conduct their business as usual in the face of the grotesquely unusual. E-Wusk and Miss Schlupe were talking in low tones in one of the cubicles. Two gesardl secretaries sat nearby, and others stood in a group near the transmitter.

Malina did not have to speak her question. Miss Schlupe looked up, saw her, and shook her head slowly. "We've looked everywhere. Now we're looking again."

"They'll be hungry," Malina said.

"That's what I'm counting on. Eventually they'll turn up at the refreshment stand."

They would be hungry. They also would be frightened and lonely. "I don't know what to do," she said. *Your children murdered a native.*

"There's nothing to be done," Miss Schlupe said. "We have an army looking for them. We'll find them."

Malina screamed silently, "Not an army—a police force." And when her children were found, they would not be restored to her arms. The law would claim them.

E-Wusk, apparently uncertain of how to greet the mother of missing children who also were murderers, spoke to her politely from a distance and waddled away. Miss Schlupe started toward her and halted when a secretary followed along suspiciously. "These dratted snoops are getting on my nerves," she announced in English.

Rok Wllon strode in, closely followed by a scurrying klo. Malina said politely, "Good morning, Arluklo." The klo responded, with equal politeness, that its name was Moluklo. Rok Wllon had obtained an interpreter of his own. With the klo's assistance, he began a lengthy conversation with the gesardl secretaries.

Malina seated herself in a vacant cubicle, and Miss Schlupe, still followed closely by the secretary, joined her. Malina asked quietly, in English, "What's going to happen?"

"Better not speak English," Miss Schlupe said in large-talk. "These characters already suspect a conspiracy, and strange intonations make them certain of it. Large-talk they can accept."

Malina repeated in large-talk, "What's going to happen?"

One of the old woman's charms was the engaging directness of her honesty. Where others would have dissembled, she delineated the situation with terse precision. "We're trying to find out. Apparently the natives have kept strictly to themselves ever since the mart was founded. The mart has no record, anywhere, of any kind of an offense against a native. From what I hear, from various sources, the situation is so unprecedented that no one knows what to do. The gesardl seems scared to death. All kinds of high-level meetings are going on right now—including that one."

She was watching Rok Wllon contemptuously. "The lousy turncoat," she said bitterly. "Trying to butter up the secretaries. He's assured them that we'll turn the children over to the gesardl the moment we find them."

"That's his mission, isn't it?" Malina asked. "To get on the good side of the natives? What sort of creatures are the natives?"

"We still don't know. I haven't found anyone at the mart who'll admit to having seen one."

Rok Wllon left the secretaries and joined them. His wide form took up an entire hassock, but he thinly perched on the edge of it. "I never imagined that you'd do such a thing to us," he said accusingly to Malina. "All of our careful plans, the fate of the universe at stake—and now, because of your children—"

"That line doesn't buy you anything here," Miss Schlupe snapped. "You're the one responsible for bringing the children."

"I had every right to expect—"

"You assured Doctor Darr that her children would be safe, and she has every right to expect your support. You weren't thinking of selling her out, were you?"

Rok Wllon looked stonily at Malina before he gloweringly confronted Miss Schlupe. "We've been interdicted," he said. "They think we're hiding the children."

"Where, when, and how?" Miss Schlupe demanded.

"That's what they think. E-Wusk isn't permitted to trade, except to dispose of perishable goods already on hand. The same goes for your business. As soon as you dispose of your stock of perishables, you'll have to close down. They've confiscated your transmitters and flyers, and none of us can leave the mart."

"Perishables be damned!" Miss Schlupe snapped. "I'll close down at once!"

She stormed away. One of the gesardl secretaries leaped to his multiple pairs of feet and followed her. Rok Wllon called after her protestingly as she vanished into the transmitter. Then he lapsed into gloomy silence. Time passed. Miss Schlupe returned looking grimly satisfied.

"Closed," she announced. "Arluklo is producing signs in all the important mart languages. They'll say, 'Closed by an illegal order of the gesardl.' We're putting them up as fast as he finishes them. We'll plaster signs on that column as high as anyone can read them. I've been feeding two thirds of the mart population, and if this doesn't produce a mild uproar, I'll consider it an insult to my submarine sandwiches."

E-Wusk waddled in and joined them. "Have you heard?" he asked.

Miss Schlupe nodded. "No trade for you except to dispose of perishables. They framed the interdiction that way so they could look noble while stabbing you in the back. Forty-nine fiftieths of them are jealous about the amount of business you've been doing. Have you got any perishables?"

"None at all," E-Wusk said cheerfully.

Miss Schlupe dropped her voice. "Get some. Quickly. Isn't there a friend who'll trade you a shipload of perishables and pretend he did it before they issued the interdiction?"

"I suppose so, but—"

"Do it! Now! If one of these multiple lynx-eyed secretaries follows you, tell him you're trying to get the deal canceled."

E-Wusk gazed at her in astonishment for a moment, and then he waddled away.

A congregation of life forms in startling variety began to erupt from the transmitter. One at a time they popped into sight, looked about them, saw Miss Schlupe, and headed determinedly in her direction. She got to her feet and went to meet them. Malina could not decide whether the group was importuning, remonstrating, or berating, but the conversation was loud and interminable, and Miss Schlupe obviously gave as good as she received. When the visitors finally took their leave, it definitely was no victory parade that plodded back into the transmitter.

Before Malina could ask about it, E-Wusk returned. He said quietly to Miss Schlupe, "It's too late. I can't get any perishables."

"Never mind," she said. "We'll do it this way. You have a shipload of perishables on the way, and if you don't trade them here, they'll spoil before you can redirect them. Explain this to the members of the gesardl and ask for bids."

"But I haven't got any perishables on the way!"

"Knowing your trading is restricted, the gesardl members will bid ridiculously low figures. Get their bids in writing. Then we'll expose this perfidious plot against us—them using their governing powers to place a false charge against the children so I'll have to surrender my business to them and you'll be forced to sell your merchandise to them at a loss. The mart should be informed about the way they attempt to profit from their own dishonorable actions."

E-Wusk's massive face was puckered with perplexity. "But if no ship arrives—"

"We'll say the captain got word of what was going on and took the stuff elsewhere. Get those written bids right now. This is important."

"If you say so," E-Wusk said resignedly. "But if I haven't got a shipload of perishables—"

"I'll help you. Draw up a list of perishables, and we'll decide which one it is."

Still perplexed, E-Wusk returned to his own cubicle.

"What'd you tell the delegation?" Malina asked Miss Schlupe.

"The complaint was that my false and misleading notices were causing turmoil on the floor of the arena. They wanted me to take them down and reopen long enough to dispose of stocks of food on hand and give the mart proper notice of closing. I told them this is impossible while my good character is tainted by unjust suspicions and rumors fostered by the gesardl. The financial loss is trifling, but my good character, my honor, is everything. Also, I suspect that the gesardl has made the false charges in an attempt to force me out so it can take over my business. I've reported this to my own government and asked for an investigation and an assessment of damages. If I do say so myself, it was very nicely put. The delegation retired in consternation."

Miss Schlupe went to confer with E-Wusk on the handling of his non-existent shipload of perishables. The gesardl delegation, considerably enlarged, made a second appearance. This time Miss Schlupe ignored it, so it conferred with Rok Wllon, pouring out a muddle of unlikely languages that Moluklo patiently put into large-talk.

Malina leaned back and closed her eyes. She should have been doing something, but if the kloa and all the others who knew the mart couldn't find her children, what chance would she have? Perhaps if she tried to imagine where they would go—surely a mother knew her own children well enough to do that—*your children murdered a native.*

Suddenly the room fell silent. She opened her eyes.

On the other side of the common, E-Wusk and Miss Schlupe had scrambled to their feet, staring, transfixed with astonishment. Everyone was turned toward the transmitter.

A man had stepped from it. A human being.

With him was an alien, nondescript among so many flamboyant life forms, but the man definitely was human—tall, blond, and blue-eyed, and even the baggy, overall-like garment he wore could not conceal a sturdy physique.

Malina leaped to her feet and stared with the rest. Startled as she was, she instinctively appraised him professionally. He looked ill. He was underweight and excessively fatigued. He swayed slightly as he stood there looking about him.

In one hand he held an enormous submarine sandwich. In the other he held a paper mug of cider. He had been eating the sandwich.

The alien who accompanied him also held a sandwich and a mug of cider, but he did not seem to know what to do with them.

The man's gaze fell on Miss Schlupe, who was still petrified with astonishment. He called in English, "Schluppy! What's going on here?"

Miss Schlupe's scream was a fervent hallelujah. "Mr. Darzek! Thank God!"

She hurled herself across the common and into his arms. He gingerly suffered himself to be embraced while safeguarding his cider and sandwich. "Take it easy," he said. "This is the first time in weeks I've had an appetite. I may lose it if I have to eat this stuff off the floor."

By the time she released him, E-Wusk had waddled forward to wrap Darzek in a multitude of limbs and further endanger his food.

"Did you just arrive?" Miss Schlupe asked.

"I've been here since yesterday," Darzek said. "I spent the night going from common to common trying to find someone who spoke a galactic dialect or had heard of a disreputable trader named E-Wusk.

No one did or had. Very disillusioning—I figured by this time you people would have taken the place over and made large-talk the official language. This morning we went down to the arena to try our luck there. At the central column something smelled like breakfast, but all the windows were closed, and of course we couldn't read the notices. I pressed my nose hungrily against a window, and behold —a former clerk of E-Wusk's was working inside. He recognized me, and pressed these samples on us, and guided us as far as your bakery, where everyone was sitting around wringing hands—E-Wusk's people have lots of hands to wring—while the bread burned."

Miss Schlupe giggled. "I told them to burn it. I wanted to find out whether they could raise enough stink to make the mart uninhabitable."

"I don't know about 'habitable,' but they've made that particular level off limits to people with noses. You weren't there, so my guide took me other places and finally sent me here. Why all the consternation?"

"Gul Darr!" E-Wusk gurgled. "You couldn't have come at a more opportune time. The most terrible thing has happened! The most incredible tragedy!"

Darzek said wearily, "E-Wusk, don't talk to me of tragedies. The word has lost its meaning."

"It's Doctor Darr," E-Wusk persisted. "Her children—"

"*Whose* children?"

"Doctor Darr's. She took them to the park, and—"

"Who is Doctor Darr?"

"The medical specialist Supreme recommended."

Darzek calmly took another bite of sandwich, and then he looked about the room again. For the first time his eyes met Malina's. He called to her, "You're Doctor Darr?"

She nodded.

"Why are they calling you 'Darr'?"

"Because it's my name."

"You come from Earth? But of course. That's the only place humans come from, isn't it? I've been in space a long time. You're Doctor Darr, and you're called that because it's your name and your profession, and you're from Earth, and you have children. Why did you bring them here?"

"She wouldn't come without them," Miss Schlupe said, "so Smith— Rok Wllon—let her bring them. He assured her they'd be safe. He hired her the same way he hired you. For a million dollars. And get this. He hired her because Supreme told him to get a skin specialist—which she is—and because her name is Darr."

Darzek was calmly studying Malina. "What about her children?"

"They're lost," Miss Schlupe said.

"Why isn't she looking for them?"

Malina felt too nonplused to speak.

"How old are they?" Darzek asked.

"Eight and ten," Miss Schlupe said.

"Then they're too large to be trampled underfoot, even in the arena. What are you doing about it?"

"Everyone is looking for them."

"I doubt that. Those zoological specimens in the arena are mostly looking for bargains in bric-a-brac and used alfalfa, but even in that conglomeration it shouldn't be easy to overlook two human children. Does she have photos of them?"

Malina hadn't thought of the photos, which weren't unpacked yet.

"That's only the beginning of the problem," Miss Schlupe said. "See those characters?" She pointed to the gesardl delegation. "The moment the children are found, they're going to arrest them."

Darzek drained his mug of cider. Then he dropped onto the nearest hassock and took another bite of sandwich. His alien companion sank down beside him and closed his eyes.

"What happened?" Darzek asked.

"These characters say the children murdered a native when they were playing in a park near here—threw a stone and hit him. The gesardl has a treaty with the native government providing that any alien involved in an offense against a native must be turned over to the native system of justice."

"There's nothing unusual about that," Darzek said. "It isn't even unreasonable."

"They have the death penalty for murder."

"So do a lot of countries on Earth. But children—"

"They make no distinction between children and adults." Miss Schlupe, too, had been questioning Arluklo.

Darzek said, "I see." He turned and met Malina's eyes again—gave her a long, searching look—and then he turned to Rok Wllon, who still stood with the gesardl delegation. He spoke conversationally. "How did you ever manage such a pyramiding accumulation of stupidities?"

Rok Wllon said defensively, "I did nothing at all without consulting Supreme. Supreme approved everything. How could I know that such barbarian instincts could mature at such an early age?"

Darzek had started to take another bite of sandwich. Instead, he yawned massively. His companion had drooped forward, obviously sound asleep. His tipped mug of cider was trickling its contents onto the floor.

Darzek turned to Miss Schlupe again. "Schluppy, we haven't slept for a week. Or weeks. I'm starved, and this sandwich tastes delicious, and I'm too tired to eat. I worked all the way here, non-stop, so I'd be ready for action when I arrived, and now I'm too exhausted to think. Give us a couple of beds. When I wake up, whenever that might be, you can tell me about all the messes you've got yourselves into."

"Of course," Miss Schlupe said. She shook the alien awake and led the two of them away.

Bitterly Malina watched them go. This was the brilliantly resourceful Jan Darzek, who always knew what to do. She sank back onto her hassock and watched the milling gesardl delegation. *Your children murdered a native.*

Some of Miss Schlupe's assistants arrived with crates of assorted sandwiches and a keg of cider. Miss Schlupe returned and went about offering food to everyone, even the gesardl representatives. "We might as well eat the surplus before it gets stale," she said.

Finally she offered Malina a sandwich. Malina said, "I couldn't—"

Miss Schlupe placed it on her lap. "Eat it. You can't help matters by starving yourself."

Malina looked down at the sandwich. Something was written on the wrapper. She recognized Miss Schlupe's scrawl and moved the sandwich so that the writing caught the light.

The message was brief. "I hid them. Eat this."

Revelation came instantly. Miss Schlupe, so admirably placed to find out everything that went on at the mart, probably knew about the tragedy as soon as the gesardl did. She somehow had smuggled the children from their beds and out of the Prime Common and hidden them. Ever since, under the suspicious eyes of the gesardl secretaries, she'd been trying to find an absolutely safe way to tell Malina what had happened.

Malina managed a smile. From across the room, Miss Schlupe smiled back. And Malina solemnly ate all of her sandwich, including the part of the wrapper that contained the message.

While she did so, she watched Miss Schlupe. *Now* it was apparent to her that the peppery old lady was enjoying this immensely, with all of the delight of one who holds nothing but trump cards when no one else knows what the game is.

Malina got to her feet. As long as her children were safe, she thought she could play a hand of her own in Miss Schlupe's game. She marched over to the gesardl delegation and, speaking large-talk, invited Moluklo to interpret for her.

"About this treaty between the gesardl and the Monturan natives," she said. "Where is it?"

Moluklo translated. The only response was what she assumed were bewildered looks.

"I want to see a copy of that treaty," Malina said. "I also want a full explanation of the legalities by which the gesardl has bound everyone at the mart to a treaty that no one has seen. Is that clear?"

Obviously it was not. Malina continued, "About this alleged murder. Gula Schlu obtained permission from the gesardl for my children to play in the park. The gesardl assured her that they would not be in danger. The gesardl would not have given that permission and that assurance without consulting the natives. Therefore I would like a full explanation of this grave offense the natives have committed by permitting their scientists to use the park while my children were there."

By the time Moluklo finished his translation, the members of the delegation were not even breathing perceptibly.

"I want to know what relief the treaty provides for injuries the natives inflict on aliens," Malina went on. "Because of that permission, and that assurance, we were entitled to assume that there would be no natives in the park. But natives were illegally present, and the resultant damage to the unshaped personalities of my children is beyond calculation. I intend to demand the maximum in damages that the treaty permits, and I'm also demanding severe punishment for the natives responsible."

Moluklo began his translation.

Rok Wllon hissed, "Surely you don't think the natives will believe that!"

"Perhaps not," Malina said. "But there's enough substance in it to make them think very seriously. By the time they've framed a reply, I'll have something else for them to think about."

## 14

Again Malina awoke to a dreary morning and aching emptiness. Her children were safe, but they would be lonely and frightened, and she couldn't risk going to them as long as the gesardl secretaries followed her everywhere.

At least she knew where they were and how they got there. Miss Schlupe had discovered a bath lounge on an underground level of their tower. It contained accommodations for every conceivable life form, with features ranging from deep pools to ceiling and floor sprays, and from chilling water to steam rooms. Malina and Miss Schlupe shared one of the steam rooms, and since this form of relaxation held no appeal for the gesardl secretaries following them, they had the room to themselves. Under the cover of hissing steam, Miss Schlupe whispered what had happened.

"I didn't dare say anything or even be seen passing you a note," Miss Schlupe said. "We aren't even safe speaking English—they may have the entire mart bugged, and one member of the gesardl is a klo. I'm betting the kloatraz can figure out any language, and if they could slip it a recording of me telling you in English where the children are, that'd be the end of it."

She had smuggled the children from the Prime Common by the simple expedient of dispatching all the assistants in the room on errands. The children had cooperated beautifully. She told them, "Come quickly—we've got to hide you." And they went.

They knew, Malina thought. *Your children murdered a native.*

Miss Schlupe had taken them by transmitter from the Prime Common to the lower level where her storerooms were located. The one moment of risk was when they stepped out of the transmitter there; but that level was infrequently used, and they met no one. From her storerooms she took them through her own transmitter to her office in the column and hid them inside the large hassock she used for a chair.

Malina exclaimed, "You mean—all the time I was sitting there—"

"Right. That's why I had you sit there. The dears performed perfectly."

She considered the children safe enough for the present. The gesardl had searched the entire column—it thought—and was convinced they weren't there. Since Miss Schlupe no longer had her transmitters, the only way into the column was by way of the door from the arena, and gesardl secretaries were watching that in case the children approached it looking for food.

"As long as they think the children aren't there and can't get in without being seen, they aren't likely to search the place again. It's a long climb to the top."

The children were comfortably established on the eleventh, twelfth, and thirteenth levels, where someone had constructed a three-level apartment. They had plenty of food, they were comfortable, and they sent their mother their love. Miss Schlupe already had taken them some clothing and a package of books, gathered up while Malina had been sleeping off her sedative. She had an excuse for daily visits to the column because of the office work involved in liquidating her business.

Three of her assistants were living on the lower levels, supposedly to guard her property until liquidation was completed. They didn't know the children were in the column, but they had strict orders not to admit anyone without Miss Schlupe's permission.

"I doubt that they could keep the gesardl out," Miss Schlupe said, "but at least no one will wander in and find the children by accident. We haven't solved anything, of course. With the column being watched, it'll be awfully tough getting them out. And if we get them out, then we'll have the problem of finding another hiding place."

Malina did not need to be told that the only permanent solution was to spirit them away from the world of Montura.

"Mr. Darzek will think of something," Miss Schlupe had said confidently.

Now, as Malina stepped around her children's abandoned pallets to open her bedroom door, she heard that gentleman's voice. He and Miss Schlupe were in the lounge, quietly talking in English. Malina was curious enough about this miracle worker to eavesdrop.

"When I got up, I tripped over URSDwad," Darzek said, "He jumped up wanting to know if it was his watch. We were in space too long. Does this world have anything resembling a bath and breakfast?"

A gesardl secretary, again posted outside Malina's bedroom door, was eying her suspiciously. Leaving the door open, she returned to her pallet. She heard Miss Schlupe tell Darzek about the bath lounge and offer him a choice of canned goods from Malina's stock or a stale submarine sandwich. He said he'd have the bath first and hurried away. Malina dozed off again while trying to devise a rescue: arena column to shuttle ship to one of E-Wusk's freighters.

Their voices awakened her. Darzek had returned and evidently was eating a sandwich while studying the view from the curving lounge windows. "It's a sick-looking world," he said. "It needs its face lifted."

"We've seen sicker," Miss Schlupe said.

"Looking down on it like this is like seeing it on a viewing screen," Darzek said absently. "I can't remember the last time I looked down on a living world that wasn't about to be murdered."

"Then what Rok Wllon said is true? You really are going to save the universe?"

"I don't seem to be doing so well. Someone better do it."

"Another sandwich?" Miss Schlupe asked. "I've got hundreds left. It's an appalling waste."

"Can't you freeze them?"

"Nope. I've got some in cold boxes, which are crude refrigerators, but they have no frozen foods. I wanted to put in a line of ice cream products, but there's no way to make ice cream when there's no ice and no cream, or even milk."

"Down, Schluppy. We aren't here to Americanize the galaxy. Where's Ceres this morning?"

"Ceres?"

"Tragic mother who'd lost her children. Wrong complexion, much too blonde, but she had all the other characteristics."

"She's sleeping?"

"What about the children?"

Miss Schlupe must have made some kind of signal, because he changed the subject instantly. "Schluppy, I never heard of this place until URsDwad brought Rok Wllon's message. What's so special about Montura?"

"We've been trying to figure that out ever since we arrived. I don't know, except that it's very special as a trading center."

"Is there some kind of advanced scientific establishment here?"

"Not that anyone has ever heard of. According to Supreme, the whole purpose of our mission is to get on the good side of the natives, and until this incident with the children, we didn't know there were any. I still don't know where they keep themselves. The world has no cities or towns, no roads, no engineering works, no nothing.

Except for the mart, there's no sign of any kind of habitation any-where."

"Then they must live underground," Darzek said.

Miss Schlupe repeated the word doubtfully. *"Under*ground?"

"This terrain looks similar to what would be called a karst plateau on Earth. It's probably riddled with caverns. That wouldn't make the natives unique, though, or even interesting. Isn't there anyone or anything at the mart that's remarkable?"

Miss Schlupe was silent for a moment. "There's the kloatraz. It's certainly unusual-looking, but it's only a computer. I've a hunch that it communicates telepathically with the creatures that work for it. Is that remarkable?"

"Probably not. Anything else?"

"There are life forms and products that confound the imagination, but that isn't what you mean."

"Anyone from this galaxy would consider them ordinary," Darzek said. "I'll have a look around."

"Mr. Darzek—about the children—"

"Mmm—yes. If we came here to get on the good side of the na-tives, that wasn't the way to do it. Have you figured out why Supreme recommended this kind of medical specialist? Not even a hint? Strange. It wouldn't be the first time Supreme has produced an enigma, but I've never known it to goof on something it stated so precisely."

"The goof was Rok Wllon's."

"It would seem so. At the very least, he should have found a skin specialist with interworld experience. If he thought he had to bring someone from Earth, a veterinarian would have been far better equipped to deal with alien life forms than a physician. I suggest that the Darr family be shipped back to Earth. The sooner accom-plished—"

"But the children!"

"I'll think about it," Darzek said.

Miss Schlupe told him about Arluklo, in case he wanted an in-terpreter, and walked to the transmitter with him.

Malina got out of bed and went to the lounge windows for her own view of what Darzek had called a sick-looking world. Miss Schlupe returned in a thoughtful mood.

"He's aged terribly," she said. "He must have had horrible experi-ences."

Malina made no comment. A miracle worker whose reaction to a problem was to send it home did not inspire confidence. She was evolving a plan of her own, and as soon as she had munched one of the stale sandwiches she went down to the bath lounge with two of the secretaries trailing after her and left them waiting outside while she had another steam bath. She intended to repeat the performance six or eight or ten times a day. Eventually they would become suspicious about all this steam bathing, especially if they investigated and found she'd never been in the lounge until her children disappeared. It would focus their attention on an area far from the real hiding place.

From the bath lounge she went to the Kloa Common. She was not particularly surprised to find Jan Darzek there, but what he was doing surprised her. He had abstracted a stool from one of the cubicles, and he sat hunched forward, elbows on his knees, staring at the kloatraz. The flickering illumination dramatically highlighted his unhealthy pallor and reinforced her conclusion that he was not a well man. He did not notice her, and she did not speak to him.

She had asked the gesardl secretaries for a copy of the treaty between the gesardl and the natives. One had been produced for her, and Arluklo had been designated to translate it for her. He escorted her to his cubicle and began to read from a formidably abstruse legal document. She understood none of it.

After a time she stopped him. "Never mind that," she said. "All I want to know right now is what it says about my children."

For the first time in her contacts with Arluklo, she found the klo speechless.

"Where does it mention children?" she asked.

"It doesn't mention children," Arluklo said.

"Then of course it doesn't apply to my children. Please inform the gesardl of that and ask it for a legal justification of this persecution it's engaged in."

She took her leave with what she hoped was an impression of smiling innocence. Jan Darzek was still perched on his stool, hypnotically concentrating on the kloatraz, and again she walked past him without speaking. Outside the common, she resolutely turned her back on the arena. If she went near the central column, the temptation to look up, to count the windows—eleventh, twelfth, and thirteenth levels, Miss Schlupe had said—would have been overwhelming. Instead, with the gesardl secretaries still solemnly marching after her, she returned to the bath lounge and took another steam bath.

She then went back to the Prime Common to wait for Miss Schlupe, who was meeting with the gesardl to discuss the uproar that still raged in the wake of her closing the refreshment stand. E-Wusk sat in his private cubicle looking forlorn—a trader forbidden to trade. A few of his assistants were lounging about in a desultory manner.

Malina joined him and patiently listened to his inventory of complaints. She wondered if, like the mythical songbird forbidden to sing, a trader forbidden to trade would waste away and die.

Miss Schlupe burst from the transmitter. She called excitedly, "I've seen a native! I actually saw one! There was a native at the gesardl meeting!"

They gathered about her excitedly—Malina, E-Wusk, and several of the assistants. The ubiquitous gesardl secretaries stood looking on blankly.

"*Now* I understand why Supreme thought the natives needed a dermatologist," Miss Schlupe said. "They wear—at least, this one wore —heavy protective clothing and a thick, tinted light shield. He looked like a monster from the nether regions. No wonder the children threw stones. If I'd met a creature like that in the woods, I'd have thrown something myself."

Malina said thoughtfully, "What we have to find out is *why* they wear protective clothing and a thick tinted light shield."

"What we have to find out," Jan Darzek's voice said, "is how a stone thrown by a child could cause the death of a creature wearing heavy protective clothing and a thick tinted light shield."

They all turned and stared. None of them had seen him come in.

"How much of the head did the light shield cover?" Darzek asked.

"In terms of a human, the area from the forehead to the nose, at least," Miss Schlupe said. "And it curved around past where a human's ears would be."

"Then the stone must have struck it on top of the head or in the back. Describe this protective clothing."

"It was white. It seemed thick. At least, it hung loosely and in folds, as though the suit were five sizes too large."

"Did it cover the head?"

"It covered everything except an opening for the eyes, and the light shield covered that."

"One would think it would give the head some protection. Has anyone seen this dead native? Is he lying in state somewhere?"

No one knew.

"As for why they wear protective clothing and a light shield," Darzek went on, "they live underground. Obviously they've adapted to an underground existence, or else they never lived on the surface. Light probably is painful to them."

"It might even be deadly if their skin lacks the necessary protective pigmentation," Malina said.

Rok Wllon arrived, accompanied by his klo interpreter. This new development was explained to him, and he exclaimed jubilantly, "Supreme was right! Supreme always is right!" He turned to Malina. "Now all you have to do is cure them, and our problem is solved. They might even forgive the horrible behavior of your children."

"Why would they want to be cured?" Malina asked. "If their condition evolved naturally, it'll be highly advantageous to an underground life. They certainly wouldn't want to make such a drastic change just so one of them could occasionally attend a gesardl meeting, or look at flowers in the park, without protective clothing. Probably most of the population never come to the surface." She turned to Miss Schlupe. "Do you want to come with me?"

"Where?" Miss Schlupe asked.

"To the gesardl. I feel a solemn obligation to pay my respects to the body of this native my children murdered."

"Good idea," Miss Schlupe said. She asked Darzek, "Do you want to come?"

He shook his head. "I've invited some traders in to see my recordings."

They started toward the transmitter. Then Malina turned and called, "Mr. Darzek. Thank you!"

He nodded and smiled. E-Wusk was emitting a low rumble, which meant that he was chuckling to himself. Rok Wllon was regarding them with what looked remarkably like panic.

The gesardl consisted of fifty variegated life forms, ranging in appearance from the diminutive klo member to several mountainous masses of quivering flesh. They filled fifty of the fifty-one elevated places around the circumference of their circular meeting room in the mushroom top of the arena column. The fifty-first, the empty place, was the one occasionally occupied by a native observer. Entrance to the room was through the transmitter frame that stood at its center.

Miss Schlupe and Malina took positions near the transmitter, and, with Miss Schlupe translating into the mart language, Malina began with a simple, polite request—to pay their respects to the dead. After several exchanges, she was flatly accusing the gesardl of collaborating in a monstrous conspiracy, and the gesardl members had attained a state of consternation that far outrivaled Rok Wllon's.

"I think we're hitting pay dirt," Malina said, looking about the room. "Tell them there's no possible way the children could have killed or even injured that native, and we insist on seeing him." Miss

Schlupe did. "Tell them," Malina said, "that Montura is the only world in two galaxies where the request would not be honored as a matter of course. We want to know why simple principles of justice are denied here. We *demand* to see that native!" Miss Schlupe did.

Eventually a messenger was dispatched. Malina and Miss Schlupe kept their places in front of the transmitter. Miss Schlupe had told the gesardl that no one else was leaving until the native was produced, and they meant that. The gesardl would have to pass over or through them or sit where it was until the native appeared.

They waited.

The messenger returned, with nothing to report except that the message had been delivered. The atmosphere of consternation became more intense. "I think," Miss Schlupe observed, "that the gesardl isn't used to the idea of natives coming when summoned. I think it's usually the other way around."

But that time the natives came when summoned.

Two of them emerged from the transmitter and stepped around Malina and Miss Schlupe before they were aware of their presence. One went directly to the circle's vacant seat. The other remained standing near the transmitter.

The native sitting with the gesardl spoke directly to Miss Schlupe, articulating the common language in sonorous, bell-like intonations. Miss Schlupe listened with increasing indignation.

Finally she turned to Malina. "This character," she said, pointing to the native who stood near them, "is our lately lamented professor of botany."

Malina stared at her. "You mean—he's the one the children are supposed to have murdered?"

"That's what the other character said."

"What kind of a farce is this?"

"That's what I intend to find out," Miss Schlupe said grimly.

It was the allegedly deceased professor's turn. He told his story at some length, speaking a similarly sonorous intonation but a different language. The klo member of the gesardl translated, and then Miss Schlupe translated the klo's translation.

"He saw one of the children throw stones," Miss Schlupe said, "but he paid no attention. He did not see the throwing of the stone that hit him, but others did. Evidently it knocked him out. When he came to, it hurt very much."

"Please convey my apologies and sympathy for the hurt," Malina said. "Then ask the rat where the stone hit him."

The question, relayed by Miss Schlupe and the klo translator, brought an answering gesture: squarely on top of the head.

"Please convey my congratulations on his rapid and complete recovery," Malina said icily.

Comment and reply traveled the same route. The professor suffered acute headaches for some time after the incident, but now he was fully recovered.

"Ask him," Malina said, "why he has made himself a party to this outrageous accusation of murder when there has been no murder. There has not even been a serious injury."

Miss Schlupe translated. The klo translated. This time the answer came from the native who sat with the gesardl.

Miss Schlupe was thunderstruck. "He says," she translated, "that there clearly was a murderous intent. And Monturan law makes no distinction between the intention and the deed."

## 15

Their fury of indignation carried them as far as the Prime Common, where they burst from the transmitter, with Miss Schlupe calling, "Mr. Darzek—" and froze in horror. They stood in an urban street, and the dead lay about them in widening puddles of purpling ooze.

Belatedly Malina remembered that Jan Darzek was having some traders in to view his recordings. So realistic was the sickening detail that when Malina and Miss Schlupe scuttled out of the projection they gingerly stepped around bodies and puddles. The two gesardl secretaries following them stumbled and fell in their attempt to keep their multiple feet unsoiled.

But there were no traders. The audience consisted only of E-Wusk and some assistants. The perplexed and horrified resident delegation of gesardl secretaries had withdrawn to the room's perimeter and was viewing the projection surreptitiously while pretending to ignore it.

Jan Darzek sat poised at the edge of the projection. He had fashioned a comfortable chair for himself by placing a low stool beside a high hassock, which gave him a back to lean against, but he was leaning forward with his eyes fixed hypnotically, wholly oblivious to anything except the simulated tragedy.

"Where are the traders?" Miss Schlupe asked.

"They did not come," E-Wusk said. "They are afraid they will be interdicted, too, if they associate with us."

"The cowards!" Miss Schlupe said scornfully. "The cowardly idiots!" She added, making it sound like an afterthought, "Our mission here is ruined, I suppose."

"Rok Wllon thinks if we were to turn the children over to the gesardl immediately—"

"Nonsense. Rok Wllon is another cowardly idiot. Anyway, how can we turn over what we don't have?" She was watching Jan Darzek. "He's been seeing this sort of thing for months—watching it happen, watching worlds and waiting for it to happen—no wonder he's aged!"

The projection changed: another world, another life form dying horribly in its frenzied flight from nothing to nowhere. Malina asked bewilderedly, "What causes it?"

"The Udef," E-Wusk said. "The Unidentified Death Force."

"That's a fancy way of saying no one knows," Miss Schlupe said.

E-Wusk continued soberly, "Gul Darr says that when it touches a world every large life form is doomed. Not one individual escapes. His scientists studied it and analyzed it and performed every test they could think of, and they had no more notion of what it is now than they had in the beginning. It's invisible. The only sounds they've detected are the screams of its victims. It's odorless and tasteless. The scientists built instruments sensitive enough to detect a puff of smoke in the atmosphere of a world, but the Udef doesn't have that much substance. Scientifically it doesn't exist, and yet it murders the population of any world it touches."

Malina looked again at Jan Darzek, who remained hypnotically engrossed in the projection. He had come to Montura in pursuit of a will-o'-the-wisp in the form of a tantalizing hint from Supreme because everything else he had tried had failed utterly. He was not a man accustomed to failing, and to fail in this, when so many innocent lives, so many worlds, were being destroyed was killing him. No wonder he looked ill.

Even if Supreme's hint had substance behind it, Darzek was about to fail again because Malina's children had murdered a native. Except that they hadn't.

E-Wusk, too, had aged. If his friend Gul Darr told him all the intelligent life in the universe was threatened, he had to believe it, and what he had seen in the recordings had shocked him out of his lamentations about being unable to trade. He had been studying a star projection upon which the known route of the Udef had been traced. "So many worlds destroyed," E-Wusk ruminated. "So many doomed. Perhaps all of them—all of us—are doomed."

Miss Schlupe, always interested in practical information, asked, "How long will it take it to get here?"

"The velocity seems unpredictable," E-Wusk said. "It rushes, it dawdles, it overlooks worlds and goes back for them, it takes leaps, it zigzags forward and backward. But over a period of time it seems to cut an enormous swath straight through a galaxy.

"Then it could be here shortly."

"Gul Darr doesn't think that likely, but he won't say it's impossible. Who could know what is impossible for a thing like this?"

"Every scientist in two galaxies ought to be recruited to work on it," Miss Schlupe said. "This galaxy should be alerted immediately. Gul Darr must show his recordings to the gesardl. It's possible to make the gesardl sit and pay attention to something. We just proved that."

"The members of the gesardl come from only thirty-nine different worlds," E-Wusk said. "Their activities are concentrated here. They have very little status except on Montura. We must reach traders who have strong links with their home planets—strong enough so that when they describe the unbelievable, they will be believed. Still, there would be no harm in showing it to the gesardl, and if the gesardl is willing to watch, then perhaps the other traders would be willing to watch also. What have you two been up to?"

They told him of their experience in confronting the murdered native. E-Wusk said meditatively, "If their law makes no distinction between the intention and the deed, whoever enforces the law has to make a presumption of intent. I wave my hand in your direction. Is it a threatening gesture, or just a gesture, or is my hand really en route to scratching an itch on my back? If I have a murderous intent, is it directed to you or at the itch? And what if the person making such a presumption has a murderous intent of his own? I don't remember ever encountering such a premise before."

"It's a legal absurdity," Miss Schlupe said. "We've simply got to get the children away from Montura."

"To be sure," E-Wusk said and added blandly, "if we can find out where they are."

"It wouldn't hurt to have a plan ready," Miss Schlupe said, dropping her voice. "Do you have any idea how it could be done?"

"It would be difficult, because the gesardl controls all the transportation."

"Think about it," Miss Schlupe said. "See if you can find a way to do it." URSDwad had joined them. Miss Schlupe said to him, "Do you have an extra projector?"

He did.

"Could you make a selection of recordings and Gul Darr's scientific data? I'd like to present them to the kloatraz. It may have data relevant to the Udef, and even if it doesn't we can ask it to evaluate Gul Darr's materials. That could be a help in persuading the traders to cooperate."

"I'll get them ready," ursDwad said.

They went to their apartment with ursDwad, and for once the gesardl secretaries did not follow. The projections they were trying not to watch had mesmerized them. While ursDwad rummaged through his luggage, Malina and Miss Schlupe sat in the lounge and whispered.

"I've thought and thought," Miss Schlupe said. "If we could get a message up to our ships—which we can't, I've tried—or if one of the other traders would help us—which none of them would, they're all frightened—or if Mr. Darzek has a technician on this ship that brought him from the Lesser Galaxy, and we could get him down here—but we can't. What I'm trying to say is that if we had a transmitter frame, or if we could fix the transmitter in our common so it would connect with a transmitter on one of the ships, or something like that, then we could transmit the kids up to a ship and escape with them."

"Would they let the ship leave?" Malina whispered back.

"No, but I'm sure the captain could find a way around that. Maybe it could make a transmitting leap from its berth or just leave without permission. The problem is to get them up there, but I can't think of a way to send a message. A transmitting frame can be put down by point transmission, but that's a touchy and very conspicuous operation and anyway we couldn't arrange to have it done without sending a message. I just don't know. Do you want to come to the Kloa Common with me?"

"I've nothing else to do except take a steam bath," Malina said, "and I've already had two today."

"Isn't that overdoing the cleanliness bit, even for a doctor?"

Malina whispered her plot to misdirect the gesardl's attention to the bath lounge, and Miss Schlupe whispered back that it was difficult and even risky to try to outguess an alien because his mental process worked in peculiar ways—the gesardl might become interested in the places she stayed away from, rather than the places she visited, and perhaps it was time Malina came to the column and helped her straighten out her books.

"I hope so!" Malina exclaimed.

"I'll think about it."

"What happened to the arena revolt over closing the refreshment stand?"

"It petered out," Miss Schlupe said disgustedly. "They're nothing but a pack of cowards."

URSDwad came in with the projector, some recordings, and the scientific data in a convenient carrying case, and they left for the Kloa Common. Two of the secretaries made the distasteful rush through the projection to follow them. Malina's parting glimpse of Jan Darzek was of an ashen-faced man staring at the death of yet another world.

Miss Schlupe told Arluklo what she wanted, and he summoned some of his fellows and quickly cleared away cubicles to form an open space near the kloatraz. Miss Schlupe set up the projector and began to play the recordings. One doomed population after another poured forth to die horribly between the kloa's cubicles.

The enormity of the thing defied Malina's comprehension, but even if it had not, she had no interest in comprehending. She was much too filled with worry about the fate of her children to be concerned about the fate of distant worlds long since dead, and she had seen enough of Jan Darzek's recordings. She turned her attention to the Kloa Common.

Except for Arluklo and a few others who were assisting him, the kloa came and went in their usual scurrying numbers and paid no attention to the projection. The kloatraz, too, seemed to be conducting the common's trading business as usual, but Malina reminded herself that a massive computer could handle hundreds or perhaps thousands of jobs at the same time.

For a time she speculated as to how it was handling this particular job. Did it have cameras concealed somewhere beneath that creamy white surface? Or was Miss Schlupe correct in thinking that the kloa communicated with it telepathetically, which meant that it was viewing the projection through the eyes of Arluklo and his fellow kloa.

She tried to imagine how such an enormous object had been constructed. One infinitesimally fine layer at a time, probably, the way an oyster secreted a pearl. More likely, a layer of microscopic, infinitely complicated circuitry, alternated with layers of creamy white insulation, sprayed or dipped. The construction would have been as much a work of genius as the design—the product of an age, rather than a moment, like a Gothic cathedral: a slow, unhurried accumulation of technology reflected in the slow, unhurried growth of that immense, creamy whiteness with its dazzling complexity of internal flickerings, its flashing and exploding lights. Occasionally the illumination seemed to change subtly in hue, becoming slightly reddish when a number of lights came on at the same time.

Suddenly she remembered that Supreme, who had thought up this incomprehensible mission for her—for all of them—also was a computer. Had Supreme sent a mission to Montura merely to get in touch with the kloatraz? She suppressed a giggle. Had it used the tragic urgency of the Udef threat as an excuse to send love letters?

An abrupt change in the nature of the projection made her turn to it again. Now it was showing a visual survey of one of Darzek's ships that had been caught by the Udef as it orbited a doomed world. Malina looked once, carefully, and turned away.

Miss Schlupe was going through a sheaf of scientific data with Arluklo when the projection of the last recording faded. The other kloa who had been watching quietly withdrew.

"Does the kloatraz have any record of a similar menace?" Miss Schlupe asked.

"No."

"Does it have any comment on the failure of the scientists' instruments to detect the nature of the Udef?"

"No. It has searched its memory fully and it has no information that would be useful in understanding such a force."

"Will the klo member of the gesardl recommend that the gesardl and all of the mart's leading traders view the recordings?" Miss Schlupe asked.

"It will recommend them to all who wish to see them," Arluklo answered.

Miss Schlupe politely thanked Arluklo and, through him, the kloatraz. She packed up the projector, recordings, and data.

"This is a disappointment," she muttered to Malina. "I expected— but never mind. Would you take these back to the Prime Common? I have work to do in my office."

They went their separate ways, each trailing a gesardl secretary.

Jan Darzek's projector had been turned off. He was still seated on the same improvised chair, but now he leaned back with his gaze fixed on the ceiling. E-Wusk had left off worrying about the Udef to worry about his assistants. He was accustomed to working them hard, and they were having difficulty in accommodating themselves to a life of leisure. Since the mart was designed for a furious pace of commercial activity and nothing else, there were no recreational facilities.

"Why not ask the gesardl if your assistants can play in the park?" Malina suggested bitterly.

Darzek's gaze left the ceiling with a snap. He straightened up and asked, "Whose idea was that?"

"Mine and Miss Schlupe's jointly," Malina said. "I wanted a

place for the children to play. She'd seen the park from the air, so she got permission for us to use it."

"Interesting that this trouble with your children happened on the day I arrived here. Who knew I was coming?"

Malina left the answer to E-Wusk, who said firmly, "No one. Rok Wllon said you might come later, but no one knew for certain or had any idea when it would be. You surprised all of us."

Malina said quietly, "It seems that my children, or one of them, really did throw stones at a native. It can't be more than coincidence that it happened on the day you arrived here. How could anyone have conspired to arrange that?"

"Someone could have been looking for an opportunity and used that one," Darzek said.

Before Malina could answer, Miss Schlupe stumbled from the transmitter. Incredibly, she looked as though she'd been crying or was about to. For a moment she could not speak. She stood staring at them.

Then Rok Wllon stepped from the transmitter, his monster face smugly triumphant. He was followed by an anxiously fluttering Arluklo.

"He gave them the children!" Miss Schlupe gasped.

"I asked the kloatraz to find them," Rok Wllon said expansively. "It analyzed the possible hiding places and detected a use of water high up in the column above Gula Schlu's place of business. It was a clever place for them to hide. The column had been searched and then watched closely, and the gesardl cannot understand how they could get into it without being seen. Anyway, the kloa have turned the children over to the gesardl, and the gesardl has turned them over to the natives, and justice will be done. We can proceed with our mission."

Malina was too stunned to speak.

Miss Schlupe turned on Arluklo. "You dirty traitor! I never thought the kloa would stoop so low."

Arluklo said plaintively, "But why would you not want to secure justice?"

"What was that about proceeding with our mission?" Darzek asked Rok Wllon.

"Since I was instrumental in finding the children, the gesardl has acknowledged that its suspicions were misplaced and the Prime Common was not obstructing justice but attempting to further it. The interdiction has been canceled. We can proceed with our mission."

"How do you suggest that we proceed?" Darzek asked.

Rok Wllon did not answer.

"There are worse things than interdictions," Miss Schlupe said heatedly. "It's possible to be ostracized and still be respected, and as long as the children were missing, there was hope that we could find a way around the problem. Now there's no hope at all, and in addition, you've made laughingstocks of all of us."

## 16

Malina saw the gesardl distortedly, as through a nightmarish warp of light and tears: she stammering a plea for mercy; the klo member translating; the native observer passive behind his concealing light shield; Rok Wllon, who had been present on some business of his own when she arrived, in a towering rage.

Rok Wllon left abruptly, not waiting for the end of her plea. And when she finished and stood facing the gesardl's foreboding indifference, he returned, still in a rage and accompanied by Miss Schlupe. Arluklo contritely trailed after them. He seemed pathetically repentant over the role the kloa had played in capturing the children, but for all that they remained captured.

"Doctor Darr claimed," Rok Wllon said resentfully to Miss Schlupe, "that *she* threw the stones. She claimed that she was the one responsible. And there were *witnesses* to the children's deed. You depraved and lying humans will destroy all of my work!"

"Put the lid on it!" Miss Schlupe snapped. "There's nothing depraved about a mother trying to save her children. We should be doing something ourselves."

Malina slumped to the floor and muffled her sobs with her hands.

Miss Schlupe spoke to Arluklo in large-talk. "I want to talk to the gesardl, and I don't want any possibility of being misunderstood, so I'll use this language. Will you translate—*carefully?*"

Arluklo made his multi-limbed gesture of assent.

"I heard a comment when I came in," Miss Schlupe said. "Something about animals that tell deliberate untruths. I answer—what kind of animals are you, to deny ultimate responsibilities?" She paused while Arluklo translated the question. There was no response. "The children were in Doctor Darr's care," Miss Schlupe went on. "In a moral society she would be fully responsible for their transgressions. Her error was in assuming that this is a moral society. I am shocked, as she was, that the morality of this planet and this galaxy is so primitive that this fact must be explained to you."

Arluklo translated, and then he translated the reply of a quivering mass of flesh that sat beside the shielded native. "Naturally visitors to the mart are subject to the law of Montura. How could it be otherwise? If each visitor chose to observe his own laws, chaos would result."

"This governing body somehow has managed to completely misunderstand the import of what is happening," Miss Schlupe said. "You're attempting to apply the legal procedures normally followed when citizens of another world are in conflict with a Monturan native. The situation here is that citizens of another *galaxy* are involved, and this brings the case under the sternly enforced intergalactic laws that unfortunately you have not taken the trouble to become familiar with. I suggest that you remedy this oversight immediately. Defiance of intergalactic law calls for harsh reprisals. I advise all of you to complete your trading commitments as soon as possible and dispose of your inventories."

She helped Malina to her feet and firmly guided her through the transmitter without waiting for Arluklo to finish his translation. They reached the Prime Common with Rok Wllon still remonstrating at their heels. Miss Schlupe told him, "Sit down somewhere and count to a million. I'll talk to you later."

In their own apartment, Jan Darzek stood looking out of the lounge windows. Miss Schlupe got Malina settled on a hassock and wearily seated herself on another. "I blew it," she announced. "I let my mouth run while my brain was turned off, and before I got the two synchronized I'd threatened intergalactic intervention. Any chance we could import your thousand ships for a weekend, just to frighten people?"

Darzek said, without looking around, "My thousand ships wouldn't be noticed. Have you any idea how many ships are docked at Monturan transfer stations this moment? Probably ten times that many. If you think the arena is a turmoil, you should watch the ships exchanging goods in space. Their techniques are worth studying."

"Then scratch the ships," Miss Schlupe said resignedly. "Is there any chance my stupid threats will have some effect?"

Darzek kept his face to the window. "The natives are the problem. You have no clue whatsoever as to how they think. And no matter how much you frighten the gesardl, you won't accomplish anything unless the gesardl is somehow able to pressure the natives. I'm afraid it isn't."

"We have one clue as to how the natives think," Miss Schlupe said. "They consider the intention the same as the deed. We've got to do something and quickly, but it's no good threatening reprisals if we haven't the means of carrying them out."

"You have the means."

"Where is it?"

"On the way. Announce that Montura will be permanently closed to all commerce and communication. Announce that the population —natives and traders—will be exterminated. If they ask you how, show them a few of my recordings." He went on meditatively, "It'll be rather interesting. On every world we've recorded, only one life form was involved. Each life form has its own innate resistance to the Udef, ranging between extremes of two to about ten minutes. On a world with a single life form, everyone is affected almost equally. On this world there'll be a tremendous variety of reactions. It'll be a genuine drama. This is the proper location for it. The place looks like a motion picture set. The mart was constructed here for the same reason motion picture sets are built in the middle of some damnable wasteland—because the land was cheap and conveniently located. As soon as the last scenes are shot, the mart will be dismantled and carted away. The landscape will be much more attractive without it. A little beauty in an ugly place is as much a blight as a little ugliness in a beautiful place."

"Why don't you say it?" Malina demanded harshly. "What does the fate of two children matter when sooner or later the Udef would kill them anyway?"

Darzek turned. "I've seen so many high civilizations destroyed," he said softly, "and so many promising worlds reduced to garbage heaps of rotting corpses, and so many innocent intelligences suddenly murdered that I find myself looking at that crowd in the arena and wondering why everyone is still alive. The danger is real enough. This galaxy next, and then ours. The only thing that stands between the Udef and all the intelligent life in the universe is time. But I wouldn't willingly abandon even one child, any more than I'd abandon one civilization. The question is what possibly can be done."

"They may be dead already," Malina said dully.

"They may be. I'd think it unlikely, but we're dealing with wholly unpredictable mentalities. They may be dead, or they may be in no danger at all. If they're in danger, Miss Schlupe's threat may have bought some time. Remember, we're as unpredictable to the natives as they are to us. If they're wise, they'll proceed slowly and carefully until they find out whether we have the means to make good the threat. Is there any clue as to why Supreme thought the natives so important?"

Miss Schlupe shook her head. "Supreme missed the mark about their needing a dermatologist. Maybe it's wrong about their being important, too."

Darzek turned to the window again. "Supreme has been accumulating its data for a long, long time, and it probably has information about Montura that antedates the mart. Supreme reasons from an accumulation of facts, but we don't know whether it weighs the possibility that some of the facts may be centuries out of date, or how it distinguishes between a reliable report and a rumor. The natives' skin condition is a fact. If the report described it as an unfortunate affliction that forced the natives to wear protective clothing, then Supreme would conclude that the natives need dermatological attention. I wouldn't say it missed the mark, though. I questioned Rok Wllon closely. Supreme said we should establish friendly relations with the natives and secure their assistance. A positive statement. And Supreme said a dermatologist *might* be helpful."

"Either way, we've blown it," Miss Schlupe said. "How can we establish friendly relations with the natives now?"

"I'll think about it," Darzek said. He started for his bedroom. In the corridor, he turned. "I've decided to send Rok Wllon to Primores. Supreme should be questioned properly."

As his bedroom door closed after him, Miss Schlupe said concernedly, "He changed. The old Jan Darzek would have taken on the gesardl the way I did, only he would have made something happen." She got to her feet. "But what *can* we do? Maybe I'd better lie down, too."

Left alone, Malina took Jan Darzek's place at the window.

If her children were to be rescued, she would have to do it herself.

She thought for a time, and then she went looking for Arluklo.

At dusk, Malina watched Arluklo stroll casually through one of the mart exits and head across the landing field toward a remote ship. Malina waited until he'd disappeared behind the ship, and then she started after him at her own casual pace. He was waiting for her on the other side, and they moved off into the gathering darkness.

Night came on quickly. Although Montura had no natural moon, the belt of storage satellites, transfer stations, and ships that surrounded the planet diffused an ineffectual moonlight that was splendidly supplemented by light from the dense cluster of surrounding stars. Malina gladly would have exchanged all of that for one serviceable moon like Earth's. She stumbled through the darkness, with Montura's crumbling surface making each crumbling step a laborious undertaking. She had worn only a light coat, and the searching wind that swept down the broad valley quickly chilled her.

She asked Arluklo if he were cold; she sensed, though she could not see, his negative gesture. But if the temperature did not bother him, the treacherous terrain was harder on him than on her despite his multiplicity of feet. Once when the encrusted surface gave way under him, he stumbled and fell. She helped him up and found his leathery body surprisingly heavy. He crunched through the brittle crust as deeply as she did.

Steadily they floundered forward. They climbed a long, barren slope topped it, descended, and climbed again. It seems to Malina that she had walked an endless distance when finally she felt soft vegetation underfoot. They climbed over the low mound that formed a boundary and set off across the park.

As the strange, treelike plants became thicker, they blotted out large areas of sky and interposed their own murky shade on the night. Malina walked with hands outstretched in front of her to avoid bumping into them. Down the slope they went and splashed into a stream of water before Malina was aware of it. With sloshing feet she trudged after Arluklo: uphill, and then downhill again.

Finally she asked, "How much further?"

"It is not known precisely."

"It isn't? I thought you knew where it is!"

"I said I would find it. I will find it."

They moved on: uphill, and then downhill. She had not realized that the park was so vast. Suddenly Arluklo turned aside, and before she could follow she heard a dull, metallic thud.

She hissed, "Careful!"

When she reached him, he stood at the side of a tall mound, his multitude of fingers scratching their way across a smooth, metallic surface. Malina bent over and attempted to scrutinize it in the dim light. It was a door, as Arluklo had promised. An entrance.

Beyond it lay the underground world of the Monturans.

She moved her hands slowly over the smooth, unbroken surface.

Arluklo had stopped his scratching. "It must open only from within," he said.

She continued to feel the smooth surface. She could detect no latch or knob or button that might control the opening. She could not even trace a crack around the edge of the door with her fingernail, so tightly did metal fit to metal.

Wearily she stepped back. "What other entrances are there?"

"The one under the arena."

"Too dangerous," Malina said. With Arluklo as a guide, she had explored in that direction earlier in the day. The way led through one of the gesardl offices and a host of working secretaries. They would be caught before they started, and that entrance, too, probably was kept locked from within. "Where else?"

"There is no other entrance near the mart."

"We should have brought a light," Malina said, again searching the smooth surface. She worked at it for a long time before she gave up.

"It must open only from within," Arluklo said again.

She sat down tiredly. "It's a dirty shame—it probably isn't used much, which makes it ideal. What about entrances that aren't near the mart?"

"There are many, but all are at a distance."

"Is there a map of them? Could you take me to one?"

"A map could be made. Yes, I could take you to one."

"Good. We'll go tomorrow night."

Resolutely she got to her feet and headed back toward the mart. This time she led the way and Arluklo followed.

Early the next morning, Malina went to the Kloa Common for a long conference with Arluklo. When finally she left, she took with her a most ingenious map on parchment—it felt like parchment—with the terrain actually shown in shallow relief so that one looking down on the map had the dizzying effect of seeing the vast plateau from the air. On this map, where Arluklo had pointed out locations, Malina had drawn X's.

She also had a second map that consisted of a maze of meandering lines drawn on a transparent film. It represented all that the kloa knew about the Monturan underground cavern world. At the center, a small circle had been drawn to represent the area where the Monturans administered their justice. The transparency, superimposed on the map, showed the location of the caverns as well as it was known.

Returning to the apartment, Malina found that Miss Schlupe had baked a small batch of fresh rolls for their own use and made up some sandwiches.

"I wish I knew some other way to use all that smoked and spiced meat I have left over," she said.

"What sort of animal does it come from?" Malina asked.

"I'd rather not know. Too bad you weren't here this morning. You missed quite a show. We had a visitation from the gesardl."

Malina raised her eyebrows.

"All of it," Miss Schlupe went on. "All fifty members. They called to throw themselves on our mercy. The natives positively refuse to even discuss returning the children to us. In the meantime, word about Mr. Darzek's recordings has reached the gesardl—some of the secretaries saw them, and the kloatraz may have sent along a report—and the gesardl has somehow got the impression that the recordings were a preview of what will happen to Montura if they don't return the children. The members think they're being unfairly squeezed in the middle. They called to suggest that we take our reprisals against the natives and leave the innocent and peaceful traders alone."

"Who turned the children over to the natives?" Malina asked icily.

"My precise question. They answered that they'd only done it because they hadn't known we could do anything about it. Their position is that we should have informed them about the reprisals before they acted and not when it's too late for them to make amends. They're scared witless."

"Good for them."

Miss Schlupe nodded. "Definitely dirty pool, and I enjoyed every minute of it, which means I've permanently blown my chance at Rok Wllon's Upright Citizen of the Galaxy award. My only regret is that it isn't likely to have any effect. The natives still have the children, and evidently the natives don't scare."

"Arluklo thinks the natives aren't worried about the Udef because they live underground."

"They're due for a rude shock. Mr. Darzek says that victims with immediate access to an exit die outside. Those too far from an exit to reach it die inside. He found dead in mines a kilometer or more underground."

"Since the interdiction is off, would it be possible to see Montura Mart from space?" Malina asked.

Miss Schlupe raised her eyebrows but made no comment. "I don't see why not. Let's ask E-Wusk. He'll know which of his ships is in the best position for it."

In the Prime Common they walked into an enormous silence. E-Wusk and all of his assistants were gaping at the center of the room, where a confrontation was in progress: Rok Wllon and Jan Darzek.

They stood facing each other: Rok Wllon with an ugly pout of determination; Darzek calmly good-natured, his smile the velvet glove on the iron fist.

"The ship," Darzek said, "is ready to leave when you are. Surely you won't have much packing to do. Here's the list of questions, and this time please don't act like an errand boy. Don't just ask the questions and record the answers. Explore them, until you understand everything Supreme says and can explain it to me."

"I suggest," Rok Wllon said icily, "that you run your own errands. Supreme has entrusted me with the Monturan mission."

"To do what?" Darzek asked.

Again they faced each other in silence. "I suggest," Darzek said finally, "that you start packing. The ship is waiting."

Rok Wllon turned away, shoulders drooping, wide form bent almost to a crease, defeated. Darzek watched him go, and then he left himself, through the transmitter.

Miss Schlupe sounded a soft whistle. "Too bad he didn't do that the moment he arrived. But it's nice to know that Mr. Darzek is still Number One. Rok Wllon is a very capable administrator—really, he is, maybe the best in the central government—but he insists on trying to do everyone's job but his own."

Malina spent the afternoon in space. The individual in charge of the ship—whether captain or janitor she could not have said—gravely studied E-Wusk's note of instructions, installed an enormous viewing screen for her in an unused compartment, showed her how to use it, and left her to herself.

She quickly learned that the minute scrutinization from space of thousands of square kilometers of a world's surface was a far more complicated and time-consuming task than she'd anticipated. She narrowed the search area as much as possible and soon discovered how to do color match-ups, but even so she had to rush to finish as night's curving shadow began to move into the area.

It was night by the time she returned to Montura Mart. She was hungry and exhausted, and the first thing she did was go to the apartment's odd kitchen and help herself to the sandwiches Miss Schlupe had thoughtfully left there. Jan Darzek came in a moment later and joined her. They sat on hassocks on opposite sides of the lounge, solemnly munching their sandwiches.

Finally Darzek said, conversationally, "How much food did you take with you last night?"

Malina stared at him. "How—"

"I followed you. How much food did you take?"

She met his eyes firmly. They were an unyielding blue, but so, she fancied, were her own, and if he considered her another Rok Wllon, she had a surprise for him. She said politely, "Would it offend you if I said it's none of your business?"

"The mart is a long, long way from any important activity center of the natives," Darzek said. "Access is probably by way of a single, extremely long cavern, and the doorway in the park probably enters that same cavern. Have you thought about the implications of that?"

"I've just been looking at the mart from space," she said dryly. "The location at the edge of the plateau makes it fairly obvious that the Monturans wanted it as remote as possible but close enough for them to collect their profits and look after their interests."

"If that door had been open last night," Darzek said, "the odds are that you'd have entered it. It would have occurred to you that the next time it might be locked, so you'd have entered. And you'd have had to walk for days. So I asked—how much food did you take with you?"

"I hadn't thought about being tempted to enter it," she said. "Thank you. The next time I go anywhere near the park I'll take food."

"Is Arluklo to be trusted?"

"I think so. The kloa seem genuinely contrite over what happened. But do I have any choice?"

"Perhaps not. Did you investigate to see whether there's any kind of compass that works on this world?"

Miss Schlupe came in. Darzek said to her, "She would have started a long underground trek with no food, no water, no source of light, no equipment, and no idea of how to find her direction or which direction she wanted to go."

"There's plenty of water underground," Malina said defensively, "and we wouldn't have dared use a light even if we had one."

"You don't know that there's water, or that the water's safe to drink. Of course you'd need a light. There may be chasms to cross. You'd need a light, ropes, tools, all kinds of equipment, and as much food and water as you can carry. You'd need blankets and warm clothing—including some for the children. Your problem doesn't stop when you rescue them. You have to bring them back."

She glared at him resentfully.

"What about Arluklo?" he asked. "You'd have to take food for him, too. What does he eat?" He turned to Miss Schlupe. "Tell her, Schluppy."

"You shouldn't be trying something like this alone," Miss Schlupe said. "It'll take everyone's combined talents to bring it off. Strange worlds, and strange life forms, can be tricky things to deal with."

"You weren't doing anything!" she said accusingly.

"We've been getting ready for this ever since Rok Wllon pulled his act. I've spent most of the day fixing concentrated foods and making packs. Mr. Darzek has been getting supplies together. With Arluklo's help he even found some infragoggles. You'll be able to see—after a fashion—in the dark."

"I still haven't made up my mind about Arluklo," Darzek said. "Maybe the kloa are sincerely trying to make amends. On the other hand, their firm is a gesard, a member of the gesardl. Does it make sense that they're contrite enough to betray their own organization?"

"Everyone at the mart snubs them except us," Miss Schlupe said. "In addition to feeling contrite, maybe they'd like to get even."

"Maybe. On the other hand, maybe they'd like to get back into everyone's good graces by blowing the whistle on this conspiracy of ours—which is bound to make endless trouble if it succeeds or even if it doesn't."

"Any suggestions?" Malina asked.

"No. As you said, you have no choice. When do you plan on leaving?"

"Tonight."

"Better make it tomorrow night. We still have some preparations."

"We?"

"You weren't listening. Pulling off something like this takes combined talents. I'm coming with you."

"That's very generous of you." She smiled bitterly. "But this is my problem, and it has very little to do with the fate of the universe. If you have suggestions I'll listen gratefully, but when I leave, it'll be my expedition. I'm leaving tonight, and I'm going alone—with Arluklo."

"We may have as much as two hundred kilometers to walk," Darzek said. "One way. We explored the possibility of Schluppy reopening her refreshment stand to get a flyer back, but of course we couldn't use it with a gesardl chauffeur, and if we tried to take off without one, flight control would push a very large panic button and alert the natives. The one thing this project has got to have is secrecy, with the natives completely unsuspecting. So we'll have to walk. Better rest up and start tomorrow."

Malina shook her head. "Tonight. Arluklo and I. Listen," she said earnestly, "we're going to rescue my children, if that's possible, and nothing else. I don't say that saving the universe isn't the most important thing in any of our lives, but it's a complicated problem that isn't likely to be solved very soon, whether you come with me or not. My children are in danger now. Once they're safe, I'll gladly do anything

I can to help with your mission. Until they're safe, I'm not having you messing up their rescue by getting the universe mixed up in it. You can satisfy your curiosity about the natives some other time."

Darzek nodded. "You're quite right."

"So I'm going alone with Arluklo."

"Oh no. I'm coming with you, but you'll be in charge. As you said, your children are in danger now, and it's your mission. Now finish your meal. You might as well start on a full stomach. It'll be empty soon enough."

"I wish I could come with you," Miss Schlupe said wistfully, "but my bunions aren't equal to two hundred kilometers."

"Someone has to stay here and pretend things are normal," Darzek said. "You can keep harassing the gesardl and try to figure out what to do with the children once we get them back here. They'll have to be hidden until the furor dies down and then smuggled off the planet. Study the more voluminous life forms and see if you can make a couple of convincing costumes that will conceal a child."

Malina said, "Do you really think we have a chance?"

"Of course we do."

She was grateful, though she knew it was an act of desperation with no chance at all.

Arluklo arrived a short time later, and they gathered around a large hassock and studied the kloa maps.

Darzek took the transparency with the representation of the caverns and held it up to the light. "This can't be complete," he observed. "The whole system will be multileveled and complicated beyond anyone's ability to represent it on a flat surface. I suppose these are the main corridors—the superhighways or superwalkways. Do they run subway trains through these caverns, Arluklo?" The klo regarded him blankly. "Do they have any kind of vehicles at all?"

"Vehicles, yes."

"But no trains. A pity. What about taxis? It'd be nice to pop down an entrance—the one under the arena, for example—hail a cab, and say, 'Tunnel of Justice, please.' We may want to stay off the main routes, but it will be a help knowing where they are. Did you inquire about magnetic compasses?"

"No such thing is known here," Arluklo said.

"Pity. I don't suppose electronic navigational equipment comes in pocket sizes, or that we could figure out how to use it if it did, or that we could use it without being detected. The next question is whether these other entrances are likely to be locked like the one in the park."

"It is thought all of them are open," Arluklo said, "but that is not known definitely. They may be open but guarded. That is not known, either."

"So the only way to find out is to go there. Next question: Is there a rule-of-thumb navigational method on this world—stars, for example —that will get us to where we want to go?"

"I will guide you," Arluklo said.

Darzek eyed him skeptically. "Have you been to any of these entrances before?"

The question seemed to surprise Arluklo. "No," he said.

"You haven't been there before, but you will guide us?"

Malina felt skeptical herself. Perhaps the kloa were so eager to make amends that Arluklo was promising more than he could deliver.

But they had no choice.

"About our destination," Darzek said. He brought out a map of his own, an enormous composite photograph, upon which certain irregularly shaped small areas were outlined. "My assistants have been studying the planet from space ever since we arrived," he said. "They've picked out certain areas where there's a distinctive color pattern. I suspect that the Monturans grow kitchen gardens around the mouths of their caverns. They probably tend them at night." He turned to Malina. "Did you notice the colors today?"

"Yes. I noticed them where Arluklo marked the known entrances, and I picked out some others, but I didn't find this many."

"One of my suspected entrances is closer by sixty kilometers than the nearest of these entrances the kloa know about. Since the one is almost on a direct route to the other, we stand to save time and a lot of walking at very small risk." He pointed. "Arluklo, can you guide us here?"

"Yes."

"We're going to carry our supplies in back packs and probably we'll hand-pack some extra food that we'll eat first. What will you need for twelve or fourteen days?"

"Need?" Arluklo echoed.

"Food. Drink. Bandages for sore feet."

"I will carry my own," Arluklo said. The response sounded testy, and Darzek questioned him no further.

Malina was studying the map: a hundred and forty kilometers to find an entrance—maybe. Then, if it wasn't locked or guarded, a long underground trek through *populated* caverns. They would be fugitives traveling crowded city streets with no hiding places. The system of caves might be horrendously complicated. If they did manage to reach their objective and rescue the children, the alarm would be sounded, the entire underground population alerted, long before they could get back to the surface. If they managed to reach an exit, the long trek back to the mart would expose them to air or ground searches or a visual search from space. And if they did reach the mart, it would be in an uproar, every potential hiding place would be a trap—and they still would have the problem of getting the children off the planet.

Darzek seemed to sense her thoughts. "Still want to go?"

She nodded.

"Tonight?"

She nodded again.

He turned to Arluklo. "Are you ready to leave at once? We'll meet you at the kurog twanlaft exit as soon as we're ready."

Arluklo agreed and politely departed.

Darzek went to finish the packing.

Malina said to Miss Schlupe, "He seems like a different person today."

She nodded. "He's been struggling so long with an unsolvable problem that a problem he actually can do something about comes as a great relief—whatever the odds." She glanced scrutinizingly at Malina. "You know how long the odds are?"

"Yes," Malina said. "But I have no choice."

17

They mingled briefly with throngs of arriving and departing traders, and one at a time they joined groups heading for ships parked near the one they had selected as a rendezvous. Arluklo went first, a comically unusual-looking klo with a large, flopping pack on his back, but no one gave him a second glance. The kloa were so ubiquitous that they went about unnoticed. Malina and Darzek carried their packs and equipment as bulky packages wrapped in cloth. Miss Schlupe accompanied them—not because she was needed, but because she desperately wanted to do something to speed them on their way.

At the rendezvous point, standing in the broad shadow of the most remote spaceship on the field, Malina and Darzek donned their packs and draped coils of rope, tools, and handlights about their persons. Miss Schlupe handed each of them a package of food to be hand-carried until it was eaten. She took the cloth used to wrap the packages, folded it up, and tucked it under her arm.

"Well—good luck," she said. She started off obliquely toward a remote cluster of ships, from which she could approach the mart from the opposite direction to the one she had set out in.

They stood for a moment, watching her go, and then they turned their backs on the soft glow of light that suffused the landing field and headed off into the chill, overcast night.

It was much darker than the previous night. The overcast blotted out the ring of artificial moonlight and the stars, and as the glow of the mart and the occasional sparks of light from ascending or descending ships slowly receded, the uncertain footing became treacherous. When Malina nearly fell while stumbling down a steep descent into a dry stream bed, Darzek called a halt to suggest, politely, that they don their infragoggles.

Malina had not thought of them. She had associated this equipment with their invasion of the caverns and placed the goggles in the depths of her pack. After an embarrassing search she found them, and the impenetrable darkness gave way to dim outlines and enough detail to make walking much easier. There were no goggles for Arluklo, but his natural night vision seemed better than theirs with goggles.

They started off again, crunching along the impacted gravel of the dry stream bed. Arluklo led the way, Darzek followed, and Malina— it was her preference—brought up the rear. The going was easy for a time, with only an occasional treacherous pothole to avoid, and Malina was able to plod along mechanically, almost oblivious to the others, and keep her thoughts on her children.

Then the stream began to meander, and gradually it curved away from their course. They left it behind and made their way along a stone-strewn valley, where in low places thick vines thrust out long, firmly anchored shoots to trap an unwary foot. Unfortunately, the infraggogles did not pick up the low-lying vines. Once all three of them went down in a heap, after which they raised their feet high when they heard the metallic clicks of vine leaves stirring in the dry, cold wind.

Darzek, who had helped Arluklo to his feet, muttered in English, "He's heavy!"

"I know," Malina answered, "but he's not indestructible. We shouldn't be walking so close together."

They changed their formation to a wedge, with Arluklo at the point and Malina and Darzek walking on either side and slightly behind him.

As they moved up out of the shallow valley and into the wind, the chill night became bitterly cold. Malina was grateful for Miss Schlupe's last-minute suggestion that she wear ski pants and a heavy jacket; but the exertion of picking her way through uncertain footing soon had her perspiring. Once she tripped and was saved from falling only when Darzek adroitly caught her. She said, "Thank you." His muttered reply was indistinct.

Arluklo did not speak at all, but he seemed to know their route unerringly. To Malina's surprise, once away from the crumbling ground near the mart, he had less difficulty scurrying along on his clusters of spidery legs than they did on their two. His pace was slower than that of a human in a hurry, but for a long trek Malina thought it much less tiring, and it might even get them to their destination faster.

At dawn the footing became much easier. They could see rocks and vines and washes of gravel and avoid them; but they went no faster, because Arluklo held them to the same steady pace.

At full daylight, Malina called a halt. She had a decision to make.

It had been necessary to travel at night until they were safely away from the mart. They still could see ascending and descending shuttle ships high above it, but it seemed unlikely that anyone aboard would observe them or—even if he did—imagine that persons abroad in that barren land would not have a compelling and legal reason for it.

Now they could travel when they chose—when she chose—but they could not travel a hundred and forty or two hundred kilometers without a rest, and neither she nor Darzek had had much rest for more than two days. Should they prepare themselves for the risky foray underground with long rest periods, or should they push on to the limit of their endurance, risk arriving at their destination in a state of exhaustion, and hope there would be opportunity for rest on the way back?

Darzek had discovered a nest of tiny, scurrying ground creatures. Little had been known about Montura's flora and fauna at the mart, so Malina went to examine these curiosities. There was something oddly familiar about them.

Then Arluklo came over to see them, and she realized what it was. The creatures looked like a klo's smaller relatives a multiplicity of times removed. Was Arluklo a native Monturan? And had the planet spawned *two* intelligent life forms, one above ground and one below?

Malina and Darzek had a few mouthfuls of food and a swallow of water while Arluklo sat nearby with the air of patiently waiting for them. Then, having made her decision, Malina made ready to move on.

They would go as fast as they could, as far as they could, and rest as little as possible. Better to arrive in time, even if exhausted, than to be well rested and late.

The decision was hers, but again she had no choice.

For daylight travel, they spread out to make themselves less conspicuous. Arluklo, his elongated pack beating a muffled tattoo on his back with every one of his multiple steps, plodded far ahead. Malina and Darzek walked on opposite sides of a ravine. Probably the infrequent rains sent torrents of surface runoff down this deeply eroded watercourse. Here and there rocks had been tumbled into heaps that formed natural dams, and the water, seeping into the porous ground, produced deep sinkholes behind them. They circled the sinkholes and clambered over the piles of rock, and the sunbaked, decaying rock often crumbled under their weights. If they'd had a year or two in which to search, they might have found a natural entrance to the natives' cavern world—or dug one of their own.

Malina, finding the responsibilities of leadership a heavier burden than her pack, wrenched her thoughts from her children and began watching the others concernedly. Arluklo's multiple limbs worked as smoothly as an infinitely complicated machine. If one foot stumbled, several others were planted to keep him moving steadily forward. Only a slide that cut the ground from under him or two clumsy humans falling on top of him would unbalance the little klo. It disturbed her that she knew almost nothing about him. How far could he walk without tiring? Did the cold night air bother him? Now the rising sun was becoming uncomfortably warm, and he was walking hatless through an unshaded wasteland. Would he be subject to sunstroke? Did his pack really carry enough sustenance to support him through their long trek? Would he tell her the truth if she asked him, or would he attempt to match strides with them until he dropped?

Jan Darzek represented a different sort of problem. She suspected that she knew him too well. His physical condition certainly was poor, but he would be even less likely to confess to fatigue than Arluklo. She could only wait and see what mental problems she might have to cope with. For the moment, he seemed completely cooperative, even submissive.

He looked ridiculous. He wore clothing of his own design, and the outer garment was a fur-lined overall. The fur, he informed her, was a discovery of his on a world whose name meant nothing to her. It had some remarkable property of keeping the body warm while not permitting it to overheat, and the garment, turned inside out, was just as effective at keeping one cool. He had a monstrous fur-lined hat that supposedly functioned on the same principle. At dawn he had ceremoniously reversed this outer clothing, and the miraculous fur was a patchy, off-color white. Now he pranced along looking like a hyperactive fur-bearing animal with a slight case of the mange.

She had noticed, though, that he did not perspire as she did; and now, with the temperature climbing, she could remove her jacket, but the ski pants were uncomfortably warm and she had brought no others.

Darzek's impulsive curiosity both irritated and worried her. It was worse than that of her son Brian. He would not conserve energy and march in a straight line. He wandered about in all directions, here examining a fungus like fuzziness around the base of a rock, there studying a plant or something resembling the footprint of an animal. Once he crossed the ravine to show her a rock that had some kind of geological significance not entirely clear to her. Brian would have brought it to her because it was pretty. It amounted to the same thing.

But all of these concerns were peripheral to the one worry that consumed her. Were Brian and Maia treated kindly? Were they fed properly? The Monturans surely had children of their own. They were a civilized people, after their own fashion. They had some kind of ethical standards, or they would not have evolved that strange doctrine of intent. She prayed that they would treat her children with kindness and consideration and understanding, and at the same time she was desperately fearful that they would not.

Darzek, who had wandered so far off course that he disappeared behind a hill, returned to halt Arluklo with a shout. She hurried to him, and he showed her the mute marks of tragedy—the large footprints of a carnivore, the small footprints of a victim, and a scattering of scales and gnawed bones.

"If it's possible to estimate size by footprints, the winner was as large as a lion," Darzek said.

There seemed to be a superabundance of footprints for one lion. She puzzled over them for a moment, and then she looked about her. "What does it live on?"

"There's always a lot more life in a place than one sees when clomping through it," Darzek said. "If its prey weren't numerous, the carnivore wouldn't be here. Did you notice that the victim seems to have four legs? That would connect it with the evolutionary line of the two-legged, two-armed natives, but how will we classify a carnivore with at least eight legs? And both of them have the same kind of foot —round, with a rim on the outside like a concave hoof. Very peculiar."

"Is the thing likely to attack us?" Malina asked.

"I don't know. We can't resemble its natural prey, which seems to be quite small. Fortunately it's a solitary hunter. A pack of these things could constitute quite a menace."

Arluklo had joined them. They questioned him, but he knew nothing at all about Montura's wild animals.

"What should we do?" Malina asked.

"There's probably very little danger during the day," Darzek said. With a swift movement he plucked a small pistol from an inner pocket. "I brought this just in case. The caliber is too small for elephants, but it makes a noise, and it's a bit more reassuring than having nothing at all. If you see one of these things, holler."

They plodded onward. When a ravine twisted aside, they mounted to the dismal plateau surface until they encountered another headed in the proper direction. Arluklo led them as confidently as a navigator with a gyroscopic compass. Even in a meandering ravine he cut across loops and seemed to deviate from his course very little.

Peering across the bleak, wind-swept plateau, Malina experienced a flash of revelation. She was looking at this land wrong side to. She was seeing what would be, in most places, the ungainly underside— because this land was upside down. The lush, watered, life-sustaining side was here to be found under the surface, in the cavern world of the Monturan natives. No wonder they rarely came to the surface!

By afternoon Malina felt exhausted, and Darzek had stopped wandering about. He walked wearily with his cycs fixcd on the ground ahead of him. Arluklo's flow of steps seemed as rhythmic as when he started, but Malina thought he had to be tiring. She wanted desperately to continue while the light lasted, because the going was so much easier in daylight, but long before dusk she realized that she could go no farther.

They stopped by a crumbling embankment that provided illusory shelter, and Darzek rolled up in a blanket and went to sleep at once. Arluklo, declining the use of a blanket, seated himself dog fashion, half leaning against the embankment, and seemed to go into a trance with his eyes open. She unrolled a blanket for herself and lay down.

Immediately she was beset with the cares of leadership. Should one of them be standing watch against multilegged lions?

She lay listening to Darzek's noisy breathing. She had half expected sexual advances from him. As a widow, she had learned to expect them, to scrutinize every friendly gesture, every tendered favor as a possible prelude to an attempted seduction. Jan Darzek, however honorable, was a man; morever, he was one who had not seen a human woman for years, and he was far too good-looking to have been a hermit on Earth. She thought she could have written his script for him: "We're all alone in the universe. It's going to be destroyed anyway. No one will know. What else matters except us?"

The heavy breathing continued with a slight, almost imperceptible snore. She tucked the blanket around her and fell asleep.

A cry awakened her. For a dazed moment she thought it was Brian's cry. She threw off the blanket and leaped to her feet. It was dusk, and she could barely see Arluklo sitting motionless against the bank. Darzek's still form was a shadow-enshrouded shadow, but his breathing was rapid and irregular. Then he cried out again, and she knelt beside him and gently shook him awake.

He sat up and stared at her for a moment. "Time to go?"

"No."

"Was I making noises? Sorry."

He flopped down again, and she returned to her blanket, wondering if some past horror had shaped his nightmare or if he were counting off the worlds that were dying while he slept—one, two, ten; banishing the universe was not enough. She should have exorcised it.

She slept longer than she had intended, and when she awoke she was still tired. She stumbled through the darkness to shake Arluklo. He made no response until she spoke his name, and then he jerked erect. Darzek heard her and began rolling up his blanket. In a few minutes they were ready to move on. She spoke to Arluklo, and obediently he started out. Malina and Darzek donned infragoggles and followed him, munching on Miss Schlupe's compressed meat candies. Malina's thoughts again were on her children. The closer she came to them, the more remote they seemed.

The terrain was changing. From the level plateau, riddled with its eroded and crumbling dry watercourses and sinkholes, they were moving into an area of genuine hills. Walking became more difficult. The watercourses were crossing their route, which meant that they were following the terrain's most rugged profile. Their pace slowed as they stumbled laboriously up ever steepening hills.

Suddenly an enormous shadow leaped up almost at Malina's feet and bolted off into the night, its flight marked by thudding footsteps and a rattle of dislodged stones. Before she could react, Darzek was at her side.

"Good show," he said, returning the pistol to his pocket. "It's afraid of us."

They caught up with Arluklo and took up their formation again.

Twenty minutes later Darzek said resentfully, "You were supposed to holler."

She did not answer.

Through the night they struggled over increasingly difficult terrain with an ever slowing pace. At dawn they stood on an eminence and surveyed the land about them. Malina saw nothing but a barren, eroded land, and although the hills seemed to gradually level toward the horizon ahead of them, she feared that it was an optical illusion.

She could not contain her disappointment. "I thought we'd be able to see something."

"What sort of thing?" Darzek asked.

She looked about her again. "It was silly of me. Just because there's a park at that entrance near the mart doesn't mean there has to be one at every entrance. I'll settle for a hole in the ground if it leads to the right place."

Darzek turned to Arluklo. "It *is* out there somewhere, isn't it?"

"The place you marked on the map. Yes. We are approaching it."

"Maybe the reason we don't see anything is because there's nothing to see. Remember—we're only guessing that there's an entrance there. Shall we go?"

Shortly after midday they found it.

They came abruptly on a steep-sided canyon. At its distant head, a dry stream bed ended where a waterfall had once tumbled precipitously into it. Below, from an enormous opening, the stream gushed forth from its new underground course and raced away between lush, cultivated fields that extended almost to the canyon walls. Machines were at work in the fields, but there were no natives to be seen.

Malina's first thought was to find a descending path that would be hidden from the yawning cavern. They walked along the cliff in the opposite direction, occasionally venturing to the edge and looking down, but the canyon deepened rapidly and the walls became increasingly steeper.

Finally they turned back, and as they approached the head of the canyon Malina thought she saw a precarious descent near the former waterfall. She led the way to it and stood at the edge of the cliff studying the tenuous hand- and footholds.

She said to Darzek, "I think you and I can make it, but what will we do with Arluklo? He's much too heavy to be carried."

"What do we do when we get down?" Darzek asked. "Go immediately into the cavern?"

"We'll hide somewhere and look the situation over and rest a little. But first we'll have to get down."

"I'd hate to leave Arluklo," Darzek said. "I respect his fortitude, and I especially admire his built-in compass. We'll need both when we get underground."

Malina turned to Arluklo. She said, in large-talk, "We're trying to figure out how to get you down. There doesn't seem to be any way."

"I can climb down," Arluklo said.

And he did. While they watched, openmouthed, he went straight down the side of the canyon wall, finding holds for his numerous limbs where none seemed to exist. Soon he stood at the bottom, a squat little brown figure looking up at them.

Watching Arluklo's startling performance, Malina thought—but did not speak—a question: How would they ever get them out? They might climb down that wall, but could they climb up again with Brian and Maia? Of course there were other exits. Perhaps they could find the cavern that led to the park near the mart. Perhaps—

Darzek was unrolling the rope that he'd carried coiled about an arm.

"Is it long enough to reach to the bottom?" she asked, as he began to tie one end about her.

He shook his head. "Halfway, maybe."

"Then let's not arrange things so that if one of us falls the other will be pulled down." She detached the rope. "We'll go separately. Promise me one thing. If something happens to me, now or later, you'll go on and do what you can."

"Of course," he said.

She turned again to study the descent, and before she was aware of it he had started down. She watched breathlessly as he felt his way from protruding rock to hollow to protruding rock. He moved slowly, but he did not hesitate, and his movements were confident. She decided, finally, that it was easier than she had thought and followed him.

When she reached the bottom, he stood waiting for her with Arluklo. They hurried behind a large rock that lay near the cliff, where she caught her breath and looked about her.

On each side of the stream a narrow road led from the cavern to the canyon wall and then followed the wall as far as they could see. All the land between the roads and the stream was cultivated.

Malina said, "Let's see if we can find a hiding place where we can look into the cavern."

Obediently Darzek moved off along the road, and Arluklo followed him. Malina turned in the opposite direction and cautiously made her way to the cavern opening.

A blast of cold air struck her as she reached it. The roads that converged there continued inside the cavern, one on either side of the river. Otherwise, for the short distance she could see into the gloomy interior, she saw nothing but the river rushing between steep banks.

She turned away and hurried to catch up with the others. Darzek had found a small cave opening a short distance up the wall and was climbing up to it. He disappeared inside, and a moment later he called to them guardedly, "Come on up!"

Arluklo went up the wall as easily as he had climbed down the other. Malina sought footholds and accepted the help of the hand Darzek reached down to her. The cave was shallow but dry and deep enough for the three of them to lie down comfortably.

"Perfect," Malina said. "We're here, and the entrance isn't guarded. The next important thing is to get some rest. We may not find many safe places once we're inside."

Obediently Darzek unrolled a blanket, made himself comfortable, and fell asleep. Arluklo crept to the back of the cave and got himself settled in the upright position he seemed to prefer.

Malina lay quietly, resisting her own desire for sleep, and studied her surroundings. The verdant canyon seemed exquisitely peaceful. A lovely park could have been made there, for children to play in. For Brian and Maia to play in. She thought of her children, for a time, and then she forced her attention back to the canyon and its sinister cavern opening. From their walk along the cliff, she knew that the cultivation extended for an enormous distance and there were at least a dozen machines in use. This was no kitchen garden, but a major agricultural project.

Finally she dozed off.

Again she slept longer than she had intended and so soundly that Darzek's recurrent nightmares, if he had any, did not awaken her. When she awoke, darkness lay about them, overlaid with the rich scent of freshly cultivated land. Occasionally, over the murmur of the rushing river, she could hear the purring of the nearest cultivating machine.

Darzek was already awake. He said, "I've been wondering if this cavern is a lower level they don't use except for access to the farm. It probably fills with water during the rainy season. The question is whether it'll take us in the right direction, but we can't find that out without following it."

"We'll have to study the map carefully before we start," Malina said. "We may not have many chances to use a light inside."

She got the map from her pack and unfolded it. Darzek called, "Arluklo."

The klo did not answer.

Malina nudged him gently with her foot and got no response. Both of them turned to the back of the cave and bent over Arluklo in alarm. The klo sat motionless in his sleeping position.

"I'm afraid he's dead," Malina said finally. "I've been worrying about his physical endurance. We must have overtaxed him. Would you hold a blanket up to the opening? We've got to risk a light."

Darzek arranged the blanket and held it, and she turned on her handlight and positioned it on a ledge. Before she tried to shift the klo's body, she decided to remove his pack. She loosened the straps and pulled them free, but the pack seemed to be caught on a trailing wire. With an effort she pulled the wire free. Then, setting the pack aside, she scowled at the end of the wire.

After a moment she felt Arluklo's back with searching fingers. A panel snapped open. She exclaimed incredulously, "He's—why, he's—"

"A robot," Darzek agreed. "Very interesting. In fact, fascinating."

"The pack has an extra battery," Malina said.

"Interesting that it lasted just long enough to get us here. Did they plan it that way? I think not. They'd know how long a battery would last. He could have suffered a malfunction. Perhaps that cliff climbing—what's the matter?"

"The kloa are slaves of the kloatraz," Malina said. "The kloa are robots. Does that mean the kloatraz is alive?"

## 18

Again the sky was overcast, and as they entered the cavern their infragoggles detected no noticeable distinction between the night without and the total darkness within. The surfaces of the roadways that ran on either side of the river were so smooth that they seemed artificial. The river rushed in a deep stone trough between steep banks, and its incessant, swirling murmur relieved them of any necessity to walk quietly. The air already seemed uncomfortably cold.

They strode along boldly, stopping at regular intervals for Darzek to take navigational sightings. He had warned Malina that the margin of error might be one hundred per cent, but he felt that they should attempt to keep track of their direction however much the cavern meandered, and she gladly gave him the job. He was attempting to record the deviation of each curve on a gadget he had manufactured for that purpose, and he was counting strides and recording the total in hundred-pace units with kernels of grain that he passed from one pocket to another.

Except for these halts, they maintained a steady, brisk pace. Eventually they would have to enter populated areas and sneak along walls and hurry from hiding place to hiding place; but until they did, Malina was determined to make the best time possible, whatever the risk of accidental encounters.

But they did not have to proceed recklessly. When they approached a curve, they slowed their pace until they could see what lay beyond it. Darzek called distances to her above the murmur of water. They were two kilometers from the entrance, three, four, eight. The cavern was beginning an almost indistinguishable large-radius curve, and he thought it was taking them in the direction they must go. One of the heavy lines on Arluklo's map roughly coincided with the route they were following. It might represent this cavern or one that paralleled it on a higher level.

"But that's only a guess," he cautioned her. "We're going to miss Arluklo's compass."

Malina missed more than the compass. Robot or not, there had been an engaging quality about the little klo, and his polite, matter-of-fact confidence had been the one solid factor in an otherwise absurdly fanciful enterprise. Darzek's calculated guesses and her own aching uncertainties were poor substitutes.

Suddenly, above the regular noise of the rushing water, her ear caught a different sound. She stopped and gripped Darzek's arm, and the two of them stood listening. Far up ahead of them, the river's murmur was acquiring a faint veneer of gurgling, pouring, and splashing. As they moved forward, the new sound became louder. Then they saw the source: a waterfall that leaped from somewhere near the cavern roof.

As they approached it, they halted again and stared. The water was carried over the roadway on a short aqueduct, from which it fell into the river, and the roadway passed under the aqueduct through the strangest archway Malina had ever seen. A massive block of rock had been carved into a delicate, three-dimensional filigree that looked like shimmering lace. She wondered how the natives preserved it intact when the rainy season filled the cavern with a roaring torrent that raged against this artistic masterpiece and brought rocks and boulders crashing in its wake.

She studied the arch thoughtfully, trying to see it as a clue to the mentality of those who had seized her children. Then, while Darzek was admiringly running his fingers over the meticulous carving, she moved through the arch and found a narrow, ascending passageway just beyond it. At the distant top of the slope, a soft glow could be seen. Motioning to Darzek to remain at the bottom, she cautiously made her way upward.

At the top, the narrow passageway opened into an enormous, vaulted room. A small stream ran swiftly and noisily through its center and vanished into an opening, from which it emerged on the other side to pass over the aqueduct and fall into the river below. On either side of the stream were large, irregularly shaped pools, fed by curtains of water that fell at the sides of the room, collected in the pools, and finally overflowed into the stream.

One of the pools was in use. Natives were bathing and disporting in and around it. Malina shrank back down the passageway and then sank to the floor, from which position she could peer into the room and remain almost completely concealed.

*Natives.* Here, finally, were those enigmatic individuals known at Montura Mart only by their bulky protective clothing and light shields. In her infragoggles they were shimmering halos of light.

When she slipped the goggles off, she saw the pool enveloped in a softly phosphorescent glow, and in it the natives were performing a stately ballet of flowing movement. They mounted rocks, they dived, they came to the surface and wove complicated patterns as they passed to and fro through the pool, and when they left the water it was with consummate grace of movement and a spattering of luminescent drops that produced the illusion of their bathing in light. Probably they continued these elaborate formations under the water, but from her position she could not see them there.

Darzek joined her. He'd had the good judgment to remove his monstrosity of a hat, and he edged up beside her to peer over the top of the slope. They could have conversed in safety because of the noise of rushing water, but speechlessness was the only possible reaction to the amazing scene before them.

The natives lacked only wings to make them seem angelic. Their skin had a golden iridescence that gave it a radiant, breath-taking beauty. Their proportions were startlingly human, and so were their features. Only with careful scrutiny could the flowing hair be seen as a crest formed of folds of skin that ran down the front of their faces to form an illusory nose. The eye hollows were oval in shape, as were the enormous, widest eyes that gave them, Malina thought, acutely effective peripheral vision, a point to remember when trying to keep out of their sight. The eyes had a long horizontal slit for a pupil. There was no body hair. The limbs, both arms and legs, seemed to be multiply jointed, which possibly accounted for their flowing movements. The bodies, too, were gracefully curved and devoid of angularity. The hands and feet looked exceedingly strange, but for the moment she could not make out the shapes.

The most prosaic scientific details—the optical principles of the strangely shaped eyes, the anatomical structure of the head crests, the mechanics of the joints in those curving limbs—such details would have fascinated, but for the moment, even to the scientifically trained mind, they seemed irrelevant. These creatures were beautiful, and the setting beautified them. They were superbly proportioned, and their golden skin appeared almost translucent in the gently glowing light. When, occasionally, several of them extended their ballet to one of the unlighted pools, it was like watching permanently glowing fireflies weave their way through the dark. Occasionally their shouts or calls echoed through the enormous room, but whether these were cries of joy or instruction or complaint Malina could not have said.

Suddenly they were gone. They filed out into a passageway at the opposite end of the room, and each one, in passing, scooped a hand into a trough that surrounded the pool they were using and withdrew it glowing with the soft light. Several of them flung handfuls of light at each other in an obvious outburst of horseplay, splashing gleaming silver drops off the gleaming golden skin. They made no sounds approximating laughter. By the time the last of them scooped up the liquid light and disappeared into the passageway, the room's glow of illumination was noticeably diminished.

They were gone. For a moment Malina gazed after them disbelievingly, and then, the spell broken, she turned to Darzek.

He spoke into her ear. "What do you make of that?"

"They're iridophores," Malina answered absently.

"How was that again?"

"The cells that produce our skin pigment are called melanophores. The natives don't have any. Instead they have iridophores or something like them."

"Is that significant?" Darzek asked.

"It's fascinating. Probably it's why Supreme said they needed a dermatologist, though there's nothing a dermatologist could do for them and nothing they'd be likely to want done in any case."

"They wear no clothing," Darzek observed.

"They wear no clothing when swimming," she corrected.

"True enough, but it's rather cold for swimming. The temperature in these caverns is probably uniform throughout the year, so they must be acclimated to a cool temperature that varies very little. That would explain the protective clothing worn on the surface, wouldn't it? It would insulate them against heat. But why the light shield? They use light here, so light doesn't bother them."

"They use a special kind of light—a cold light," Malina said. "Regular light might be blinding to them. Sunlight certainly would be deadly. Without melanophores a few minutes of exposure to the sun would cause serious illness or death."

"The fact that they do use light could be helpful," Darzek said. "It means that with our goggles we may see as well in the dark as they do. If we can avoid their lights, we might have an advantage."

"It won't be much of an advantage. Those large eyes may mean they once got along without any light."

"If there's any advantage at all, we ought to accept it gratefully. Have we learned anything else that's useful?"

"I don't know how useful it is, but they may be amphibious. Did you notice their strangely shaped hands and feet? They looked webbed."

Darzek turned quickly. "Not webbed. Have you forgotten our

many-legged lion? Its feet were oval discs, just like the natives' hands and feet, but probably nothing like as well controlled. The natives' hoofs—that's what they really are—seem flexible enough to serve as hands and fingers for many purposes. Anything else?"

"They may be telepathic. They have a spoken language, or at least sounds of expression, but they do things in unison without any verbal communication."

"Point well taken," Darzek said. "Useful to know, but not helpful in the sense that we can do anything about it. The first native to see us may be able to warn the entire native population, and we won't even hear the alarm. Did you make note of any other cheerful potentialities?"

"No, except that you probably guessed right about their living on the upper levels. That passageway leads upward. We could follow them, but I'm for sticking to the lower cavern as long as it seems to be going in the right direction. We can't assume that they never go down there—obviously they do—but I'd rather travel that river road than tippytoe through their bathing chambers and bedrooms." She backed down the passageway until she could stand without being visible from the room beyond. "Shall we go?"

They walked beside the roaring river for the remainder of the night and most of the next day as well as Malina could calculate—she reset her watch every twelve hours to compensate for Montura's longer day. In the stygian tunnel it was a futile exercise, because day and night had lost their meaning.

Frequently they saw passageways angling upward, some of them as wide as the roadway, and several times they encountered aqueducts that carried streams over delicately filigreed archways to plunge into the river with foaming roars. One of the streams was enormous, and the passage under its aqueduct a tunnel within a tunnel.

They saw no other sign of the natives until they rounded a curve and sighted a distant glow of light ahead of them. They slowed their pace and approached it cautiously. Abruptly the river cavern enlarged into a room of breath-taking proportions, and the instant they entered it a massive glow of light blinded them. They jerked off their goggles and used their hands as blinders to race through the enormous room to the safety of the dark passage beyond.

Only then did they attempt to contemplate the glowing mass that filled the room on both sides of the river. It had blinded them because they had come onto it from the dark and because of the sheer mass of the luminous material, but the light was not brilliant. It was the same soft, faintly bluish illumination they had seen the bathers using.

"What is it?" Malina asked.

"Maybe some kind of phosphorescent fungus," Darzek suggested.

"Whatever it is, they brew their liquid light from it. Let's get out of here."

They hurried their pace until the glow was lost behind the river's next curve. Then they stopped to rest and munch on Miss Schlupe's compressed meat, and Darzek made a tent of their blankets so he could translate his navigational observations into a line on the map.

When he emerged, he shouted into Malina's ear, for the river was deafening there, "We're all right."

They walked on—past more passageways, under more aqueducts, for an hour, two hours, four hours. Malina had long since passed the point where she could go no further, but she willed herself to continue. Finally the roadways left the river canyon to slope upward on long ramps and vanish into arched passageways. Malina stopped to look up at them apprehensively, but Darzek moved on, following a narrow path along the river. Beyond the roadway's ascending ramp, the bank widened again, but there the river shore was irregular and strewn with rock. When Malina overtook him, he had picked out a place of concealment where they could rest.

They munched their rations in silence.

"It's been too easy," Malina said finally.

"Maybe. But maybe it's been easy because it's the first time anyone has tried it."

"I can't understand our coming so far without meeting anyone. It's asking too much of coincidence."

"However we did it, we're here, and I think we're fairly close to where we're trying to go."

"To the circle on the map? The place of alleged justice?"

Darzek nodded. "Up that ramp, and then—do you want to rest first?"

"No," she said firmly. She pushed herself to her feet. Then she sat down again. Silently Darzek handed her a blanket and took one for himself, and Malina found a place to lie down where the rocks did not seem too formidably inhospitable.

But though she rested, she could not sleep. Probably Darzek did not sleep either, for he got up the moment she did. It was only an hour later by her watch when they donned their packs and started the long climb up the ascending roadway.

At the top, they found themselves abruptly in another world. The slanting passageway ended in a wide archway fashioned of the same delicate filigree that they had seen below. Behind it hung draperies woven of some tough, hard fiber. They overlapped at the center of the arch. Cautiously Malina parted them.

The light from the corridor beyond blinded her. It was the familiar cold blue light they had seen twice before. They removed their goggles and took turns glancing through the draperies until their eyes had become accustomed to the light.

Darzek whispered to her, "According to the map, this corridor is perpendicular to our route."

She risked a brief foray to look down the corridor in both directions. There were no natives in sight, and she saw, in the distance, what might be a main intersection. She withdrew again and tried to decide what to do. Behind them, there was no hiding place closer than the bottom of the passageway. The moment they moved into that well-lighted corridor they were helpless. They could not go ahead; they could not remain where they were.

Darzek waited patiently, saying nothing at all. The decision, for better or for worse, was hers to make, and there was no point in waiting for a more opportune moment. In this dilemma there would be no way to recognize opportunity until it had passed them by.

She parted the draperies again. There still were no natives in sight.

She hissed, "Come on!"

She slipped through the draperies and started along the corridor at a loping run. Darzek quickly overtook her and ran at her side.

If the broad corridor had once been a natural formation, it was no longer recognizable as such. The floor had been leveled and covered with a soft material of startling resilience. Walls and ceiling had been smoothed, the ceiling arch made symmetrical, and both covered with finely woven, bright-colored hangings. The liquid light flowed or was contained in troughs along each wall. The natives' underground world was the opposite of the murky habitat Malina had expected. It was a world of dazzling brilliance.

They hurried along noiselessly, passing innumerable arched doorways, all of them covered with draperies. Suddenly a drapery parted a mere ten meters ahead of them and a native stepped through.

As he turned toward them, Malina halted. She was too stunned to take another step or even to think. Should they run? But where? Should they overpower him? But how? She gripped Darzek's arm; he seemed calm but equally uncertain.

In the instant that they hesitated, the native walked past them, large eyes focused straight ahead along the corridor, apparently unseeing. He looked exactly as the natives at the pool had looked—no clothing, golden skin, head crest—

Darzek, scowling perplexedly, had turned to look after him. Malina, still gripping Darzek's arm, pulled hard and hurried him forward.

They came to the intersecting corridor and turned, and abruptly the corridor was filled with golden-skinned natives. They poured from every archway, some turning one way, some the other. It was as though a whistle had blown for quitting time or a school bell had sounded dismissal. Before Malina quite grasped what was happening, they were filing along the corridor with a crowd of natives and passing another crowd headed in the opposite direction.

And the natives ignored them. They looked past them; they looked at them with large, staring eyes that might have been blind. They brushed against them in total unawareness. Experiencing a sensation of icy roughness and finding her fingers in contact with a native's golden skin, Malina stared at them in disbelief. She walked along mechanically, wondering whether she or the natives were mad.

As abruptly as it had begun, the rush was over. The natives began to turn aside and disappear through draperies. Twice they had to stop and wait for the corridor to empty ahead of them while the natives made a calm and orderly exit.

They were alone. Malina felt limp and ready to collapse. She glanced at Darzek and found him grinning at her. She grinned back at him and stepped up her pace. Perhaps what they had just witnessed was a miracle, but she would have to work out the theology at a more favorable time. They hurried side by side along an empty corridor.

At the intersection with a smaller passageway, more natives appeared. These quickly overtook and surrounded them. No sounds were uttered; no signals were given; no restraint was suggested. They continued to hurry along the corridor, but now there were natives on both sides of them and in the rear.

They were caught.

Far ahead, at the end of the corridor, one native stood as though waiting for them. As they approached, he came slowly to meet them. Malina had the impression of immense age, though he did not look old except for a slight stoop to his lithe body. He greeted them. There could have been no other word for it, though the strange disc-hands gestured meaninglessly. He invited them to follow him, again with gestures.

Malina staggered and would have fallen if Darzek had not caught her. The days and nights of exertion, the lack of sleep, the worry, the unending suspense of their search, had brought her close to physical and mental collapse. She forced her legs to move, and with Darzek supporting her they moved on.

They turned off at the end of the corridor, turned again, passed through an opening from which the drapes had been drawn aside, and ascended a ramp. At the top, they found themselves in a vast, well-lighted cavern room. They were on a balcony. In response to another gesture, they stepped to the stone wall that ran along its edge and looked down.

Malina caught her breath. She tried to lean forward. If Darzek had not instantly gripped her arm and compelled silence, she would have cried out.

Below them was a park, with treelike plants and the soft purple ground cover underfoot. In the park were three figures: two human children—her children—and a native swathed in protective clothing.

The native was performing elaborate gestures. The children seemed to be sullenly ignoring him. Finally the native took Brian's hand as though to lead him away. Brian shouted, "You leave me alone!" and kicked at him viciously.

The native collapsed onto the soft turf and lay there unmoving.

The two stunned children stood looking down on him. Then Brian dropped to his knees beside the prone body, crying bitterly.

This was Monturan justice. The natives were not punishing the children; they were curing them.

## 19

In the Prime Common, conferences involving E-Wusk usually took place in his own office cubicle, it being easier to move the conference to him than him to the conference. Five of them had gathered there: E-Wusk, Miss Schlupe, Darzek, ᴜʀsDwad, and Malina. Brian and Maia were safely and snugly asleep and none the worse for their experience except that they were extremely tired. Malina already had looked in on them twice, and she went a third time and tucked in a blanket where Brian's restlessness had tugged it loose.

When she returned, Darzek was discussing the natives.

". . . no science, no industry, no technology. Their civilization is a physical culture cult with subcultures of sculpture and philosophy. Their main interest used to be agriculture, and the establishment of their surface farms, which they had to work by night, must have been high adventure requiring courage and resourcefulness and a stupendous amount of work. They still may be the most talented mushroom or fungus culturists in three galaxies, but otherwise their agricultural talents are stagnating. Their cut of the mart profits brings them everything they need, including automated agricultural machinery to operate farms they keep going more as a matter of habit than necessity. So they have unlimited time for play. Many of the elders see this as a sad deterioration of a once self-reliant society and advocate the expulsion of the mart—which is why the gesardl panicked over the missing children. It didn't want to provide ammunition for the dissident minority."

"But what about the Udef?" Miss Schlupe asked. "Don't the natives understand that it threatens them, too? Won't they help us?"

"They're intelligent enough to realize that this is something completely beyond their understanding, so they refuse to worry about it. They'd help us if they could, whether it threatened them or not. Since they can't, they wish us well and go about their business and leave us to go about ours. If we wish to make our business something that neither we nor they understand, that's our worry."

"They're smug, conceited hypocrites," Miss Schlupe announced. "Look at that silly system of justice. Intention the same as the deed —balderdash!"

E-Wusk spoke for the first time. "As you described it, it seemed like a remarkable system of justice."

Malina turned to Darzek. Since the tumultuous climax of their invasion of the caverns, she'd had no opportunity for private conversation with him. She said resentfully, "You knew all the time. Why didn't you tell me?"

"I didn't *know*," Darzek said. "I suspected. A people who'd make that much fuss over an intention would either be exceptionally stupid and cruel or exceptionally wise and lenient. The choice was between waiting to see which they were or going to find out."

"But why didn't they let me know what they were doing?"

"They wouldn't have harmed the children under any circumstances, so naturally it didn't occur to them that you could possibly imagine that they would."

"But they have the death penalty! Arluklo told me so!"

"Ah—but when you asked Arluklo you really were asking the kloatraz, and one has to be exceedingly careful how one puts questions to a computer, even when the computer is alive. Exactly how did you phrase the question?"

She thought for a moment. "I think I said—what penalty does the law permit?"

"And he answered, 'Death.' No doubt the law does 'permit' death, but that penalty may be carried out only under the most extraordinary circumstances, and I'm confident that it's never applied where the offender is a child or the offense is only an intention."

She said resentfully, "You sound as though you think they actually did the right thing."

"Brian did throw the stones. The native could have been injured severely. They considered the boy desperately in need of help, and they felt they had both a moral and a legal obligation to give it to him. They couldn't understand your attempts to prevent that. From their viewpoint—"

"Never mind their viewpoint. What's yours?"

"That Brian was behaving like a spoiled brat, and you should be grateful to them."

She kept her anger firmly in check and her resentment to herself. It was the least she could do. He had abandoned his own mission and worked as hard to save her children as she had, and now he should be able to get back to saving the universe without petty distractions furnished by her.

Darzek had resumed his discussion. "The natives can't help us, but at least they won't put obstacles in our way. They'll encourage the gesardl to cooperate, but now that the gesardl understands the menace, it doesn't need encouragement. ᴜʀsDwad will set up a factory to duplicate my recordings and manufacture projectors. Our objective is to alert all the scientists and engineers of this galaxy."

"What about the governments?" Miss Schlupe asked.

"We'll leave it to the scientists and engineers to decide what should be done about their governments."

E-Wusk would be in charge of the outfitting of an initial thousand ships that would be used to disseminate recordings, projectors, and related information, and ᴜʀsDwad would assist him. The two of them happily set to work. Miss Schlupe was thinking about reopening her refreshment stand, and she had work of her own to attend to.

Malina and Darzek took their conversation to their apartment's lounge, where they wouldn't disturb the workers. Malina said, "It seems to me that you're not furnishing much information to these scientists and engineers—just the recordings and some negative data."

"We'll give them all the facts we have," Darzek said. "We hope a few of them will be inspired to do some original thinking. It wouldn't do to muddy things with speculations from nonscientists such as myself."

"What are your speculations?"

"The Udef," Darzek said soberly, "is a mindless entity. It has a brain but no mind at all, which I consider to be the ultimate form of insanity. It drifts through the universe in search of the mind that it lacks. When it finds one, it destroys it. The logical questions are how an entity can be mindless and without substance and still have a brain, and how it can destroy the minds of an entire world in such a short time, and I say logic can't be applied to this. It is a mindless brain, and its essence is pure, horrible force, and it has no physical substance at all."

"That would muddy things," Malina agreed. "If the Udef's nature defies all scientific principles, scientific research isn't likely to be helpful. What you need is inspiration. If you'll pardon the expression, you need a brain wave."

Darzek stared at her. "What a singular way to put it! Brain waves are electrical, aren't they? Do they broadcast, like radio waves?"

"I know nothing about electroencephalography beyond the basics, and the little work I've done with it involved electrodes in contact with the head."

"But surely there are sensitive instruments that could detect brain waves from a distance, aren't there?" This was a new Jan Darzek— alert, intense, eager. "If there aren't, there's nothing theoretically impossible about the existence of such an instrument, is there?"

"I suppose not."

"And if the brain wave of one individual is a rather feeble emission, would there be any kind of cumulative effect with the brain waves of a billion billion individuals? Would the waves be mutually supporting, or would they tend to cancel each other out?"

"I haven't the faintest idea."

He was paying no attention to her. "Does a world emit a characteristic brain wave which is a summation of all of the brains of the lives it supports? And what if the Udef were a life form attuned to, and stimulated by, brain waves? Or what if it's a brain wave carnivore, going about consuming them for nourishment? Since the results are impossible, we're in no position to quibble about the improbability of the causes. The first thing we'd have to decide is whether this death force has the ability to detect brain waves at a distance and home in on them until it locates the world they emanate from. Does every world with intelligent life send out a signal that says to the Udef, 'Brains here!' If so, perhaps the only way we can save the intelligent life of the universe is by developing a brain wave filter."

"It wouldn't necessarily have to be waves," Malina said. "Thought produces chemical changes in the brain. The by-products—"

"Then the Udef could be a chemical analyzer instead of a brain wave detector."

"I can't believe either one," Malina said. "It would take a fantastically refined apparatus to register such chemical changes."

"Or to detect brain waves across the light-years?" Darzek suggested.

"They're comparable fantasies," she agreed. "What about telepathy?"

"Definitely a possibility, but in that case we'd have to assume that any creature possessing intelligence emits some kind of telepathic signal. Are there thought waves, as distinct from brain waves?"

"On a world where the natives are telepaths, we shouldn't have to speculate on the nature of telepathy. Why not ask them?"

"Ah! But our friends the Monturan natives couldn't explain how telepathy works any more than a gymnast could explain what makes his muscles function. We also have the kloatraz, which communicates telepathically with its robots even at distances of a hundred and forty kilometers, as we know. Does it also communicate with the natives? We definitely must investigate the kloatraz." He yawned. "Excuse me. Tomorrow we definitely must investigate the kloatraz. What are your plans for tomorrow?"

"I'm taking my children to the park," Malina said.

He stared at her for a moment and burst into laughter. "Good thought. Do you have permission?"

"No, and I don't intend to ask for it."

Miss Schlupe hurried in excitedly. Darzek asked, "What about you, Schluppy? What do you have planned for tomorrow? Are you ready to return to Earth?"

"Certainly not. I'm sticking around. If all the intelligent life in the universe is going to be destroyed, I want to be one of the first to know. Anyway, I've decided to reopen my refreshment stand, but I'm cutting the gesardl's share of the profits to ten per cent, the bums."

"Have you told them that?" Darzek asked.

"I certainly have. I gave them a choice: ten per cent of my business, or fifty per cent of no business, and they decided to take the ten per cent."

"Then it's business as usual." Darzek yawned again. "Excuse me. Submarine sandwiches and games in the park. And the kloatraz. I wonder whether the kloatraz could communicate directly with one of us if it wanted to."

"I wonder if Supreme knows about the kloatraz," Malina said.

Darzek nodded. "That's one of the questions Rok Wllon will ask it."

In the morning Malina borrowed the flyer and chauffeur directly from the gesardl, "for personal use." The gesardl may have winced, but the request was acceded to without comment. She flew to the park with Brian and Maia and accompanied them in their play as far as the mysterious door, and when they encountered a pair of natives studying the tree plants, Brian and Maia marched boldly up to them to make ceremonial presentation of gift-wrapped packages of spices from the mart, something one of the gesardl members had assured Miss Schlupe the natives were fond of.

Brian bowed; Maia curtsied albeit she was wearing trousers; and the natives, their reactions hidden by the light shields, performed gestures either of perplexity or gratitude. Malina felt satisfied. A mon-

THIS DARKENING UNIVERSE 169

strous nightmare had been exorcised, for herself if not for the children.

They returned to the mart, and she got out the children's textbooks and made assignments. "From now on," she announced, "five days of seven will be school days."

She left them at their books and went looking for Jan Darzek.

As she expected, she found him at the Kloa Common. He sat on a hassock near the kloatraz, withdrawn, oblivious to his surroundings, while all of the trading bustle generated by the army of kloa flowed around him. Beside the looming whiteness of the kloatraz, with its spectacular flashes, he seemed an utterly drab, inconsequential figure. Miss Schlupe sat nearby. She jumped to her feet as Malina approached. "Thank God. Now you can be the subject. I have work to do."

"What sort of subject?" Malina asked.

"You'll find out. It's painless. Come and see me when he's finished with you."

She hurried away. Malina took her place and waited, and eventually Darzek became aware of her presence. "What are you doing?" she asked.

"Trying to communicate with the kloatraz telepathically," he said.

He raised a finger, and Arluklo materialized from somewhere nearby, his mechanical breakdown fully repaired. "Does the kloatraz know the ages of Doctor Darr's children?" Darzek asked.

Arluklo gestured negatively.

"Doctor Darr is going to think the names and ages of her children. There will be two names and two numbers, with a pair of primary relationships. She will think the numbers in this language I'm using, which we call large-talk. I'd like to know if there is any leakage at all. Ready?"

"Ready," Arluklo said.

Darzek said to Malina, "Think their names in English and follow each name with the large-talk number for the age. Do that over and over."

She did so, concentrating furiously; but after a few minutes Arluklo announced, "No. Nothing at all."

Darzek lapsed into moody silence.

"What was supposed to happen?" Malina asked finally.

"I wanted to see whether the kloatraz had any more success with your thoughts than with mine or Miss Schlupe's. We humans seem to be thoroughly unexceptional where telepathic talents are concerned."

"But—there are many humans who have telephathic talents!"

"Unfortunately we don't have one here to test. The kloatraz says telepathic leakage can occur with any life form, but it is random, uncontrolled, unpredictable, and usually done without the awareness of the individual doing it. Telepathic communication is something quite different. But you'll notice I said humans *seem* to be unexceptional. The kloatraz said it got no leakage from you. Does a kloatraz lie?"

She stared at him. "But why—"

"Miss Schlupe and I studied a bit of its history this morning. First we asked the kloatraz about its early life and it said it didn't remember."

She continued to stare. "Didn't—remember?"

Darzek grinned at her. "I have to keep reminding myself, too. It's alive. It's an intelligent life form. It may possess the most monumentally brilliant brain in our three galaxies. But does it lie? How much do you remember of events when you were a baby? Maybe it was abandoned here by its parents. Maybe it was a seed from outer space that grew here. Or an egg some undefined life form left here to hatch. It says it doesn't remember, which probably is true. It also professes to remember very little of what happened before the mart was built, and that certainly is false. So Miss Schlupe requested an interview with one of the rare native linguists who knows the mart language she learned, and we explored the early history of the kloatraz as far as the natives remember it. They aren't much for written records. Since they lack Earth's long history of political and military squabbles, it must seem to them that they've had very little to record. According to their oral tradition, the kloatraz always has been here. Their earliest recollection has it present as an outside mind located they knew not where that participated fully in the telepathic life of their community. Their tradition also says that when they finally located that outside mind—remember, they rarely came to the surface except to work their fields at night—it was a plant growth shaped like a rock and the size of two of their peculiarly shaped hands."

Malina gazed upward dumfoundedly at the glowing mass.

"It's alive," Darzek said. "It grows. It's still growing. Tradition may exaggerate, but undoubtedly it once was quite small."

"Then it really is a plant?"

"Precisely. It has roots. It's always been where it is now. It did not come to the mart; the mart came to it—was built around it. When the natives first found it, it had the appearance of one more rock in a wasteland of rocks, although an unusually beautiful one. The natives quickly discovered that a living computer has its uses. All of this happened hundreds if not thousands of years ago, mind you. When neighboring worlds developed space travel and visited Montura, the kloatraz's fame spread to the stars. Other worlds sent delegations to consult it. In time this became a convenient place to exchange goods while awaiting a turn with the computer oracle, and the result of that was Montura Mart—conceived, designed, promoted, and brought to reality by the kloatraz. All this time the natives were stuck with the job of providing interpreters for non-telepaths consulting the kloatraz, which must have been quite a bore for them. They weren't much interested in commerce and still aren't."

"Where did the kloa come from?"

"The world of Klo—a world with a unique expertise in manufacturing robots. It brought some here to trade. The kloatraz became interested and designed its own robots, which the experts on Klo built for it. They turned out to be uniquely designed robots, each with its own personality and individual capabilities—Arluklo's is languages, for example—and all of them have the ability to communicate telepathically with their owner. Not a bad achievement for an overgrown vegetable. It makes one wonder what else the thing could do if only it would condescend to put a few of its circuits to work for us. Maybe it could design some instruments that would help us figure out what the Udef is. Unfortunately, it doesn't seem interested. Anyway, that's how the kloatraz got its name. The robots from Klo were called kloa, and their owner—or master—became the kloatraz."

"Doesn't the kloatraz realize that the Udef is a threat to it, too?" Malina asked.

"My very question. The answer is no. Its own physiology is entirely different from that of the victims it saw in my recordings, and it considers itself invulnerable to such a force. Further, it's far too busy with trading ventures at the moment to devote time to figuring out something that doesn't interest it and for which there's almost no data to work with."

"How much trading does it expect to do after the Udef passes through here?"

"Likewise my question. Obviously the implications haven't penetrated. We've got to stop thinking of this thing as a computer and think of it as a fallible living intelligence."

"But it does have a sense of ethics," Malina mused. "Remember how eager the kloa seemed to be to make amends after they found Brian and Maia for the gesardl?"

"Was that from a sense of ethics or an awareness that the incident might provide bad publicity for the mart? Too many unjust legal complications on Montura would encourage traders to found another mart and trade elsewhere. That would effectively put the kloatraz out of business. I see it as an extremely selfish genius that's looking after itself. The problem is to convince it that by helping us it's also helping itself."

"How are you going to do that?"

"I'm going to *try* to talk the natives into announcing the closing of the mart—ostensibly so the participating worlds can get to work planning the defense of the galaxy. That may make the kloatraz realize there's not going to be any trade at all unless the Udef is dealt with. It may even make it realize that the universe is likely to be an insufferably dull place if it's the only intelligent life form that survives. If it realizes that, perhaps it'll gives us some grudging cooperation."

Miss Schlupe already had reopened her refreshment stand, and she was happily looking down on the throng of customers when Malina arrived in her office. She asked how Malina had made out with the kloatraz, and Malina told her about Darzek's plan to stimulate the kloatraz's imagination.

"Close down the mart?" Miss Shlupe exclaimed indignantly. "When I've just reopened?"

"I don't think he actually intends to—"

"Mr. Darzek ought to know better. That's no way to practice alien psychology. He's been in space too long."

"I thought he seemed much improved."

"He's got a long way to go yet. Come on. We've got to get there before—"

She was gone. Malina chased her through two pairs of transmitters and failed to catch up with her until, in the arena, she had to stop to extricate herself from the involuntary embrace of a multi-armed life form she had collided with. They walked on together.

"What are you going to do?"

"Space or no space, Mr. Darzek ought to have more sense than that," Miss Schlupe said, still being indignant. "Tell that curdled Christmas tree you're going to close the mart, and it'll immediately start scheming to keep the mart open. We've got to remember that the dratted thing is a *brain*. It might even succeed, and where would that leave us? Putting it in opposition to us when we could have it on our side is just plain stupid."

They swept into the Kloa Common and cornered Arluklo. "Tell the kloatraz we need its help," Miss Schlupe panted. "Immediately."

"In what way?" Arluklo piped politely.

"I've just reopened my refreshment stand, and reordered all my supplies, and found a producing orchard, and got my cider crew on location and working, and finally I have the whole operation going smoothly again—"

She paused for breath. Arluko, still being distantly polite, asked, "In what way do you need the help of the kloatraz?"

"It's got to help us keep the mart open. I don't want to have to close down again and take another loss and then go through the strain and expense of opening up a third time. It'll understand that."

"Keep the mart open?" Arluklo piped blankly.

"Surely you know about the Udef—the death force. You saw all those recordings. If it isn't stopped quickly, the traders will dispose of their inventories and head for home. A lot of them won't wait to dispose of their inventories. They'll want to warn their own worlds about what's coming. The closer the Udef gets to us, the more business we'll lose, and long before there's any real danger here, the mart will close down completely. How can we keep it open?"

"The kloatraz will consider your question," Arluklo said.

"Can we count on its help?"

"Of course."

"I was afraid maybe it'd be running off to warn someone or find a safe place for itself like all the other traders."

"It does not think the Udef offers any danger to such as itself, but it agrees that the mart must be kept open, and it will consider ways to do that."

Miss Schlupe expressed gratitude and profound relief. "If the kloatraz says it'll help," she announced, "then there's nothing to worry about. The mart won't close."

They were in their apartment lounge an hour later, mediating an argument between Brian and Maia over a geography lesson, when Jan Darzek came in. He said blankly, "The kloatraz has changed its mind."

"Changed its mind how?" Miss Schlupe asked.

"Changed its mind about helping us with the Udef." Darzek was elated and at the same time exasperated. "Not only is it willing to help us design new instruments, but if we can find a way to take it with us, it's willing to go off and meet the Udef in person. It says it would like to experience this death force itself. And I hadn't even got started on my scheme to close the mart. Now why would it do an about-face so quickly?"

Miss Schlupe affected nonchalance. "You know how fickle these alien intelligences are."

## 20

"I talked with Mr. Darzek," Miss Schlupe said. "He says there's no reason why you shouldn't go home any time you want to."

"Thank you," Malina said.

"But right at this moment he can't spare a ship to take you all the way to Earth. If you don't mind waiting, he'll have Rok Wllon escort you when he returns."

"I'm sure we can manage without an escort."

"I'm afraid you can't. Earth isn't a member of the Synthesis, and getting there takes very special arrangements. Of course we'd love to have you and the children here as long as you're willing to stay. And if you'd like a job, temporary or permanent—"

"I'd love to have a job," Malina said. "Practicing medicine."

"I'm afraid I can't help you with that. Want to come sightseeing with me? E-Wusk has found a ship big enough to transport the kloatraz. It's due in this morning, and I'm going up to have a look at it."

"A ship that big would be worth a look," Malina agreed.

A special shuttle ship had been placed at their disposal, and Miss Schlupe and Malina joined Darzek and E-Wusk for the inspection visit to the ship Darzek already had dubbed the Behemoth. The suggestion that the gesardl maintained space-to-ground transmitters for its own use proved to be a malicious rumor.

"The fact is," Darzek said, "the gesardl is making a very tidy profit on the shuttle service and sees no reason to change."

Even at a distance and against the backdrop of space, the Behemoth looked enormous. The moment it achieved orbital perfection, their tiny ship swung to a docking position as it would have at a transfer station—for such a monster could not use the regular transfer stations and thus constituted a special station of its own. They filed into the control room and proceeded by interior transmitter to a cargo control room somewhere in the depths of the ship. It was a small cargo holds. The cargo master, a tiny life form with four inordinately long arms and as many short legs, stood at a control panel. He seemed to enjoy being a center of attention.

"They're dressing the ship," Darzek said. "They have to hold it at a precise inclination when they eject the cargo."

There was nothing to be seen through the transparent walls except the ends of cargo compartments, so Malina watched the cargo master. She never before had been close to the controls of anything larger than an automobile, and she was prepared to be dazzled by the complexity of such a formidable-sounding undertaking as ejecting cargo at a precise inclination; but the controls looked childishly simple.

The cargo master turned a dial until its calibrations lined up with the proper hieroglyphs. Next he positioned a pair of indicators. One pointed to each cargo hold; therefore, Malina concluded, the contents of both holds were going to be ejected.

Finally, at a shout of command through an amplifying system, he lifted a clamp that held a meter-long lever in place and swung the lever through a half circle. There was a sudden *whoosh*.

Malina turned and caught a fleeting glimpse of the cargo compartments disappearing into space. Both holds' openings closed automatically, and the cargo master cheerfully returned the lever to its original position and restored the clamp.

"Very neat," Darzek said. "Now the compartments are conveniently stored in orbit until called for. The gesardl has a special fleet of these giants."

"But why do they need such huge ships?" Malina asked.

"To take advantage of special economies in transporting huge cargoes. For example, they could transport a world's grain surplus with one trip and park it in orbit here, and any world with a grain shortage could come directly here to buy whatever it needed. Needless to say, the gesardl's business is very big business indeed."

They stepped to one of the transparent walls and looked into a hold. It was now a vast, empty cavity. Malina flattened her nose against the wall to look upward into uncertain dimness. The place seemed enormous, but so was the koatraz. "Is it big enough?" she asked.

"Just," Darzek said.

On the far side of the hold Malina could see window walls similar to the one she was looking through, some of them filled with unlikely faces. Again she turned her attention to the hold. "How will you get it here?"

"You have unerringly singled out the problem," Darzek murmured.

"Don't be facetious," Miss Schlupe snapped. "I'd feel a lot better about this business if we had some of our own transmitting experts here. What if those nincompoops launch the poor thing into space?"

"They'll manage," Darzek said. "All they have to do is build a transmitter that's big enough."

They returned to the mart, and Miss Shlupe went to her business, Darzek to his transmitting engineers, and Malina to her children. She heard their lessons and then took them on another outing to the park, and while they played and looked about for unsuspecting natives to deliver presents to, she held a debate with herself: to wait for Rok Wllon, or to insist on leaving now?

She asked the children if they would like to go home, and they chorused disgusted negatives. There was still the charm of novelty about the mart, but very soon, she thought, they would become as bored as she was now. To wait, or to insist on leaving? She did not think Darzek would refuse if she insisted.

She delivered the children to Miss Schlupe for an hour or two of work at the refreshment stand, and on her way back to the Prime Common she stopped off to see how Darzek was making out with his engineers. She finally found him at the deepest level of the Kloa Common, supervising an excavation: soil was being removed from around the kloatraz.

He paused to explain the problem to her. The kloatraz's weight was unknown even to the kloatraz, and grappling hooks or clamps or any such devices were out of the question. Thus it was impossible to move the kloatraz through a transmitter frame, so the engineers had devised an arrangement whereby a transmitter frame would be passed around the kloatraz. The openings around the kloatraz in the various floors of the Kloa Common had to be enlarged—a major construction project. Scaffolding was to be set up and supporting members put into place for the tracks that would accurately guide the transmitting frame on its fall from the roof to a level below the deepest basement.

The excavation was to make it possible for the frame to drop past the kloatraz's base. It was a delicate process, exposing masses of the creature's roots. These ranged in size from slender ropes to cylindrical growths a meter in diameter—and thus far the main roots were concealed far beneath the kloatraz.

"Are you going to cut them?" Malina asked.

Darzek shook his head. "It says it will disengage itself at the proper time. I don't know how it proposes to manage that, but we have no choice except to take its word for it."

Malina was scrutinizing the kloatraz's massive base. Here, at the very bottom of its bulk, the rippling lights seemed dim. She had never been so close to it before; the balustraded openings on the upper levels kept spectators at least three meters from the creamy surface. She was curious about the cellular structure of whatever it was that served as its epidermis, and she also wondered if it was correct to call it a plant merely because it had roots. Animal, vegetable, or mineral?

Just above her eye level, the surface shaded into a shadowy spot a couple of meters in diameter. She moved a few steps and picked out another. And another. They varied in color from dim gray to noticeable brown, and the shapes were highly irregular. From close up, the creature's base had a distinctly mottled appearance.

Cautiously she reached out to touch a spot.

A shout rang out—Darzek's—and at the same instant she experienced searing pain. She jerked her hand away; the tips of the three middle fingers were burned severely. Several of the kloa converged on her, talking excitedly, and Jan Darzek was confronting her sternly. She ignored the lot of them and examined her fingers with professional detachment. Second-degree burns.

She spoke before Darzek could. "There's heat involved—you can feel its warmth when you come close to it—but there isn't enough heat to do this. It must secrete a film of some corrosive substance."

"An acid?" Darzek suggested.

"Acid or alkali. Something with an extreme pH."

"It's probably a defense mechanism," he said. "A creature like this would be terribly vulnerable to enemies or even curious passers-by. But if that's what you wanted to find out, why didn't you use just one finger?"

"I didn't know it was dangerous," she said. "I wanted to examine it."

"Examine—"

"I think your precious alien life form has a skin disease."

She identified Arluklo among the fluttering kloa—Miss Schlupe, tired of mistaken identities, had tied a ribbon around his neck and he continued to wear it. She said, "Please tell the kloatraz that there are areas on its lower surface that look unhealthy. Ask it if it is aware of any pain or irritation there."

Arluklo piped a negative with his usual politeness, and Malina retired to the Prime Common with no small chagrin to bandage her fingers.

The following day she stopped in again at the Kloa Common to see how the work was progressing. As she approached, the transmitting frame hurled downward, unpowered, on a dry run. The frame struck the ground and flew apart. The engineers, who represented a spectacular diversity of life forms, gathered up the pieces in a mute agony that she found comical. "Back to the drawing board," she murmured.

She seated herself on one of the scaffolding braces and studied the kloatraz. Darzek came over and sat down beside her. "Same diagnosis?" he asked.

"Those spots certainly look unhealthy."

Darzek thrust out an arm and rolled his sleeve up a few inches. He pointed at several large freckles. "Those spots certainly look unhealthy, but if I couldn't see them I'd never know they were there."

"Unless a nosy dermatologist called them to your attention," she suggested.

"Right. If that happened, I might start worrying about them."

She turned quickly. "You mean—the kloatraz—"

"It now decides that it's afflicted with an itch. Thus far it's being noble about the amount of pain involved. When pressed, it confesses to experiencing a painful irritation. Any suggestions?"

"If the pain is phychosomatic, none at all. Kloatraz psychology certainly would be a fascinating study if we had a lifetime, but that would delay your expedition. If the pain is wholly somatic, then the problem is slightly more complicated. Is the pH different in the areas of pigmentation? I'm not sure that I know how to find out, but if the kloatraz doesn't mind, I'm willing to try a few things."

"Ask Arluklo," Darzek said. "If the irritation or pain is psychosomatic, the fact that the creature is receiving attention may help the situation."

Malina consulted Arluklo, and then she went for her medical kit. With Arluklo standing by, poised to pipe a warning if anything she did made the situation worse, she selected the largest spot she could conveniently reach and took skin scrapings. Then she took scrapings from an area that looked normal. The surface was hard, but the scrapings came easily. Neither the kloatraz nor Arluklo made complaint. Malina thanked them both and returned to the Prime Common. For once she felt grateful to Rok Wllon—his lavishness with medical supplies had enabled her to include a microscope. Excitedly she prepared slides and took her first look at the cells of genus kloatraz.

They certainly were unearthly, but she disregarded that for the moment and made her comparisons. She found no abnormalities in the cells from her control area, but many of the cells from the spot looked necrotic. She quickly identified an acid condition, and she thought the scrapings from the necrotic area had a lower pH than those from the control, though she had no means of precise measurement.

Neither did she have any notion of what to do about it, but she had told Darzek she was willing to try a few things. She made up a phosphate buffer solution and returned to the Kloa Common. She summoned Arluklo, and then she soaked a bandage in the solution and cautiously applied it to one of the spots, holding it in place with forceps. The moisture evaporated almost at once, and before she could react, the bandage had become uncomfortably warm. When she jerked it away, the under surface was charred.

She retreated in confusion and seated herself on the scaffolding.

"What did it feel?" she asked Arluklo.

"The same. Only in greater quantity."

Her medical thermometer, with its upper limit of 42°, was useless. She dispatched Arluklo on an errand; he probably had to tour the mart to accomplish it, but eventually he returned with a boxlike object with protruding radii and a strangely graduated dial. Since none of her medical sources indicated a normal surface temperature for a kloatraz, she would have accomplished nothing in trying to convert the graduations to centigrade. She first grasped a pair of radii, which enabled her to establish the reading for human surface temperature as a reference point and also to convince herself that the thing worked.

Then she pressed several of the radii against the kloatraz. Arluklo assured her that it felt nothing at all, so she proceeded with her experiment. With the help of the engineers, who raised and lowered her on the new transmitter frame they had built, she established that the kloatraz's surface temperature at its base decreased steadily all the way to the top, where the temperature was little more than half what it was at the bottom. She could detect no measurable difference, at least on this thermometer, between the spots and the surrounding area.

She was pondering this when Jan Darzek returned. "Found out anything?" he asked.

"Several things, but I don't know what they mean. Did anyone notice these spots before?"

"Probably not," he said. "Until we started our excavations, no one but kloa ever came down here. If they'd noticed them, the kloatraz would have known about them."

"The spots definitely are getting darker, and there are more of them than there were yesterday. Now that I know what to look for, I can pick out a multitude of them in incipient stages. I think your kloatraz is on its way to becoming extremely ill."

"You *think* so," Darzek said. "Are you willing to swear that the spots aren't a cosmetic affliction like freckles or even a sign of robust good health?"

"Of course not. All I can swear is this: if you intend to haul the creature off across two galaxies and you want it alive when you arrive, you'd better give some thought to its health before you start."

Darzek said despairingly, "Worlds are dying, and you want to deprive us of the only potential weapon we have while you play nurse. I'm willing to take the risk if the kloatraz is."

Malina smiled. "If neither you nor the kloatraz cares, I don't see why I should. I certainly haven't established any kind of a doctor-patient relationship with it."

She packed her medical kit. As she was leaving, Darzek's gloomy countenance made her burst into laughter. "If it's any consolation," she said, "eighty per cent of the sick get well whether they have medical attention or not—though I couldn't say whether that figure applies to kloatrazes. If it's been here as long as you say, the spots may be a symptom of senility."

She returned to the Prime Common and looked again at the kloatraz's cells. And when, later that day, she took the children to the park, she met a native by special arrangement with the gesardl, and he carefully cut specimens for her of several kinds of Monturan vegetation. Back at the microscope, she quickly established that the kloatraz, plant though it might be, had no apparent relationship with Monturan plant life.

There was one further experiment she could perform. She had brought no culturing equipment with her—the standard BAP's would not have survived such a long trip, and in any case she had expected that the ultramodern city she was to practice in would have competent medical laboratories to perform chores that were beyond either the competence or interest of most dermatologists. Now she went down to Miss Schlupe's sandwich assembly line and abstracted a few pieces of pseudo salami. These she boiled into a thick broth, and she prepared three cultures: one with the normal skin scrapings, one with the necrotic cells, and a control. "And," she told herself, "I'll pray that nothing grows in any of them, because if it does I won't have the faintest idea what it is."

Early the next morning Darzek came for her. The dark spots were enlarging, there were more of them, and the kloatraz, whether for cause or because it merely wanted attention, was complaining. Would she please come back and have another look?

She made another buffer solution with a higher pH, and this she sprayed on several of the kloatraz's larger spots. According to Arlu-klo, the kloatraz noticed nothing different about that area, but at least the medication did not evaporate as quickly as the previous solution. She could not venture a guess as to how long it would take before she knew whether or not it was helping.

She spent an hour minutely scrutinizing the kloatraz's base, and then, after repeating the spray, she joined Darzek, who had been watching her from his own favorite seat on the scaffolding. She said bluntly, "If you're taking it anywhere soon, I think I'd better come along."

He shook his head. "You saw the recordings. You know how dangerous it is. If we make one bad guess, or have a few seconds of bad luck, you'll enhance your medical education by experiencing first hand an extremely unpleasant way to die."

"The kloatraz is the real reason Supreme sent a mission here, isn't it?" she asked.

"It must be."

"Has it occurred to you that the kloatraz may also be the reason Supreme sent a dermatologist here?"

He studied her gravely. "No. That hadn't occurred to me."

"Then think about it."

"What about your children?"

"I'm sure Miss Schlupe would be delighted to look after them, and she'll do it very capably. It'll be a rewarding experience all around. The children have no close relatives, and she's never had young children in her family. They're calling her 'Auntie Effie,' and she reacts as though she's been awarded a medal."

"There really is a good possibility that the children would be orphaned a second time. What about that?"

Was it foolish of her to feel completely indifferent about the danger? E-Wusk was fond of saying, with his booming laugh, that Gul Darr was indestructible. No doubt Darzek's reaction would be explosive if she told him she would feel safe because he was along.

"The question," she said slowly, "is whether this is genuinely important. I undertook to do a job when I came here. If this is the job, and there is as much at stake as you say, then there should be no other consideration than the fact that it's got to be done."

"Let's go see Schluppy," Darzek said.

"Not now. I want to see if I can teach Arluklo to apply this spray. When were you planning on leaving?"

"There's the question of how the kloatraz will react to being unrooted—that's its term, unrooted. Then there's the problem of transmitting it to the ship. Once there, we should conduct some tests to see how it will react to low gravity and the artificial environment of a spaceship. And then we'll have to evaluate this ailment it has, if it is an ailment. I'd say that when we leave is entirely up to the kloatraz's personal physician."

## 21

In the Kloa Common, the transmitter frame was poised at the top of its tracks, ready to plunge to the bottom. In the ship, the receiving frame surrounded a bed of soil that had been placed in the bottom of the largest hold for the kloatraz to rest on.

Malina was watching from the cargo master's control room, which was crowded with engineers. They consulted their instruments, the word "Ready" was spoken, translated through several languages, and finally relayed to the mart.

Suddenly the kloatraz loomed before them. It looked unchanged and none the worse for being unrooted and snatched into space. The rippling lights flashed as Malina remembered, but there were far fewer of them. Without an army of kloa and a trading empire to direct, the enormous vegetable mind had much less to do—for the kloatraz had turned its unfinished business over to other members of the gesardl, and the Kloa Common was closed.

Malina went into the cargo hold to scrutinize the pigmented patches, and Darzek followed after her and waited patiently while she conducted her examination. The spots she had treated seemed unchanged. Some of the others obviously were enlarging, and each time she looked there seemed to be more of them.

"The cargo master's living compartment is adjacent to his control room," Darzek said. "You can take it over, if you like, since you'll be the cargo master on this trip."

"Thank you. May I have Arluklo?" She felt silly in asking. Now that she knew the kloa were robots, there was no reason to prefer one of a category to another, but Arluklo's real or fancied personality appealed to her.

"Of course," Darzek said. "He'll be permanently assigned to you. We're taking a hundred kloa along. If the kloatraz is able to help us, each scientific project will need a direct link with it, and we want plenty of spares on hand in case of mechanical failure. As soon as you're ready, we'll try some experiments."

"I'm ready if the kloatraz is."

Darzek had the temperature, air pressure, and gravity moderately raised and lowered, and the kloatraz seemed not to notice. "Tomorrow we'll do it more drastically," he told Malina.

With her patient restored to her, she spent hours circling the massive form and making sketches. No system of photography available at the mart was able to delineate the spots to her satisfaction, so she produced her own map and divided it into zones so she could test and compare the effectiveness of different medications. While she worked, the rippling lights continued to wax and wane. All of the recordings Darzek had brought with him were being shown in a special scientific common in the forward part of the ship. The kloatraz had asked to see them, and it was viewing them through the eyes of a circle of watchful kloa.

When Malina finished her drawing, she initiated her first therapeutic regimen. She carefully instructed Arluklo in the application of sprays and ointments, and as soon as she was satisfied that he could proceed without supervision, she returned to the mart. She wanted to spend as much time as possible with her children before she left. She also wanted to visit the Kloa Common again and see the roots left behind by the kloatraz.

She took Brian and Maia with her, and the three of them prowled about the mammoth excavation. Darzek's scientists had been there ahead of them to lay bare the upper ends of the roots and study them. The central root was a gigantic protrusion some ten meters across, and the center one third of all the roots was hollow and lined with clusters of fine filaments.

Maia said suddenly, "What smells, Mama?"

Malina bent over and took a careful whiff. Then, with the children scrambling after her and asking what was wrong, she dashed off to find Jan Darzek. "Those roots have started to rot!" she exclaimed.

He scratched his head perplexedly. "Does it matter? The kloatraz won't be needing them again. It says it can grow new roots when it gets back."

"Don't you know what happens to vegetables when they're picked? Sooner or later, if they aren't preserved in some way, they rot."

Darzek pursed his lips to form a long, silent whistle. "But wouldn't the kloatraz be aware of that and tell us if there was any danger?"

"How could it know? It's never been picked before. I'd suggest no more experiments with high temperatures. As quickly as possible we should establish a low-temperature environment for it."

Darzek said slowly, "Of course it's true that most bacteria would be inhibited by cold, but that doesn't mean—"

"It means we'll play the odds," Malina said. "There isn't time to study all of a kloatraz's bacteria, and even if there were I wouldn't know how to begin. I have a couple of fine collections, grown from skin scrapings, and if those specimens had heads and tails I still wouldn't be able to make head or tail of them. Most bacteria are inhibited by cold temperatures, so we'll play the odds."

"All right. But remember—the condition you're trying to treat was present before the kloatraz unrooted itself."

"I'll remember. Let's not do anything to make it worse."

The arena no longer seemed the same. The kloa, so easily overlooked when they were numerous, now were startlingly conspicuous in their absence. Malina had to take Miss Schlupe with her everywhere, as an interpreter. The two of them prowled about the arena seeking out life forms that professed to have smatterings of medical knowledge and quizzing them about products available at the mart that might have medicinal qualities. Darzek had given Malina a special cargo compartment for medical supplies, and she laid in huge stocks of everything she or anyone else could think of that might be useful. The quantity of her own medical supplies, which had seemed so lavish back on Earth, already was proving sadly inadequate. When she'd made her selections, she hadn't considered the possibility of having to experiment on acres of epidermis of unknown structure.

Between speculations in extraterrestrial herbal medicines, pondering the strange bacteria that continued to grow in her pseudosalami cultures, and enjoying her children, she made regular visits to the spaceship Behemoth. A series of careful experiments established the kloatraz's preference for a temperature a few degrees above freezing and an atmosphere of twenty per cent Monturan normal.

"Its range of tolerance must be highly unusual for a life form," Malina observed.

"The highly unusual shouldn't be surprising in a creature we already know is unique," Darzek said.

Suddenly it was time to leave. Her patient was neither better nor worse for its change of environment, and Montura Mart could offer nothing more that seemed of any possible use. Malina took her children for a last romp in the park and was both delighted and pained at the brave manner with which they parted from her. Miss Schlupe embraced her and wished her luck, and E-Wusk fluttered his limbs at her in what she assumed was a benediction.

While they were meeting the Udef head on, E-Wusk, with URS-

Dwad's assistance, would direct the operation planned to alert a galaxy. Miss Schlupe would continue to run her refreshment stand. It was an invidious comparison. If it hadn't been for the children, Malina thought, Miss Schlupe certainly would have insisted on coming along.

She put Montura and its mart behind her and moved into the cargo master's living quarters; and she was already at work on her patient when the ship made its first transmitting leap.

She quickly settled into a routine. In the low gravity she could have inspected much of the kloatraz's surface by leaping, but tabulating conditions while floating past the patient was not her idea of how to conduct a medical examination. The ship's crew ingeniously rigged a chair for her that was suspended from an oblong spiraling track at the top of the hold. Once she had mastered the controls, she could raise and lower herself and move completely around the kloatraz. She had a small staff of crewmen and scientists, life forms with varying physical and mental talents, to call on when she needed them, but she preferred to work alone with Arluklo. Bundled up heavily because of the low temperature, wearing a special oxygen mask because of the thin air, she spent most of her waking hours in the cargo hold.

The kloatraz was constantly alert, its lights rippling and flashing, and in each of the rooms with transparent walls overlooking the cargo hold, Malina could see an assortment of diligent monsters hard at work—presumably in response to instructions originating in some part of the pattern of flashing lights as interpreted by the klo that worked with each group. These scientists, and others Malina could not see, were producing working drawings of mysterious, horrendously complex and incomprehensible instruments. These were to be translated into unlikely-looking gadgetry in the ship's instrument shop, and once the kloatraz had approved them they would be produced in quantity for distribution to the ships of Darzek's fleet.

When Malina stood at her own transparent wall brooding over her patient, she could see engineers and scientists in some of the rooms on the opposite side of the hold also looking out at the kloatraz and performing their own brooding. But what they were brooding over did not concern her, and on the infrequent occasions when she saw Jan Darzek, she was not interested enough to ask him what progress he was making.

Her patient's spots were slowly enlarging, and it had begun to slough skin. The discard, a parchmentlike membrane of dead cells, quickly became putrefied in the cargo control room, which she had converted to a laboratory. The kloatraz's stoic, almost non-committal acknowledgments that it felt discomfort in the sloughed areas came more and more frequently—and no wonder, since the sloughing left raw, denuded areas that oozed a strongly acid, colorless fluid.

She still had no inkling whether the disease centered in the outer epidermis or whether the condition she was treating was only a symptom. She systematically concocted sprays and ointments with which to treat the spots. These she tested experimentally, several at a time, in different zones of her map, and several at a time she rejected them. The spots continued to enlarge and slough alarmingly.

With a human patient, she would have inquired into his diet. She began to wonder about the kloatraz's diet. Since it had roots, it must have derived its nourishment from the soil—but what nourishment, and how could it survive now, without roots?

She asked Arluklo and learned that Jan Darzek already had investigated this point. The kloa had been adding nutritional supplements to the soil the kloatraz rested on for longer than anyone could remember. They would continue to do so. Once every ten days, Monturan time, several bags of a powdery substance would be spread about the base of the kloatraz on its bed of soil and thoroughly soaked with water. When Malina asked Darzek what the substance was, he answered, "Fertilizer." She asked Darzek's scientists for a chemical analysis, but their terminology and symbols were incomprehensible to her. At least she had the assurance that there had been no recent change in her patient's diet.

The one positive thing she learned was something she should not do. She applied a steroid compound to a spot, and the gigantic form instantly blazed with light while Arluklo suddenly shouted at the top of his piping voice, "No! No!"

She worked frantically with swabs and sprays to dilute the compound and remove it, and the light gradually subsided. Darzek came and watched her and said nothing at all, for which she was grateful. The brown spot she had been treating turned a flaming red and the following day was encrusted. When the scab detached, the spot had vanished, but she did not know whether she had cured it or merely eradicated it by permanently damaging the tissue.

She had learned a lesson. After that she never tried anything without having several countermeasures on hand and ready to use.

She continued to perform experiments. She would ask Arluklo to shout the moment the kloatraz felt anything, and then she would apply medication in small quantities: a drop of oil to a sloughed area; a drop to a nearby unaffected area. The kloatraz seemed to feel nothing at all unless the reaction was violently painful. If anything eased the discomfort it felt in the increasingly hideous, raw, oozing sores left when the skin sloughed, she was unable to find it.

Scientists and members of the crew came occasionally to watch her work, sometimes arriving in the cargo control room by transmitter, and sometimes entering the hold by way of a door on the opposite side. Her own routine centered on the kloatraz, and she went nowhere except the cargo hold, the cargo control room, and—to eat and sleep—her living quarters. She had brought a stock of the Earth canned goods with her. She hastily prepared a light meal when she felt like eating; she slept only when exhausted.

Otherwise, her patient obsessed her. For hours at a time she sat on a hassock in the cargo control room, worrying; or, bundled up and wearing her oxygen mask, she slowly circled the kloatraz at a dizzying height in her suspended chair or stared long at one particular spot, trying to think of some new experiment to perform. She had to have a piggyback seat made for Arluklo so he could ride aloft with her—she could not hear his piping responses from so far below.

As she worked, she questioned Arluklo incessantly: Did the kloatraz feel anything when she applied this spray? Had it ever tried to *move* an area of epidermis? Did it have muscles or anything comparable that could control a part of its body? Could it feel the swab she was using? Could it light its lights at will?

This last question so intrigued her that she pretended to need more light for a special experiment she was conducting and asked the kloatraz to light up the hold for her, but it could not or would not.

They were traveling across the Large Magellanic Cloud in enormous transmitting leaps; her own progress seemed non-existent. Having failed utterly with ointments, she returned to sprays with an equal lack of success until it occurred to her to try a *heated* buffer solution. For the first time the sloughing seemed to be arrested, and the sloughed areas very slowly began to form crusts.

Then Jan Darzek came and asked her, "Have you been doing anything different lately?"

She described her new technique and its results. She thought she had succeeded in stabilizing the kloatraz's condition in the test areas, and she was about to try the technique on a larger scale.

"It's virtually stopped working for us," Darzek said.

"What do you mean?" she asked.

"It was evolving an interlinked instrumentation, stage by stage, and my scientists thought they were finally on the way to something really significant. Suddenly it reversed itself and started redesigning what it had done earlier."

Malina withheld her special treatment. To her complete mystification, the healing process she thought she had started spread to untreated areas. To Darzek's mystification, the kloatraz seemed unable or unwilling to return to its grandiose instrumentation project. "It seems to have lost interest," he said.

Malina was in the cargo hold meditating methods of applying heat directly—was there, anywhere on board, the equivalent of a kloatraz-sized hot water bottle?—when Darzek, bundled up and wearing his own oxygen mask, joined her. He was carrying a focused-beam handlight, and he stepped back and aimed its spot illumination at a point midway up the kloatraz's side.

"Don't say anything," he said. "See that place?"

"I—"

"Don't say anything! Are you looking where the light points?"

She nodded.

"Keep watching that place." He switched off the light. "Now—say something."

She spoke resentfully. "What do you want me to say?"

"Did you see it? No? Then say something more. Recite a poem."

She said, feeling ludicrous, "Mary had a little lamb. Its fleece—"

Now she saw it. When she spoke, light flashed dimly in the area Darzek had picked out with his light.

"It does that every time you speak," Darzek said.

"Nonsense! What could it hear with?"

The light swelled softly and was gone.

"We don't know," Darzek said. "That isn't the question. Do you realize that this unmentionable lump of undefined tissue is in love with you?"

"Ridiculous!"

Again the light swelled and faded.

"The kloatraz," Darzek said, "is almost as old as the hills, and in that long lifetime it has met millions or maybe billions of intelligent life forms, and every individual among them wanted something from it—information, assistance in some project that benefited everyone but the kloatraz, and so on. Suddenly it has encountered an intelligent being wholly dedicated to its own welfare. Every question you ask it is about itself. How do you feel? Does this hurt? Is the itch any better today? Which salve do you like best? Can you wiggle your boils?"

"They aren't boils!" Malina said indignantly.

"All of your waking hours are devoted to nothing but this monstrosity's health," Darzek went on. "Or the lack of it. You ask nothing at all for yourself. You've turned the thing's mind inward. A life form that's mainly brain is hardly aware of its physical existence, but you've made it aware. Now it's thinking of itself to the exclusion of everything else except you, because everything you do makes it more aware of itself."

"What do you want me to do?" she demanded. "Quit?"

He looked at her levelly. "That's a good idea. Let's try that."

She thought for a moment. The notion that the kloatraz was in love with her seemed like a typical masculine fantasy, but she could not deny the possibility that the kloatraz's illness was psychogenic. As with a human patient, if illness brought about a desired result, the patient would remain ill and very likely become worse.

"All right," she told Darzek. "But strictly as a medical experiment."

She moved to the most remote compartment available, and one of Darzek's assistants took over her nursing chores. Once a day—and once only—he applied her selections of medications to the areas she indicated on her map. Otherwise, the kloatraz's problems, physical or mental, were left strictly alone.

The kloatraz showed no improvement on any level. Its physical condition became worse; the Udef identification system remained incomplete. Finally Darzek gave up and told Malina to do what she liked with her patient. She returned to the cargo control room and saw the kloatraz for the first time in more than a week.

Its spots had multipled; the sloughing had increased. The entire lower one third of that vast, looming form was fast becoming a composite mass of enormous, oozing, fetid lesions.

Again she tried the heated buffer solution that had been briefly successful. She began to achieve positive results almost at once. Crusts formed on the worst lesions, but this time they seemed to have an alarming life of their own. They grew and merged and became massive lumps of hardened matter; and then, to her amazement, they began to be absorbed. When they had completely disappeared, the formerly smooth surface had pronounced irregularities, with a visible nodule at every healed ulcer.

But an epithelized nodule was a definite improvement over an oozing lesion. She was pleased with her progress. She wanted Darzek to see for himself this refutation of his feckless fantasy, and she sent Arluklo for him; but he was busy and unavailable. Perhaps he preferred his fantasy.

Later she sent Arluklo again, and Arluklo returned with the information that Gul Darr was on another ship. At first she could not comprehend. Theirs had been a self-contained universe for so long, and she had been so intensely preoccupied, that she had forgotten where they were going and why.

"What do you mean—another ship?" she asked.

"We have reached the fleet, and Gul Darr is giving the captains of the other ships their instructions."

"I see," Malina said.

It meant that whatever instruments the kloatraz had completed were being distributed to the fleet, and soon they would go chasing about trying to corner the Udef and make it perform for the new instruments. It seemed like a tiresome waste of time and energy.

And, she reflected, when a doctor had a patient to care for, it could be an intrusion and a damned nuisance.

## 22

The relapse came with startling suddenness.

Malina had been treating the entire base with a daily application of a heated solution. The healed area had enlarged, and all of the ulcers seemed to be encrusting nicely. Abruptly new spots began to appear; the ulcers developed a creamy discharge, teeming with bacteria, that resembled pus; and even the area that had seemed completely healed began to slough again. The base of the kloatraz quickly reverted to a suppurating mass.

Malina, glumly meditating this worsening condition, realized with a start that she'd forgotten her children, just as she'd forgotten the Udef.

She said aloud, "Brian. Maia."

Light flickered in the area Darzek had pointed out to her. It seemed much brighter now, but that could have been because the massive form remained almost completely dark. The brain was becoming dormant, and it no longer sparkled with visual flashes of thought.

She feared that her patient was dying.

She had noticed another area of the surface that lighted dimly when she entered the cargo hold and then faded when she left. Both areas lighted whether or not Arluklo was present as the kloatraz's eyes and ears. Was the kloatraz able to see as well as hear, or did it perceive her presence and her voice in some other way?

She transmitted to the ship's control room to tell Jan Darzek about her rapidly failing patient. The captain, an extremely tall life form with arms and legs that tripled at the elbow and knee, gravely informed her that Gul Darr again was in conference on another ship.

As she turned away, he remarked, "You can join him there if it's important." He gestured at a transmitting frame.

Was it important? Darzek had considered the kloatraz their one hope against the Udef. On that premise he had brought it, and her, on this interminable journey across the light-years. Now the poor creature was too sick to work for him, and he had lost interest. He seemed not to realize that if it recovered it might be able to work again.

She thanked the captain and stepped through the transmitter.

She was in the control room of another ship. There was moisture on the floor, and she slipped and nearly fell. Regaining her balance, she tripped over a corpse. One of Darzek's scientists caught her as she went headlong. Politely he set her upright and helped her to a corner where the floor was dry. Then he returned to the corpse he had been examining.

The bodies of six different life forms—in her benumbed state of shock she absently counted them—were sprawled about the room, their variously colored body fluids running stickily together. In the corridor beyond, other corpses lay.

"The Udef?" she asked.

The scientist answered non-committally. "Yes. Udef."

The ship had been in remote orbit, he explained, waiting to perform tests if the Udef struck that planet; and the orbit had not been remote enough, or the ship had the bad luck to be squarely in the Udef's path on its approach. Either possibility had an identical, inevitable result: one crew lost; one ship that needed extensive cleaning.

When Malina had insisted on accompanying the kloatraz, Darzek had told her that there were three or four chances in a hundred that the Udef would strike the ship she was on. She'd answered brightly that her chances of dying accidentally on Earth were only slightly better than that. Ever since, she had seen her outlook for survival as a mathematical ratio. Now she saw it in terms of blood-spattered ships crewed by corpses.

She watched the scientist for a few minutes. He had a cluster of tentacles at each shoulder, and each tentacle terminated in a cluster of fingers—equipment any human pathologist would have regarded with envy.

"Where is Gul Darr?" she asked finally.

"Down," the scientist said.

"Down?" she echoed blankly.

The scientist pointed to a viewing screen she had not noticed. A group of Darzek's scientists in bulky protective clothing were cautiously picking their way through a nightmarish scenario of which the scene surrounding Malina was only a minor echo. Corpses lay everywhere in grotesque clusters and heaps.

"If it's urgent, you can go down," the scientist said. "There are extra suits in the lockers."

It hadn't been urgent to start with, and it was seeming less so with each passing minute. She was about to return to the other ship when Darzek's assistant, URsGworl, entered.

The scientist said, "She's looking for Gul Darr."

URsGworl nodded and motioned her to follow him. The protest was on her lips; her curiosity was more compelling. If she was laboring to save the universe, perhaps she should see first hand what she was saving it from. URsGworl measured her with a glance and handed her a suit of baggy clothing. She donned it thinking of the Monturan natives. On the third try they found a helmet that fitted her. URsGworl swiftly outfitted himself, gestured, stepped through a transmitter frame. She followed him.

Instantly she wished she hadn't. One body could be a study; ten, a tragedy; a hundred, a disaster. But a million corpses were merely ten thousand disasters lumped together in gross redundancy. It was impossible to feel ten thousand times as stunned and indignant over a million corpses as she would have over a hundred. She wished she were back in the peaceful dimness of the cargo hold worrying about the kloatraz.

And the carnage she was viewing represented the fate of only one city of one world. She remembered Jan Darzek's answer when Miss Schlupe asked him if he really was going to save the universe: "Someone had better do it." She breathed a fervent "Amen!"

Gingerly she stepped over and around the clusters of dead, hurrying after URsGworl, and eventually they overtook Darzek and his scientists. At this late date there was little that another pile of corpses could tell them about the Udef, so their work was almost finished. Darzek did not recognize her in the protective clothing, and she was content to follow after him anonymously. He walked along quietly, listening to his scientists; and their remarks, turned to thunder by an amplifier in Malina's helmet that she didn't know how to adjust, sounded like cryptanalysis in a strange language.

Finally they marched in single file to the transmitter frame, and through it to a decontamination chamber, and through that to the room where Malina had donned her suit.

As she removed her helmet, Darzek suddenly became aware of her presence. For a long moment he seemed to have difficulty remembering who she was.

"What are you doing here?" he demanded.

"Sightseeing," she answered coolly.

With him glaring at her reproachfully, she wiggled out of her protective clothing, returned it to a locker, and left. She refused to try to explain her unimportant important mission. He carried the staggering burden of trying to save the universe; she was only trying to save a dying kloatraz that he'd forgotten about.

She returned to the hold; she spoke. The appropriate areas lighted dimly. With Arluklo trailing after her, she circled the kloatraz despondently. The condition of the festered base now was so completely beyond her control that she lacked the courage and patience to try further medication.

"Poor old kloatraz," she murmured. "While you were the universe's one hope, everyone gathered around to see how you were doing. Now there's no hope at all, and the universe is in as bad a shape as you are. And here are the three of us—alone."

Again she wondered to what extent—if any—the illness was psychogenic. Darzek's scientists had discarded the kloatraz the moment it could make no more progress with its instruments. The brain that had handled dozens or hundreds of trading operations simultaneously was left without mental stimulation. Was the sudden physical decline an inevitable result of that?

She turned to Arluklo. "When is the kloatraz going to finish the instruments it was designing for Gul Darr?" she asked.

Arluklo answered promptly, "It did finish them."

"But it didn't," Malina protested. "It was advancing the complexity of the designs by steps and suddenly it stopped. Why didn't it finish them?"

"It did finish them," Arluklo said.

She could think of nothing more to ask. Perhaps Darzek could have given her enough information so she could pursue the subject, but the possibility of achieving anything was so obviously dubious that she decided not to mention it.

She felt the throb of transmission. The ship was under way again, off to investigate another dead ship or dead world. Her brief excursion—the effort of getting about in the awkward clothing and the physical and emotional strain of avoiding corpses and their ooze—all of that had exhausted her. She went to bed and fell asleep at once.

It was the heat that awakened her. The living quarters suddenly seemed stifling. At the same moment a strange dizziness seized her. She lurched to her feet and staggered into the cargo control room.

Shielding her eyes against a blinding light, she attempted to look through the transparent wall into the cargo hold.

The kloatraz was ablaze with heat and light. Crowds had gathered at the transparent walls she could see on the opposite side of the hold. She hoped desperately that Jan Darzek was among them—someone had to do something and quickly—but because of the intense light she could not make out who was there. While she was peering across at them, one of them dropped to the floor, and then another. Her own dizziness was increasing, and she had difficulty in standing.

Then she realized what was happening. The Udef had found them and was attacking the kloatraz, and the heat of that battle filled the cargo hold.

Desperately she looked again at the transparent walls opposite. Now she could see no one there. All of them had fallen. Even while occupied with the kloatraz, the Udef had enough force left to kill them. "Brian!" she cried. "Maia." She wanted to run, to escape the thing within her that tore at her brain. She put a hand forward to steady herself and felt the transparent wall yield at her touch. It was almost at melting temperature.

The pain from her burned fingers momentarily aroused her. She staggered to the control panel, unused since the cargo master had emptied the holds at Montura. How had he done it? A twist of the dial—she twisted it all the way. Position the hold indicator—she positioned both of them. A pull of the lever—but the lever would not move. Sobbing, she applied all of her strength. Then she remembered the safety catch. She released it and hauled at the lever. She was barely able to move it. Another tug, another—

A sudden, shrieking *whoosh,* and the kloatraz was gone. The hold opening closed automatically. The normal light that remained seemed the edge of darkness. Malina forced the lever back and even conscientiously locked it into place with the safety catch before she fainted.

She came to with an awareness that the floor was uncomfortably warm to lie on. She struggled uncertainly to her feet and looked about her.

The hold was empty. The transparent wall bulged with the impressions of her fingers. Arluklo sat against the wall waiting for her voice to activate him. She spoke his name and repeated it twice, but he did not respond. Had he suffered another internal malfunction?

"He's lost his brain," she sobbed.

She stepped through the transmitter to the ship's control room.

There were several bodies on the floor, but those in the room who were still standing—Darzek among them—were paying no attention. They were watching the ship's viewing screen.

On the screen, the kloatraz was drifting against the deep black of space with a fierce, blinding light that rivaled a sun.

"I just got here," Darzek said. "What happened?"

She did not answer. There was a dazzling flash, the kloatraz's light momentarily filled the screen and then faded, and the screen was empty.

"So it lost," Malina said bitterly. The irresistible force had met the immovable object, Udef crashing headlong into kloatraz, and the kloatraz had been vanquished.

"I wonder if maybe we gave up on it too soon," Darzek mused. "Even if it lost, that was quite a struggle."

A heroic struggle, Malina thought. A struggle to the death by a lonely, sick creature. Even now she could manifest no affection for the brain-bound monster, but she could pity it, and she had and did.

"Was it you who ejected it?" Darzek asked.

She nodded.

"How'd you happen to know how?"

"I watched the cargo master. Back at Montura."

"Incredible. You're probably the only one on board who knew how. We never figured on it leaving the ship except by transmitter. You saved everyone aboard, including yourself."

"What about them?" she asked, indicating the bodies on the floor.

"I think they're all unconscious."

Malina turned again to the empty viewing screen. "I suppose we wouldn't have stood much of a chance if the kloatraz had blown up in the cargo hold."

"You wouldn't have survived long enough to die in the explosion," Darzek said. "The Udef was here. In no more than another minute or two, everyone aboard would have been dead. Two things saved you. You ejected the kloatraz, and the Udef, or most of it, went along. And the captain, who was asleep when the Udef struck, managed to stagger in here and hit the transmitting button, which we keep permanently set for a short escape leap when we're in Udef territory. He must have done that seconds after you ejected the kloatraz."

"So only the kloatraz died," Malina said. "And that was entirely unnecessary."

"What do you mean?"

"If you hadn't been in such a rush to leave Montura, the kloatraz could have designed your instruments there—all of them—and maybe solved this Udef riddle. But you had to unroot it and bring it all this distance in an artificial environment that was about to kill it anyway, just so it could die spectacularly fighting the Udef. It wasn't even a fight in a good cause. It was just a stupid loss because no one took the time to sit down and think."

She turned and stepped through the transmitter to the cargo control room. There, seeing Arluklo still sitting against the wall with the empty cargo hold behind, she wept.

## 23

When Malina could stand its presence no longer, she picked up Arluklo's body—strangely light under the ship's low gravity—and carried it through the transmitter to the control room. One of the captain's assistants showed her the compartment where the other kloa had been placed for storage and helped her to arrange Arluklo's inert form among them. With a nod of benediction, Malina left him.

"Is there any chance of reviving them?" she asked the assistant.

He did not know. Their instrumentation was bewilderingly complex, and though the scientists thought that much could be learned from it, at the moment they were preoccupied with other things. Some of them feared that the kloa could be activated only by a telepathic power such as the kloatraz possessed.

Malina asked about Gul Darr. He was in conference again, this time on this ship. If Gula Darr wished to join him—

Darzek, the captain, and at least a hundred scientists had gathered in one of the ship's smaller cargo holds. The variegated life forms sat, or reposed, or lounged, or sprawled while keeping their organs of vision fixed on a screen that had been installed in a far corner.

Lines moved across the screen. Some were almost straight, with only a slight quaver, and others meandered wildly. When finally the tape or recording came to an end, most of the lines stopped abruptly. At the bottom of the screen, several drooped and dribbled slowly into nothingness. The screen went blank.

"Let's have it again," Darzek called.

After a brief interval, the lines again began their parade across the screen. Darzek came over to the entrance and stood beside Malina.

"What is it?" she asked.

"Records charted by those instruments the kloatraz designed for us. They measure quantities and qualities we weren't able to measure before. Unfortunately, we haven't been able to figure out what it is that the quantities and qualities are of, except that it's the Udef. This is a synchronization of the readings taken at various times and locations. All of them are quite similar except the one at the bottom, which is the record of the Udef's encounter with the kloatraz."

Malina studied the parade of meaningless lines for a moment. "Then you have two questions—what are the instruments measuring, and what is the significance of the differences?"

"Right. There are five different instruments, supposedly recording five drastically different things. So each group of five lines represents one encounter with the Udef."

Compared with the others, the five lines at the bottom were wildly eccentric, and these were the ones that slowly drooped and dribbled away when the others cut off sharply.

"Again!" Darzek called. He said quietly to Malina, "I'm waiting for some inspired individual to invent a theory."

She smiled. "To see if it matches the one you already have?"

He made no comment.

"Has there been any sign of the Udef since its encounter with the kloatraz?" Malina asked.

Darzek shook his head. "It may have limped off to lick its wounds. Or it may have taken one of its enormous leaps. There's no way of knowing or even guessing which way or how far. All we can do is scatter the fleet and search."

"I suppose you won't know whether you've made any progress until you find out what the kloatraz's instruments are measuring."

"We know that they're measuring the Udef, and that's phenomenal progress. They let us know when the Udef is nearby. We've only lost one crew since we distributed them, and that because the captain forgot to turn them on. Of course we almost lost this crew, but that was a comparable goof. The instruments were turned on, but no one was watching them. A ship had never been attacked in deep space before, and everyone thought there was no danger."

Malina pointed at the screen. "What's your theory?"

"That the Udef and the kloatraz destroyed each other. In all the other encounters, the graphs terminate abruptly. The Udef finished its work and went—zip—somewhere else. But in this last encounter, the graphs slowly drop to zero. The Udef didn't go anywhere. It died."

"But your scientists don't see it that way?"

"I hire them to tell me their theories, not to listen to mine."

Malina excused herself—there really was nothing there for her to do—and returned to the cargo control room. It was time she thought about getting back to Montura, and picking up her children, and going home. She couldn't claim to have earned her million dollars, because the only task she had found for herself had proved to be vastly beyond her ability, but she had done her best in a difficult situation, and she could retire with conscience unblighted, beaten but not dishonored.

"Like the kloatraz," she thought soberly.

She glanced at the corner where Arluklo so frequently had sat leaning against the curving side of the ship when he was not needed. She turned away sadly.

Then she looked again and stared.

On the floor lay a tiny, creamy white object.

She stooped to pick it up and snatched away a seared finger. After treating the burn, she tried again, with forceps, and placed the object in a cotton-filled box from her medical supplies.

Then she studied it. It looked like a small bead, badly chipped or broken on one side. Gazing at it intently, she almost thought she could see lights flashing within it.

She stepped to the intercom. "Please tell Gul Darr that Doctor Darr would like to see him at once in the cargo control room."

He stepped through the transmitter a moment later. "What is it?"

She held the box under his nose. When he reached out for it, she pulled it away and said, "Just look. Don't touch. I burned myself trying to pick it up."

"Where'd you find it?"

"On the floor." She pointed a toe at the spot.

"It must have holed the hull," Darzek said.

"I beg your pardon?"

"That was quite an explosion, and this piece had enough velocity to come through the side of the ship. It happens occasionally with small meteoroids, which is why the ship has a self-sealing hull. I hadn't realized that the bodily substance of the kloatraz was that hard. Have you finished with it?"

"What do you want it for?"

"I'll have the scientists do a proper analysis of it."

She pulled the box away from him protectingly. "No. That would destroy it. I have a better use for it."

"What?"

"I'm going to plant it."

He backed over to the one hassock remaining in the room and sat down. "Tell me more."

"Back on Montura," she said, "a silly idea occurred to me. Since Supreme is a computer, and the kloatraz was—we thought—a computer, I wondered if Supreme had sent a mission to Montura just so it could get in touch with the kloatraz. I wondered if we were unknowingly carrying love messages from one computer to another."

Darzek made no comment. His eyes were fixed on her face; his manner was alertly, intensely curious.

"So perhaps this is merely another silly idea," she went on, "but it occurs to me that opposites attract."

He scowled. "*Every white will have its black, and every sweet its sour.* Perhaps. Though when humans remark that opposites attract, the opposites referred to usually have more in common than in opposition."

"In many species, the two sexes are drastically opposite."

Darzek's scowl became fierce. "Then—this fragment that holed the ship is a seed? Or an egg?"

She nodded. "If you don't mind an oversimplification. More likely it's a fragment of a creature that reproduces by multiple fission or combines reproduction and regeneration or something like that. We shouldn't be discussing the reproductive system of an alien in human terms."

"You're absolutely right. Go ahead and discuss it in nonhuman terms."

"I can be just as reckless with a theory as you can," she said sharply. "Say a fragment similar to this one came drifting through space and reached the world of Montura—and grew there."

"Having somehow survived its collision with the atmosphere."

"What's impossible about that?" Malina demanded. "The kloatraz underwent tremendous heat but it didn't burn up. It exploded."

Darzek shrugged. "It reached the world of Montura—"

"Yes. Relatively few such fragments would ever reach hospitable worlds on which growth would be possible. The one on Montura had the additional incredible good luck to find a telepathic life form it could communicate with and which could be of service to it in many ways. Its history may be unique. It was able to develop its mental powers fully. It came to the same end, though, as if it had grown up as an unthinking vegetable. It reached sexual maturity and went to seed."

Darzek said slowly, "Then the spots you were trying to cure could have been an indication of sexual maturity? And when it came into estrus, it sent out a signal?"

"If you don't mind a terrestrial illustration, the female luna moth releases a scent that attracts males from kilometers away. There probably are better examples."

"Then we'll say the kloatraz sends out some kind of emanation when it reaches sexual maturity: a scent, a radio signal—"

"Not a very precise signal," Malina said. "But it serves."

"I'd say highly precise, considering the size of the universe. The Udef was attracted to the correct galactic system and only missed its objective by one galaxy. Then your theory is that this fragment is the offspring of a violent sexual union, and that given proper opportunity it'll grow into another kloatraz. That's certainly an original theory."

"I'm also wondering if the Udef exploded the same way the kloatraz did and scattered its fragments."

"The female gives birth to females and the male to males?"

"You're still viewing the reproductive system of an alien in human terms. Why shouldn't each partner give birth to offspring of its own sex? That's much more logical than our untidy system."

"Let it not be said that I raise my voice against logic," Darzek murmured. "Then those oscillating lines on the graphs represent the climax of a sexual union, after which the partners subsided and then vanished by giving birth. It's a good theory. It's even a lovely theory. I'm going to break a personal rule and pass it along to the scientists. It'll make them flip, which will be healthy for them. They'll start worrying about those millions or billions of kloatraz and Udef fragments floating about the universe. They'll wonder whether on some obscure world in one of our three galaxies, another kloatraz is about to reach maturity and start signaling. Sobering thought: did the kloatraz stop designing instruments for us because it realized that we were trying to destroy its intended husband?"

"Here's a more sobering thought," Malina said. "Was the kloatraz helping us, or was it using us for transportation?"

"I don't think it was consciously using us. I doubt that either kloatraz or Udef had a conscious awareness of the other's existence, and I'm certain that such a marriage has never taken place in space before. Normally it would happen on the ground, where the kloatraz was growing, and perhaps the explosion serves to throw the particles into space. That's another theory that'll make the scientists flip. They're already flipping over the explosion. It definitely wasn't atomic, but they've no notion what it was. Let's talk about the Udef."

"It was driven by its mating instinct," Malina said. "Since the kloatraz was an enormous brain, the Udef's instinct was to treat each brain it encountered as a potential mate. Or perhaps it attempted to treat an entire world population as a potential mate. Whatever the kloatraz was emanating must have approximated the emanations of a world of normal brains. When the Udef realized its error, it left the brains destroyed and continued the search."

"I vaguely recall a story out of India," Darzek said, "about a tiger in estrus that forced the closing of a major highway by attacking everything in sight."

Malina smiled. "Apparently nature operates everywhere to produce inconceivable differences and appalling similarities."

Darzek got to his feet. He had seen her finger indentations in the transparent wall, and he went to examine them. Then he stood looking into the empty hold and spoke meditatively. "Somewhere in the universe, there may be a galaxy, or a galactic system, or a group of systems, where Udef and kloatraz are the dominant life forms. No other intelligent life form could develop in a system where Udefs are numerous. One kloatraz seed or spore or fragment, from one of those remote unions, drifted an incredible distance across the universe and reached the world of Montura. And except for another unlikely accident it would have lived out its life there and perished unmated: it encountered a life form it could communicate with and make use of —and that led to the mart, and its own robots, and wealth, and the means to indulge itself with a regular application of its favorite fertilizers—with the result that it attained an immense size and in the process probably delayed its sexual maturity. When maturity came, its signal was powerful enough to attract a mate from an enormous distance."

"And now we have the danger that kloatrazes and Udefs may become numerous in this galactic system," Malina said.

"And we—perhaps—have a defensive weapon in the instruments the kloatraz designed." Darzek reached out and took the box with the kloatraz fragment. "I'll see that this is planted and tended with care. But of course nothing may happen. There may be no substance to your mating theory."

"And even if there is, you'd still have the problem of finding a way to cope with the next Udef that happens along."

Darzek nodded. Again he gazed meditatively into the empty cargo hold. "And the universe certainly holds stranger mysteries and ghastlier horrors than kloatrazes and Udefs. . . ."

The intercom clicked. The captain spoke above the babble of excited voices. "A special emissary from Primores. Just arrived."

"Send him in," Darzek said. He turned back to Malina. "Where was I?"

"The mysteries of the universe."

"Yes. The next Udef may be something entirely different. Perhaps it's just as well that we don't know all the dangers the universe contains."

Rok Wllon stepped through the transmitter frame.

They greeted him warmly, but he was wasting no time on conversational clichés. He panted, "Supreme says—"

"Sit down," Darzek said, guiding him to the hassock. "Relax. You look as though you'd run the last three light-years."

Rok Wllon refused the hassock. "Supreme says—"

"Sit down," Darzek said firmly. "Take a deep breath. Doctor Darr has solved all of our riddles, and whatever Supreme says comes too late."

Rok Wllon seated himself reluctantly. "Supreme says the natives of Montura have an unusual computer that is alive. It might be capable of different patterns of thought and able to devise a defense—"

"But we discovered that ourselves right after you left," Darzek said. "The computer that was alive was the kloatraz, which now is dead. You'll have to go back to Primores immediately to bring Supreme up-to-date. You also must tell Supreme that it goofed badly in recommending a dermatologist, and that the dermatologist it shouldn't have recommended has solved our problem."

Rok Wllon gazed from one to the other with a blankness so exquisitely expressive that both Malina and Darzek burst into laughter.

24

# MALINA DARR

Montura Mart no longer seemed the same fantastic trade center, and Doctor Malina Darr felt substantially changed herself. Instead of a dermatologist bewilderedly in search of nonexistent patients, she now was an official emissary with impeccable credentials.

Jan Darzek had entrusted her with the mission of notifying the gesardl of the death of one of its members and of requesting cooperation and assistance in a planned multigalactic sweep to insure that the Udef, if not deceased or disintegrated, at least was not lingering in the vicinity.

Maia and Brian greeted her overwhelmingly when she stepped off the shuttle rocket. A beaming Miss Schlupe stood looking on. The gesardl's delegation, on hand to accord Malina the status she was deemed entitled to, hovered sedately in the background. Malina took her greetings and honors in stride, controlled her pride in her offspring—both children seemed taller and more mature than when she'd left them—and plunged at once into the necessary conferences. The gesardl, too, had changed. There was no klo member, and Malina sadly missed having a politely hovering Arluklo waiting for instructions. Miss Schlupe served as her interpreter, and together they conveyed Gul Darr's reports and his request for assistance. The conferences were tedious and seemed interminable, but eventually they secured the gesardl's pledge of full cooperation.

In celebration, Malina took Brian and Maia for a romp in the park. Miss Schlupe had been taking them there daily, and they had made a tradition of their ceremonial presentation of gifts to any natives they encountered. The children enjoyed this thoroughly, and Miss Schlupe suspected that the natives had appointed a special committee to receive gifts from the Darr children; they never failed to find at least one native in the park.

Much later, after the children had been put to bed, Malina settled down for a long talk with Miss Schlupe.

"As I understand it," Miss Schlupe said finally, "the kloatraz was sending out signals that started the Udef on a rampage, wrecking world after world because it wanted a mate and couldn't find one. And the Udef was sending out signals that made the kloatraz break out in boils. If that's sexual maturity, they can have it. I suppose they would have gone right on sending signals until they got together, even if they had to wreck a dozen galaxies to do it. Poets keep saying that love is grand, but you'll notice it isn't the poets that have to sweep things up afterward. Well—Mr. Darzek will see that it doesn't happen again."

Malina smiled. "I'm sure he will. What are you going to do now?"

"I'm thinking maybe I'll stay here," Miss Schlupe said brightly. "I've got this nice business, and I'd hate to walk off and leave it. And that store I had in Brooklyn was a drag from the day one. So I think I'll stay. I've got this idea for building up a franchise system. Some of the traders think my submarines and cider would do well on their worlds, so we're working out the details. If the thing's a success, I might expand to pizza and hamburgers."

"No fried chicken or tacos?" Malina asked, heroically keeping her face straight.

"Maybe tacos. But fried chicken requires chickens. I've thought about it, and I've done some experimenting, and all the substitutes come out fried-something-else. And where could I get enough chickens to feed a couple of galaxies? On the other hand, hamburger can be made out of anything."

"Just like on Earth," Malina suggested.

"Exactly like on Earth. Except that each franchise would develop its own special kind of hamburger out of the meat available locally, so my hamburgers would have a distinctively different taste everywhere you went—unlike those chains on Earth where the food's the same everywhere only more so. A Schlupe hamburger would be a gourmet surprise no matter what world you bought it on. Are you really going back?"

"My medical practice on Montura didn't flourish the way your refreshment stand did. There's nothing to keep me here."

"I thought maybe you and Mr. Darzek—you made a handsome couple, you know. Didn't you like him?"

"He's very attractive, especially when he's joking. Otherwise he's a bit overwhelmingly serious. I'm afraid he's not the kind of person I'd want to be a couple with. I've had a husband I loved, and who loved me, and I know what that means. I'm sure Mr. Darzek is warm and considerate, but every now and then he goes completely blank on you, as though he's put up a barrier in his mind to keep you from interrupting while he solves the problems of the universe, and that wouldn't be tolerable if you were a couple. Besides, I'd always be suspicious that he considered me one of the problems."

Miss Schlupe sighed. "Maybe the poets should be doing a better selling job."

"Look at the bright side," Malina said. "Here's one case that won't require any sweeping up." She added thoughtfully, "He does have a very nice laugh, though. It's too bad he's so overwhelmingly serious."

## ROK WLLON

Because he sat alone in the official residence of the Eighth Councilor, there was no witness to his discomfiture, but this did not prevent his squirming with embarrassment.

He had indited the report with his usual diligence, but Supreme was having difficulty in understanding how a massive, rocklike life form was able to mate with an invisible force. Rok Wllon had not been able to explain the process even to his own satisfaction—he found it totally incomprehensible—but it was his solemn duty to attempt to elucidate whenever and whatever Supreme asked. So he had made the attempt.

And Supreme kept asking for more details, which were unavailable, and for further explanation, which Rok Wllon was unable to provide.

Grimly he began again, for the fifth time, to indite a description of the mating of the kloatraz with the Udef.

## SUPREME

In its data storage banks were detailed descriptions of the reproductive processes of every known life form in its galaxy and of many life forms in the adjoining galaxies, but the process referred to by the Eighth Councilor differed in so many significant aspects that Supreme found it unclassifiable and therefore suspect. It digested the Eighth Councilor's latest attempt and again processed it through data storage.

And again it asked for more details and further explanation.

# JAN DARZEK

He remembered Malina Darr's laughter long after he placed her on a ship for Montura. He could not recall the last time he had heard anything so joyously carefree. He had been entrapped in a nightmare of death. Everything he touched, every world he looked at, died.

Now he was awake. There was no sign of the Udef anywhere. There was, there always would be, death, but it no longer surrounded and stifled him.

He even was able to joke with URsGworl about an error in a fleet-maneuver plan. In large-talk script, a *9* was very similar to a *3* when written carelessly, and URsGworl had produced a carelessly written plan guaranteed to temporarily lose sixty ships.

"We would think the Udef now was devouring ships as well as crews," Darzek remarked, making the correction. "If the error wasn't discovered quickly, I'd be recalling Doctor Darr and preparing to start the investigation over again. Only this time it would be spots before your eyes she'd have to treat instead of spots on a kloatraz."

URsGworl thought it discreet to change the subject. "When does Doctor Darr return?"

"She doesn't," Darzek said. "She only came here as the kloatraz's doctor, and, as we now know, it didn't need one. Her assignment was on Montura, but she wasn't needed there either. She'll stop there briefly, to pick up her children, and then she'll go home to Earth."

URsGworl screwed up his unhandsome face perplexedly. "Among your kind, is she not thought attractive?"

"Highly attractive," Darzek agreed. "Especially when she laughs. Otherwise, she tends to be a bit on the serious side."

"We thought she had come as your mate. Seriousness is a defect?"

Darzek grinned at him. "It depends on what one is serious about. Doctor Darr has children and a career, and she's extremely serious about both, which is proper. But I'm afraid she'd be equally serious about a mate, and I've already got too many people taking me seriously."

URsGworl reflected. "Perhaps she is serious about the wrong things. I remember she was more concerned about spots on the kloatraz than about the worlds the Udef had destroyed."

"Well—they were her spots. She was medically responsible for doing something about them, and the worlds were my responsibility.

Seriousness is all right in its place, but I don't think I'd want a mate looking at me the way she studied those spots." He added thoughtfully, "She does have a very nice laugh, though."

URSGworl departed with his corrected maneuver plan. Darzek turned to the pile of unfinished business on his desk. There was Udef research to continue, a seedling kloatraz to nourish and study, and the incredibly complex question of what should be done about, or for, or to the devastated worlds that littered more than half the Lesser Galaxy. So much knowledge to be gleaned; so much beauty to be preserved . . .

For the first time in a couple of years he had been sleeping well; and now that he was fully awake, there was work to do.